Nancy Madison, a former corporate librarian for an international accounting-consulting firm, lives in Texas with her husband.

WAIT FOR ME

Claire Stanhope returns to Bowness in the Lake District after a five-year absence. But what begins as a peaceful family reunion at her aunt's small hotel turns into a cat-and-mouse game. A professional assassin is in the village, searching for the truth about his brother's disappearance. Tony, the hotel's charming handyman, soon becomes Claire's friend, but she loathes Max, the new manager of the local paper, even before they meet. Will Claire realise which man she can trust with her life, and her heart, before it's too late?

Books by Nancy Madison
Published by The House of Ulverscroft:

CLUES TO LOVE
NEVER LOVE A STRANGER

NANCY MADISON

◆

WAIT FOR ME

Complete and Unabridged

ULVERSCROFT
Leicester

First published in Great Britain in 2005

First Large Print Edition
published 2005

This book is a work of fiction. Names, characters, places, and incidents are either the product of the author's imagination or are used fictitiously, and any resemblance to actual persons, living or dead, events or locales is entirely coincidental.

The model for Kings Grant Hotel was the charming *Lindeth Fell Country House Hotel* in *Bowness-on-Windermere, Cumbria.*

British Library CIP Data

Madison, Nancy
  Wait for me.—Large print ed.—
  Ulverscroft large print series: romantic suspense
  1. Lake District (England)—Fiction
  2. Romantic suspense novels 3. Large type books
  I. Title
  813.6 [F]

ISBN 1–84395–739–6

Published by
F. A. Thorpe (Publishing)
Anstey, Leicestershire

Set by Words & Graphics Ltd.
Anstey, Leicestershire
Printed and bound in Great Britain by
T. J. International Ltd., Padstow, Cornwall

This book is printed on acid-free paper

1

'Stop him! Stop him!' The shrill cry pierced the quiet October morning.

Waiting for a train at a small Devon station, Claire Stanhope turned. A woman was running down the platform in her direction, chasing a little boy.

The child darted by Claire and reached the front of the platform. He tottered on the edge then fell onto the tracks.

Each of the other travelers near Claire reacted differently. The withered elderly woman in a wheelchair gasped and her male nurse bent to calm his patient. The woman seated next to them dropped her knitting. While all three seemed frozen into position, a British Rail train appeared around a bend in the track, racing toward the station.

Mindless of her own safety, Claire leaped from the platform to the tracks below. She grabbed the child. Holding him tightly in her arms, she rolled away from the tracks.

Seconds later, the express train roared by, missing Claire and the child by mere inches. Now that the danger was past, the boy burst into tears.

The station master appeared out of nowhere to kneel at the platform edge. Holding out his hand, he helped Claire and the child climb back onto the platform.

The child's mother clutched her son and Claire. 'Thank you. Thank you.' She sobbed, too overwhelmed with emotion to say more.

'Mommy, you're hurting me,' the little boy cried, pressed between the two women. His mother released his rescuer.

Claire wiped at what had been her favorite navy wool pantsuit. Surveying the soiled fabric and a small tear in one sleeve, she made a mental note to take the outfit to the cleaners. Then she realized how much worse her condition might have been and felt the urge to laugh and cry at the same time. Since the Stanhopes frowned on displaying emotion in public, Claire contented herself with a childhood habit. She sucked in her breath and gnawed her lower lip.

Claire shivered as her pulse slowed toward normal. Death had come too close for comfort. In an attempt to soothe the other woman, Claire patted her on the arm. 'Please don't thank me,' she murmured softly. 'You'd have done the same.' She managed a shaky smile before stepping away.

A spontaneous burst of applause from the crowd of curious onlookers now gathering on the platform prompted Claire to search for a way to escape the unwanted attention.

The WC signs on the side of the station caught her eye. Without a moment's hesitation, she pushed open the door marked 'Ladies' and dove inside.

As luck would have it, the restroom was deserted. She conducted a quick survey of her body in the privacy of a stall and was relieved to find nothing worse than a few minor scrapes and bruises. Soaking a paper towel in cold water, she dabbed at her worst wound, a scrapped left elbow. Hopefully, the little boy had fared no worse.

By the time Claire stepped from the restroom, she was pleased to find the crowd had dissipated. The mother and child had also left. She'd hoped to see them again so she could make certain the lad was all right.

Perhaps the last person to witness what had happened, an old lady with a backpack patted Claire's arm in passing. 'Good for you, lass,' she said in a thick Scottish brogue.

Like a magical chariot, Claire's own train chose that moment to glide to a halt at the platform. It was a most welcome sight.

No porters appeared to help so she manhandled her trunk aboard and left the heavy suitcase just inside the car marked '1' for First Class. Avoiding the seats marked

'Reserved,' Claire slumped into an unticketed seat.

As the train pulled out of the station, she discovered she was the only passenger in the First Class car. That was fine with her. After what had happened in the Devon station, Claire needed some quiet time. She still couldn't believe she'd acted so boldly. But she had no choice. No one else had moved a finger to help.

Claire frowned. How surprised her brother would have been if he'd stood beside her on that platform when the child's mother screamed. Most likely Charles would have hung back, waiting for someone else to respond.

In her head, Claire could hear her brother's comment as clearly as if he'd been seated beside her. 'Dear, you just can't get involved with people. It's really none of our business.'

Charles's attitude had been one of indifference to most other living creatures on the earth. If he were still alive, he'd have been the first to admit his concerns were limited.

His list of priorities had been short. He came first followed by Claire. With a sigh, she admitted she'd been more than a priority. Her brother had been obsessed with her.

Next came their property and investments then Kings Grant, Uncle Stephen's home.

Their deceased father's older brother had promised King's Grant to them. No one and nothing else mattered to Charles.

Looking back over the years, Claire admitted Charles's attitude had never swerved. He had always been selfish.

A question had burned in her brain since her brother's death. Could she have saved Charles? Needing to resolve the past, Claire counted on her aunt. It was time she moved on with her life.

The swaying motion of the train lulled Claire and she dozed while British Rail continued on its route. Following a number of shorter stops, the train halted in Euston Station, London's main terminal for rail travel to northern England and Scotland.

Several young men and women wearing BritRail uniforms boarded at Euston. Laden with supplies for the buffet, they bantered back and forth with each other. Soon two of them served Claire her lunch from a trolley. The meal was edible though it didn't come close to the home cooking she was already anticipating when she reached her destination.

Within a few minutes, the train started again. Its final destination was Glasgow, several stops beyond Oxenholme where Claire would leave British Rail for the shuttle to Windermere thirty miles off the main line.

The train picked up speed until the scenery seemed to leap by her window. Raindrops from a brief passing shower splattered the glass, blurring the view while she recalled her last hours at home. It'd rained that day, also.

Her departure from Bowness would remain forever etched in her memory. To avoid a prolonged goodbye, Claire had packed her bag and crept from the hotel early that morning. If she waited until the others woke, she knew they'd insist on driving her to the station. Or worse still, her Aunt Kate would make a last-ditch effort to convince her to stay.

Kate had stood beside her during a terrible time. Claire's throat tightened as she considered how Charles had brought danger into her aunt's uneventful life.

Though she tried to relax, Claire's nerves remained taut. It had been five years since she'd fled to Devon, a long time to be away from the people she loved. Closing her eyes, she could see their faces, Kate, Nick and Mattie.

Only Charles would not be there to greet her this time. Thoughts of him brought a dull ache in the direction of her heart until she forced herself to think of something else.

As Claire recalled what had happened, she

was still amazed that Kate didn't hate the very sight of her. On the contrary, her aunt had been loving and kind. She'd sent Claire many letters during her stay in Devon and they all ended with the same words. 'When are you coming home? I miss you.'

Almost home. Soon she'd be able to gaze upon the old familiar scenes, the autumn-brown bracken on the fells, the village streets quiet without the crowds of summer tourists, and the steamboats plowing Lake Winder-mere, pursued by the ever hungry gulls.

The train reached a station north of London, halting a few minutes for passen-gers. A polite cough resounded behind Claire as they got underway again.

★ ★ ★

In Bowness-on-Windermere, Max Bronsky swore in exasperation at the antiquated printing press that was the heart of the Bowness Bugle. If he hadn't wanted to sample a mug of Arubian beer, he wouldn't be in this annoying situation.

Nine days ago he'd flown into Aruba in the Caribbean for a short vacation following the completion of his last assignment. A cable waited for him at the hotel, the message brief and to-the-point. Max was needed right away in the Lake District of northern England. His vacation would have to wait.

That evening he paid his first and last visit to the hotel bar for a mug of Aruba's famous beer.

A broad-shouldered, middle-aged man in an expensive-looking tweed suit climbed onto the next stool and ordered the same beer.

'Are you here on holiday?' He glanced in Max's direction.

From the man's accent, Max thought he was a Scot. 'Yeah,' he said. 'You?'

'I made my reservation for a week's stay before falling in the shower and breaking this.' The Englishman gestured to the cast on his right arm. 'It seemed a shame to cancel my holiday so I came anyway.'

'It is a lovely spot,' Max agreed. 'I can see why you were reluctant to change your plans.'

The other man smiled boyishly. 'Oh, no. I wasn't about to do that.' He leaned toward max. 'May I tell you a secret?'

'Sure.' He never ceased to be amused at the way travelers confided in perfect strangers. In his line of work, it could cost him his life.

'You might say I'm playing hookey,' the other man confided. 'I've run away from my new business.'

'I see,' Max replied, politely. 'What's the business?'

'Fiona, my third wife, thinks I've gone bonkers to buy a business without knowing anything about it,' the man began, pausing for a moment to motion to the bartender for seconds. 'A friend cried on my shoulder until I agreed to buy him out. So now I own a daily newspaper with no idea how to run it.'

'I'm a free-lance journalist myself,' Max said. That was his cover story anyway. 'I just finished an assignment in Belgium.'

'You don't say.' The older man raised an eyebrow as if impressed. He put out a well-manicured hand. 'Peter King here.'

'Max Bronsky.' He shook the other man's hand. 'Good to meet you, Peter.'

'I suppose you're on your way to another assignment?' King peered, curiously, at Max from under shaggy eyebrows.

'No, I'm not.' Max shrugged. 'I like to hang loose, take my opportunities as they come.' His employers would love hearing him say that.

'My little paper needs someone to build up circulation and report the local news, and I have no idea where to start. I'm in sheep,' King declared as if that were explanation enough. 'I don't suppose you'd consider taking on the Bugle for a few weeks? I'd make it well worth your while.'

'I've never published a paper.' Max

hesitated, not sure how to answer. When he'd come to the bar, he hadn't expected to get more than a beer.

'If you're accustomed to writing for large papers all over Europe, the Bugle would be a piece of cake for you. And it'd be a pleasant change,' King said. 'Have you ever been to Cumbria?'

'No, I haven't.' He neglected to say he was flying there in the morning.

'Well, it must be the most beautiful part of England,' King said enthusiastically. His eyes sparkled as he described his favorite place. 'Picture this, small mountains that we call fells, beautiful lakes left over from the glaciers of the Ice Age, lovely sheep everywhere and limestone walls around lush green meadows.'

'It's clear that you're fond of the area,' Max said.

'I'm making myself homesick just talking about it. It's so lovely, I find it difficult to leave,' King concluded, sipping his beer. 'The problem is I have to make up my mind soon whether I want to stay in the newspaper business. Having someone run the Bugle on a short-term basis would give me time to decide.'

'I don't know . . . '

'You'd be doing me a big favor.' King pressed him to accept.

'Where's this paper anyway?'

'Up in the Lake District, Bowness-on-Windermere. Have you ever been there?'

'No, I can't say that I have.' It wasn't often that such an opportunity came along. The location was where he needed to be for his new assignment, and a cover as a newspaperman would be perfect. Also, a small paper wouldn't be much trouble. It would give him time for the real reason he was there.

Max could think of no excuse he could make to refuse King's offer. Before they parted, he let King talk him into managing the Bowness Bugle for a few weeks.

And here he was, running the paper and trying to figure how to make it successful. Within the last week he'd toured the area, talking to local residents in an attempt to find interesting news he could publish. With the tourist season past, Bowness and Windermere were quiet and there wasn't much going on. Except sheep. There were a lot of sheep in the area. Apparently sheep were very important to the local economy.

Max was tired of hearing about sheep and writing stories like the one he had just finished. His lip curled in disgust as he scanned the article on his desk.

The headline read *Farmer Sues Tourist Over Sheep*. The gist of the story was a tourist had run over a farmer's prize sheep. The tourist swore the stupid sheep was lying in the middle of a country lane on an extremely dark night. The Windermere police officer appearing on the scene found the motorist drunk.

Max threw a few darts at the board on the wall opposite his desk. He'd acquired a taste for English beer and darts the last few days. When one dart hit the bull's eye, he grinned.

Max considered the article again. One possible alternative to more sheep articles might be a human interest story on one of the local residents.

What secrets lurked behind the surface of these bland-faced people? The prim little spinster in the florist shop or a hotel owner might each have a secret life beyond imagination. Why not select one person and see what he found?

Max smiled at his foolishness, expecting to find anything unusual in the locals. But anything would be better than staying in the small office, puttering with the press and answering the telephone when it rang, which wasn't often.

The fact was he needed to establish his cover, so for the last few days, he'd spent most of his time at the Bugle, while his Yard counterpart kept him posted on Antonio. So far, the man appeared to be playing tourist, riding the steamboats on Windermere and visiting Beatrix Potter's Hilltop Farm. Maybe he'd move on. If he did, Max would be right behind him.

The phone rang and he grabbed it. 'Bowness Bugle. You make the news, we report it.' He winced, hearing his own voice chortle the paper's insipid motto. 'How can I help you?'

'Charley Stanhope's brat Clarissa comes home today,' a gravelly voice said. 'If you ask me, Bowness's been a heck of a lot better without the likes of her. Too bad she had to return.'

2

'Mmmm, . . . why do you say that?' Hearing a name he recognized, Max clutched the Bugle's office telephone tighter. He tried to keep his caller talking. Given enough time, he might be able to identify the voice.

'Those Stanhopes were never worth much,' his caller said. Resentment slid into his voice. 'Them with all their fancy ways and big homes. They always did what they damn well pleased.' The line went dead abruptly.

What a weird call. Max replaced the receiver. The man had confirmed what he'd already heard. Clarissa was on her way home. Why was she coming? To see family or was there another reason?

Max's growling stomach interrupted, reminding him that he'd missed breakfast by coming to work early. He checked the wall clock and found it was almost noon.

Eager to escape the small office, Max shrugged into his jacket, locked the door and hurried down the street to the pub. High overhead, a flock of geese honked as it headed south, drawing his attention. He stared after them.

Would he still be in Bowness when winter arrived? It didn't make much difference if he was. His only living relative was a retired cousin who lived in a small condo in Florida, supplementing his retirement income by taking tourists deep sea fishing. They exchanged Christmas cards every year.

Max still missed his parents. His father, a jovial baker always full of jokes and good will, and his sweet-dispositioned mother had never given up hope that their son would find a 'nice girl and settle down.'

It had been ten years last week since an intoxicated Brooklyn driver had killed the two people most dear to him. For a few moments, Max's grief mingled with a smoldering anger. Losing those you loved hurt too much. He'd be wise not to love anyone else. It was always possible he'd lose that person as well. Max pushed away his memories and focused on the present.

As he stepped into the smoky historic pub, Max gazed at the sparse group of men lounging there. One of these locals might be willing to talk about Clarissa's family.

Scotland Yard suspected Clarissa might be a link to Tony Grambello. Mario Grambello, Tony's ailing father, was now serving a life sentence in Dartmouth Prison. Tony went free until the authorities could prove he was

15

Antonio, the assassin.

In the pursuit of information, Max let another man win at darts before picking up the tab for a round of beers.

Standing with his foot on the bar rail, he chatted with his darts opponent. He wondered if any locals besides his caller felt bitter toward the Stanhopes.

When the conversation lagged, Max casually asked, 'Does a family by the name of Stanhope still live around here? Someone mentioned their name the other day.' He addressed the man who'd won their darts game.

Jeremy, a florid-faced ex-sailor in his mid-thirties, and the proud owner of the video shop down the street, took a swig of beer. Setting his mug on the bar counter, he wiped his mouth on his shirt sleeve before answering. 'Any bloke who grew up in Bowness would be able to tell you about that lot.'

'What'd they do? Rob the local bank?' Max grinned. Though he joked with the other man, he coolly observed his companion's movements and remarks.

'Nah, nothing like that. My relatives knew the family. Aunt Bertie worked as cleaning lady for old Mrs. Stanhope until Bertie won the lottery and ran off to Spain. Her

16

ex-husband's still around, though you wouldn't want to meet the sorry sod. Uncle Nigel still blames the Stanhopes for destroying his marriage.'

'Why is that?'

'He's crazy.' Jeremy shrugged. 'Nigel says if Auntie hadn't worked, she wouldn't have had the cash for lottery tickets.'

Maybe that's who called me. Max nodded and concentrated on steering the conversation back to the Stanhopes. 'The family was quite wealthy?'

'Rather. Old Stanhope had King's Grant built so his wife and boys could escape the summer heat in London. He'd work at his father's bank in the city then come up here weekends.'

'That sounds like a pleasant life.' Max waited for his new friend to tell him more.

'Yeah. Stephen, the older son, was a nice enough bloke, even if he did turn out a stuffy banker like his old man. Charley, the younger lad, was always in trouble. And he married an Italian. That upset his father.'

'Why?' Max's curiosity wasn't all due to his training.

'Old Mr. Stanhope hated Italians. I think he fought in World War II.' The other man shrugged. 'It's been a long time. Auntie always said young Charley was the splitting

17

image of his father. He ended up bad, too.'

'And Clarissa? How's she related to this bunch?'

'Ah, you heard about young Charley's baby sister. I fancied her myself when I was fifteen, not that it would ever have come to anything. The Stanhopes might as well have lived on another planet, they were so far above us common folk.

'Clarissa was a pretty blonde but very shy. If you ever saw her around the village, her big brother was always there, watching over her.

'I was away in the military when young Charley died. My mom sent me articles from the paper. Sad business, that.' Jeremy tilted his beer mug and drained it. Belching, he patted his stomach. 'Thanks, mate. Got to get back to the shop. Ta.' He walked out of the bar.

Interesting people, Max had to admit. An idea struck him. Use the Stanhopes as the subject for a newspaper story. It sure beat writing about sheep.

The bar help didn't object to wrapping his roast beef on rye so Max hurried back to his office, lunch in hand, and turned on the computer.

Though he took an occasional bite from the sandwich, he could have been eating hardtack for all the attention he paid his food while entering and searching the Papers section of Internet. Several older articles on the Stanhopes appeared, most in the 'Society' section of the Manchester Chronicle. It was disappointing not to find any current news on the family. One article gave brief mention to young Charley's drowning in Morcambe Bay five years ago.

That particular year nagged Max until he unlocked his desk drawer and glanced through his notes, confirming what he had suspected. Tony Grambello's brother had vanished that same year.

With his notes at hand, Max typed a rough draft on his word processor. All the while, his mind searched for angles.

He'd start with a brief mention of a few world-famous aristocrats with family problems then narrow the geographic area to Cumbria and discuss the Stanhopes, members of the local aristocracy. Maybe he could write more than one article on the family. Of course he must be careful not to print anything he couldn't verify.

He'd call Kings Grant Hotel later and ask Clarissa to let him do a human interest story on her return. It was possible she'd come to meet Antonio. The Task Force was most interested in knowing why Antonio was in the Lake District. If he made one false step, the authorities would be on him. He'd been lucky so far, eluding the law. Still, even his luck could run out.

★ ★ ★

That same afternoon Claire turned from the train window. A ruggedly attractive older man was staring at her from the aisle. His large hands twisted and turned the dapper tweed hat he held.

'Is this seat taken?' He gestured to the space beside her.

'Why . . . no, it's not.'

'Do you mind?'

Before she could suggest he sit somewhere else in the coach, he settled into the seat beside hers. Claire admitted privately that she was glad to have some company. Before he came, she'd been alone in the car.

'I wonder if you can help me?'

His accent was unmistakably American, a slight twang in his speech reminded her of the actor John Wayne. At least this American had good manners. Arranging her features into a courteous expression, she braced herself for the usual barrage of questions tourists asked. 'Yes?'

'Can you tell me the time? I just flew into Gatwick this morning and need to set my watch forward.'

'I'm sorry. I'm not wearing a watch.' That was the truth.

'Oh?' Doubt resounded in his voice. 'Never mind. I'll ask the conductor next time he comes around checking tickets.'

'I never wear a watch.' Claire held out her left arm, showing a bare wrist. For some reason, she felt compelled to give this stranger an explanation. 'There's almost always a clock handy, so why bother with a watch?' She smiled.

'That's a nasty scrape on your elbow,' he observed, pointing to her injured arm. 'Did you have an accident?'

She smoothed her sleeve down over her arm. 'It's nothing.' Claire wasn't about to tell him she'd hurt her elbow throwing herself off a railway platform.

He reminded her of a tutor she had once as a young girl. The man had been friendly to a point, yet he never let her forget he was her instructor and she was his pupil. 'Are you a teacher?'

'Is it that obvious?'

He held her attention now. 'Well, I guess so. Let me see.' His direct manner and his bearing prompted her to ask, 'Do you teach in a boys' school?'

Resting his head on his seat back, her new

companion flashed an amused grin, then his expression turned serious. 'Actually, I'm a psychology professor at a small private college in Virginia.'

'I'm sorry,' Claire said. 'That was just a wild guess.'

'No problem.' He patted her hand and gracefully shifted the focus of their conversation. 'I've been listening to you speak. If you don't mind my saying, you have a delightful, lilting accent. Are you from Cumbria?'

She nodded. 'I've been living in Devon but Bowness is home.'

'That's a beautiful place.'

'Oh, have you been there?'

'No, this is my first time. I'm up here, birdwatching. I once had a relative who resided near Bowness.'

Claire waited for the professor to elaborate. He didn't. 'Has it been a long time since he lived there?'

'Yes,' he said. He'd been quite chatty while they were talking about her or the area. Now that she was asking the questions, he seemed more reserved.

'My family has made their home in the village for years. Tell me your relative's name, perhaps I'd know him.'

The professor shook his head. 'He's deceased now.'

They rode on in silence until he put his hand over his mouth, masking a yawn. 'Excuse me.' He got to his feet, stretched then moved across the aisle.

Before she could tell him it wasn't allowed, he'd loosened his tie and removed one of the reserved signs. Her face must have mirrored her concern.

'Please don't look so distressed. I know these seats are reserved. To tell the truth, one of them happens to be mine. I sat beside you because I like company.' A yawn later the professor slipped off his loafers and lay back in the seat. 'Jet lag has caught up with me again. I never sleep on planes.'

'If you want to take a nap, go ahead,' she suggested. 'I'll wake you when we're approaching Oxenholme.'

'Thanks.' He lay back in his seat, closing his eyes.

Claire resumed watching the passing scenery from her window. The sight of herds of white sheep with black faces grazing in green fields lulled her until her own eyes grew heavy. Before she could doze off, the conductor walked briskly through the coach, pausing by her seat long enough to check her ticket and announce Oxenholme was the next stop.

Her traveling companion still slept in his

seat across the aisle. With his mouth half-open, he snored lightly. Since she had offered to wake him when it was time to leave the train, Claire called, 'Professor, wake up. We're almost to Oxenholme.'

His eyes popped open and he answered her in an alert voice. 'All right. Thank you, dear.' His ability to instantly switch from deep sleep to full consciousness amazed her.

Through the coach windows, Claire had observed the sky during their journey. Other than a brief shower, it had been a pleasant autumn day, so she assumed the temperature hadn't changed much since she boarded the train that morning.

As soon as they stood outside, Claire found the weather was much cooler in the Lake District. A brisk October wind was busily pushing fallen leaves, empty drink cans, candy wrappers and anything else in its path along the platform.

To escape the weather, Claire led the professor to shelter inside a tiny hut that'd been erected next to the Oxenholme station in honor of the Queen's Diamond Jubilee.

Her hands and feet grew colder by the minute. It was a relief to see the Windermere shuttle arrive.

The professor and Claire joined a few others who climbed aboard the three-car train. They again shared adjoining seats for the half-hour ride to their final destination.

During a pause in their conversation, the professor asked, 'Why did you move to Devon?'

'I needed a change of scene.' That was her usual answer. She didn't mention Charles or what had happened before her departure.

'I see,' he commented. 'And now you're on your way home. Will you stay in Bowness, or is this just a visit?'

That question struck her as a little too personal. She didn't even know the man's name. Claire became evasive. 'Well, I am quite fond of my aunt and I look forward to meeting my new cousins.' Why was this man so interested in her?

As the train pulled into the Windermere station, she smiled and waved to the tall auburn-haired woman waiting for her.

3

Claire stepped from the train into Kate's embrace.

'You look a lot better than last time I saw you,' Kate said. 'I like the way you're wearing your hair.' She touched Claire's sleek ash blonde hairdo. Kate's hair was arranged in a twist.

'I've been wearing it short since . . . ' Claire's voice faltered. Charles had always insisted she keep her hair long.

'I know.' Kate's expression was fond and understanding.

They walked down the platform and through the small station to Kate's waiting silver Range Rover. While climbing into the vehicle, Claire couldn't help noticing the back seat full of children's toys.

Kate checked the rear-view mirror before backing out of the parking slot.

The professor waved to Claire from across the parking lot as he climbed into a local taxi. The vehicle quickly sped away.

Kate stared. 'Who was that?'

'An American who sat by me on the train. I didn't get his name.' In retrospect, Claire marveled at her ease in talking to the professor. Remnants of shyness still lingered from her childhood. She wasn't comfortable with strangers, especially men.

'Is this his first time in the Lake District?'

'Yes. A relative of his used to live here,' Claire said. 'Stop acting like a policeman's wife.' She grinned.

With a laugh, Kate avoided another vehicle and changed lanes. 'Don't look now, but this policeman's wife will celebrate her fifth wedding anniversary this Chistmas.'

'Is everything all right in that department?' Though Claire couldn't put her finger on it, unflappable Kate seemed a little bemused. Also, there had been dark circles under Kate's green eyes when she'd removed her sunglasses to locate the car keys in her shoulder bag.

'Sure, other than the universal complaint, not enough time. Nick's busy at work and your niece and nephew keep me jumping.'

'I can't wait to meet them.' Claire had been tempted to return four years ago when the babies were born. Then she'd reconsidered. To make up for her absence at a time she knew Kate would have appreciated her company, Claire had sent two Stieff teddy bears for the children and a silk floral arrangement in a Waterford vase for Kate.

Claire again blessed her mother for her inheritance. Thanks to Charles' foolish investments, that was her only source of income except for The Folly. Should she sell it?

'I'll be right back,' Claire's aunt said as she parked outside a Safeway. Leaving the motor running, Kate ran inside for milk and bread. Soon they were moving again.

Kate gave a left turn signal by a stone wall where an elegant bronze sign announced King's Grant Hotel. The vehicle passed through the open gates onto a curving private road flanked by ancient boxwood hedges.

★   ★   ★

From a nearby field, Tony, the new hotel handyman, watched Kate's vehicle entering the hotel grounds through his binoculars. He focused on Claire in the passenger seat.

'What a pretty woman. And she's blonde. This may be more pleasant than I expected.'

★   ★   ★

Kate drove up the driveway, parking outside a gracious stone mansion once owned by her first husband, Claire's Uncle Stephen.

'It's just as I remembered it,' Claire

murmured. The old limestone building brought back bittersweet memories. Charles used to day-dream out loud about their living in that residence when Stephen was gone. It seemed a lifetime ago. 'I bet when Grandfather Stanhope built his summer home, he never dreamed it'd be converted into a hotel. You must be so proud.'

'One thing's sure,' Kate said. 'I couldn't have done it without Mattie, Diane and Chris. They're all gems.'

'Mattie hasn't retired, has she?'

'She wouldn't dare. We need her.' Kate smiled. 'Besides, Mattie loves running the place. With the help of two or three village girls, she keeps the hotel in pristine condition.'

'Does Diane still help you plan the menus?'

'Sure. That was my lucky day, meeting her at the newspaper in New York. If anyone had told me a New Yorker like Diane would fall in love with growing carrots and potatoes, I'd have fallen down laughing.' Kate chuckled. 'And before you ask, let me assure you that Diane remains in charge of our vegetable gardens.'

'I won't even bother to ask about Chris then,' Claire said. 'He was so head-over-heels in love with Diane, there's no way he'd leave as long as she's here.'

'Chris's so busy with the grounds and hotel repairs, I've talked him into hiring an assistant.'

'Did you ever get rid of Uncle Stephen's old car?'

'Are you kidding?' Kate grinned. 'So far, Chris has been able to keep the Rolls running. We don't ask how, though I suspect magic. However he does it, it's great for transporting guests.'

'It must be wonderful to have such loyal friends.' Claire tried not to sound envious, though she was. She had no close friends in Bowness or anywhere else.

'We're also business partners,' Kate reminded Claire. 'Give yourself a chance. You'll have some friends here before long.'

Kate turned off the ignition. Before getting out she said, 'I wrote you that we're remodeling our home?'

'Yes. So you're all staying in the hotel?'

'Right, in some rooms upstairs not in use for the hotel. It's like camping out, without the tents. Living in two rooms with a husband and two four-year-olds is a real challenge.'

'I bet the kids love being at the hotel. Mattie must spoil them rotten.' Claire recalled how the housekeeper had intimidated her when she was a small child until she found that under Mattie's stiff, starched apron was a kind, generous heart. Also she baked wonderful cookies.

'When I'm not around.' Kate sighed.

Worry pricked Claire again. *What's wrong with Kate? Never mind. I'll find out sooner or later.*

'Most of the other small hotels are closed now. Everybody's ready for a rest after last summer,' Kate said.

'Have your guests all left?' If that was the case, Kate would be free to spend more time with her. Claire scolded herself for being selfish. Still, she'd missed their camaraderie. They'd been friends since Kate had married Claire's Uncle Stephen. Nine years older, Kate had always seemed like an older sister.

'A climber left the hotel this morning,' Kate replied. 'He may be the last guest this season, though you can never tell. There's always a chance a few stragglers will come by if the good weather holds.'

'I hope he knows what he's doing. The steeper fells can be treacherous for novices.' Claire remembered hearing about accidents on the fells, even a few deaths.

'I think this man knew what he was about. He had the usual gear for climbing. And I caught him scanning the weather on television and taking notes.' Kate reached over and squeezed Claire's hand. 'I'm so glad you're home. It should be just the family for dinner tonight.'

Claire nodded in agreement. Kate thought of her staff as family. And in a way they were. If being fond of someone and liking their company meant you considered them family, she supposed Mattie, Diane and Chris were her family, too.

As Kate unlatched her seat belt, preparing to get out of the car, Claire hastened to say, 'Please try to remember I've changed my name. I'm Claire now. Clarissa belongs to the past.'

'I won't forget.' Kate led her inside.

A quick glance around the ground floor assured Claire that no major changes had been made in her absence. There was new wallpaper in the reception area. The cream background and blue floral pattern brightened the dark half-paneled hall.

A pretty girl in jeans, white shirt and a crisply starched blue pinafore came out of the office and handed Kate a note.

Smiling, Kate read it and passed it to Claire. 'Didn't I say not to worry about not knowing people here? You've just arrived and already a reporter from the Bowness Bugle has called, asking for you.'

'Bowness Bugle?' Claire grinned. 'What a ridiculous name.'

The phone rang. Kate leaned over the front desk to answer it. 'King's Grant Hotel. Just a moment.' With an amused expression on her face, Kate offered the receiver to Claire. 'It's the Bugle for you.'

Claire took the phone, listened then responded. 'No thank you. I can't imagine why you'd want to do a story on me.' She returned the phone to Kate who hung up the receiver. 'What nerve. I haven't even unpacked my suitcase yet a reporter wants to see me. How did the word get out that I'm back?'

'Your guess's good as mine.' Kate shrugged. 'It wasn't a secret. Maybe one of the girls who works here told a friend who also told a friend . . . You know how word spreads.'

'This man's American at its worse, the instant friend type, said his name's Max and he'll see me around town.' Claire couldn't help feeling annoyed. 'Not if I can help it. What a creep.' She wasted no time changing the subject. 'Where's everybody this afternoon? The place appears deserted.'

'Diane and Chris went house-hunting with a real estate agent this afternoon. I didn't see their Honda so they mustn't be back yet.' Kate replied. 'Mattie's car just pulled into the parking lot behind the hotel. She may've needed something from the new Safeway

33

where we stopped. The kids usually go with her. They nag her into buying them candy.'

Claire peered out of one of the windows, eager to get a glimpse of the housekeeper and the children. The back door opened and closed, then Claire heard footsteps and children's voices. A light giggle drifted to her. 'Well, my feelings are hurt.' She spoke in a loud voice, her hand gesturing towards the next room. 'I come all the way from Devon to see Nicky and Kayla and they aren't even here.'

Kate nodded. 'Maybe they went upstairs to take a nap.' She winked at Claire.

A small figure dressed in a brown and gold Winnie-the-Pooh top and slacks burst into the room.

'We're not napping,' the auburn-haired boy yelled, laughing like he was amused.

Claire swung Nicky into her arms. 'Ouch, you're a big guy,' she said, setting the sturdy little boy back on his feet. 'Where's your baby sister?' Nicky had been born first.

Kayla appeared. 'I'm not a baby,' she said, hiding behind her mother's skirt.

Claire smiled when Nicky's fair-haired twin sister approached and let her aunt give her a hug. 'No, you aren't.' If she believed in fairies, Claire would've sworn her niece Kayla was a changeling. Born to dark-haired parents, the child's flaxen locks were unusual.

Now Claire was doubly sorry she hadn't been there when Kate's children were born or learned to walk. 'I have presents for both of you.'

Nicky's large brown eyes stared at his new found relative. 'Is it a puppy?'

'No,' Claire said, ruffling his dark hair. 'You'll like it. I'll get it for you later.'

'Let me call Tony, our new handyman.' Kate picked up the phone and started to dial the number of the workroom. 'Your trunk is too heavy for either of us to haul upstairs.'

A moment later she replaced the receiver. 'I don't know where my mind is these days,' she admitted, shaking her head. 'I just remembered Tony doesn't join the staff until tonight.

'Chris asked him to start work yesterday. Tony begged off due to some personal business,' she said. 'If he doesn't show up soon, I'll get Chris to carry your luggage upstairs when they get back. Now, let me get you a cup of tea and we can talk.'

Before long Kate and Claire sat on the patio, enjoying Kate's own blend of peach nectar tea. The autumn breeze brought a sweet fragrance from the rose garden below where a few brave holdouts still bloomed.

While Claire and her aunt talked, the children entertained themselves coloring pictures and munching biscuits.

Later Kate escorted Claire to her room at the top of the stairs, the children trailing along behind.

Once the room had been Kate's. The day King's Grant Hotel had opened, the newly-dubbed Windermere Room and the Grasmere Room down the hall became master bedrooms for hotel guests.

Claire gave her young cousins a hug and promised to read them a story before their bedtime. 'See you later,' she called. Blowing them a kiss, she closed her door.

The spacious room was now decorated in yellow florals with a mock canopy over each twin bed matching the drapes. The decorating was forgotten once you reached the double windows.

What a glorious view. Claire watched a brief flurry of golden and crimson leaves cascading from the giant oaks and maples that trailed down the fell towards the lake.

She stood mesmerized until someone slammed a door downstairs, breaking the spell. Closing the drapes, she eased off her shoes and lay down on the bed to rest for a few minutes.

Years ago, Charles and she had discovered a short cut that reduced the distance between the hotel and their home to one mile. The rough path dipped into a thicket of evergreen forest then hugged the side of the fell, ending behind the Folly. Uncle Stephen had made them promise they wouldn't take the shortcut in bad weather since the path could be dangerous when slick.

Her family home, The Folly, an elegant pink brick mansard-roofed mansion, was closed now and dark. The splendid furniture was draped with sheeting, its windows dark and empty.

Who knew what ghosts roamed those empty rooms? A shiver ran down Claire's spine.

Enough of that, she told herself. Claire burrowed under the comforter on her bed like a small woodland creature finding shelter and closed her eyes. Just a brief rest before unpacking, she promised her weary body.

Later, a commotion in the hall interrupted her slumber. Groggy with sleep, Claire stumbled to the door, expecting to see Chris in the hall. Instead, she gaped in surprise at a stranger.

4

'Miss Stanhope?'

Tall, dark, from what she could see he appeared good looking. The light in the hall wasn't the greatest. His accent wasn't English. 'Yes?'

He gestured at the over-sized trunk resting on the floor at his feet.

So that was the noise she'd heard. He'd been carrying her trunk up the creaky old staircase and must've bumped against the wooden paneling. Claire hoped he hadn't damaged the walls. She fumbled mentally for the name of the new handyman. 'Tony?'

He nodded. 'I'm sorry you had to wait. I just got to work. Miss Kate asked me to bring your luggage to you.'

'Do you live in the village?'

'No, Miss.' A boyish smile slid across his face.

Tony neglected to mention where he was from. Claire didn't want to appear nosy yet he aroused her curiosity. She'd seen a number of handymen, none with a face like his. She fumbled mentally, searching for an apt description. A Botticelli angel. That was what came to mind, gazing at him. A tad annoyed at his reticence, she found herself returning his smile.

From Tony's appearance, Claire was sure he'd be popular with the local girls. It wouldn't take long for him to find a girl friend with those broad shoulders, black hair and boyish face. None of her business, of course.

She opened the door wider and he stepped inside. 'Thank you,' she said, fishing inside her shoulder bag for her change purse to give him something. She must've moved too slowly since by the time she located a tip, he'd gone. She stood in the middle of the room, holding the coin and feeling a little foolish.

★ ★ ★

Dinner was chaotic with the twins playing around and under the table while the adults tried to carry on a conversation.

Chris dropped by in time for dessert.

'Welcome home,' he said to Claire. Standing behind her, he squeezed her shoulder before pulling an extra chair to the table to sit between Nick and her. Kate and Mattie busied themselves, carrying servings of Kendal Mint Cake to the dining table from the kitchen.

'Where's Diane?' Claire had looked forward to seeing her.

Chris started eating his dessert as soon as Kate served him.

'Gatehouse,' he managed to say, pointing to his full mouth. It was obvious that Chris still enjoyed good food.

He poured himself a glass of water from the pitcher on the table. Wiping his mouth, he elaborated. 'Last I saw her, Diane had already started packing. If I know my wife, by this time tomorrow, we'll be ready to move to our new home.'

'So you did find a house,' Kate said, slipping back into her own chair. 'This place won't seem the same without you two living down the hill.'

'There won't be much difference,' Chris commented. 'We'll both still be here at work almost every day.'

Moving her dessert plate out of Nick's reach, Kate shook her head at him. 'I guess we need to find a new tenant.' She turned to Claire. 'What do you think? Should I ask the Bowness Bugle to run an ad?'

'I . . . guess.' Claire hadn't cared for the nosy Bugle reporter who'd called earlier.

'When do you plan to move, Chris?' Kate inquired.

'As soon as possible. The house's empty

right now. Our realtor just needs a deposit and I plan to take that to her office tomorrow, bright and early.'

'So if I place an ad in the Bugle, I can say the gatehouse will be available next week?'

'Before that, if I know Diane.' Chris's happy smile was a dead giveaway that his wife wasn't the only one delighted with the prospects of owning their first home. 'Thanks for the dessert. I'll see you all in the morning.' Chris patted Kayla and Nicky on their heads as he passed them on his way out of the room. Both children smiled at him. Stepping into the hall, Chris turned on his heel and asked, 'Where's Tony?'

'He needed to make a call and his cell phone wasn't working so he's using the office telephone,' Kate said. 'I invited him to have supper with us. He told me he'd already eaten. There's plenty of food left in case he changes his mind.'

'I just happened to walk into Porto Bello Restaurant the other day when the owner was ranting at Tony,' Chris explained to Claire. 'Mario was about to call the police because Tony was a little short of cash for his lunch.'

'That would've been a little harsh,' Kate said, adding, 'Tony seems to have good manners. Can you tell us any more about him? I know you said he'd hiked around

41

Cumbria until he ran out of funds. Has he given you any references you can check?'

'No, and I didn't press him. He was a student until this fall.' Chris scratched his head. 'The kid had tears in his eyes when I offered him a job. In a way, he reminded me of myself when I was younger.' With a wave, Chris left.

'You shouldn't have trouble renting the gatehouse.' Having visited there as a child, Claire remembered the little flat. It must have been tight quarters for two adults.

The children became wilder as their bedtime approached. Nicky chased Kayla around the dining table and the little girl tripped, fell and burst into tears.

Kate appeared weary of their antics. 'Okay, guys. Time for a bath.' She ignored Nicky and Kayla's loud complaints while herding them upstairs.

'I promised them a story.' Claire called after them.

'We'll see how they behave in the tub.' Kate's voice floated downstairs after she and the twins disappeared.

Mattie began clearing the table.

'Let me help you.' Claire started to rise.

'No, lass.' The housekeeper shook her head. 'You've had a long day.' She carried a stack of dishes into the kitchen.

'She's amazing, isn't she?' Claire watched Mattie through the open door to the kitchen. As always the older woman's posture was ramrod straight. Age had brought a few more wrinkles and more gray in her black hair. Still, she was the friend Claire remembered, tall and erect, strong-willed and determined.

'Yes, she is. She makes me weary sometimes, she's so energetic,' Nick said.

Kate's husband appeared tired and quiet. Claire reminded herself that the position of Superintendent of Police must be most demanding.

She studied Nick, not missing the few streaks of gray in his dark hair. He'd aged since she'd seen him last. And gained a few pounds. No wonder with Kate's cooking. Somehow, Nick didn't appear as dashing a figure as she remembered. She reminded herself that she'd been younger and more impressionable when he'd come into their lives.

Claire recalled Kate and Nick's meeting. The first weekend King's Grant Hotel was open, an older Cornish guest had been found dead in his room. The local police department had sent Nick Connor, their youngest Detective Chief Inspector.

Nick investigated the crime and soon concluded the intended victim was Kate

43

rather than the Cornishman. Thrown together by his assignment, Kate and Nick soon fell in love.

Later, tragedy stuck. Charles had come close to killing Kate. He lost his own life in the process.

A deep sigh escaped Claire's lips.

'Are you all right?' Nick asked.

'I . . . guess. I was remembering when we met.'

'That's all in the past.' Nick's tone became gentler as he added, 'Now's the time to look forward to the future.'

'You're right. And I love being here with you, Kate and the children.' She put away her memories. 'I just hope you don't mind my staying here while I decide what I want to do.' The last thing she wanted was to be a nuisance.

'Of course I don't.' Nick paused before asking, 'Have you made a decision about your home?'

'Not yet. I haven't been there yet.' She hadn't slept a night under her own roof since Charles' death. Sometime soon she must visit The Folly, if for no other reason than to see what condition the house was in. Maybe she should sell it.

'Under the circumstances, I can see why you wouldn't be in too big a hurry.' Nick frowned, as if remembering the time that had been painful for them all. He reached across the table and touched her hand. 'Don't sell the place until you're sure you won't regret it later.'

'I won't,' Claire promised. 'But the way I feel now, I don't know if I can live there again.'

'Maybe you could redecorate,' he said.

Kate came back downstairs with a flushed face and her clothing damp. 'Claire, if you meant what you said, the kids would love a story.'

'Let me get the books I brought them from Devon,' she said and hurried from the room.

Starting up the stairs, Claire heard the deep rumble of Nick's voice.

'Kate, have you decided what you want to do?'

A little ashamed to be eavesdropping, Claire nevertheless paused to listen. Kate either didn't reply or her response was too low to hear.

Claire hurried upstairs, found the picture books, and carried them to the temporary nursery. 'Are you ready?'

'Sure,' Nicky said from his youth bed. Almost a miniature of his father, his shiny clean face beamed at her.

In her letters to Claire, Kate had said her

children were as different as night and day. Nicky was outgoing and gregarious while Kayla was quiet and shy, though she knew how to get her way with her brother. All the little girl had to do was shed a few tears and Nicky would give in, do whatever she wanted.

Oh, well. People were different, even twins. Claire read the stories then kissed Nicky and Kayla's rosy cheeks and wished them good night.

'We need to kiss Mommy and Daddy, too,' Nicky informed her.

'All right, I'll tell them.'

Once Nick and Kate appeared, the children went into what appeared to be a regular bedtime routine.

'Can I have a glass of water?' Nicky asked.

Kayla fretted, looking under her covers. 'Where's my dolly?'

At first Claire marveled at Kate's patience, then hearing a trace of weariness creep into her aunt's words, Claire stepped in to help. 'If you go to sleep, you both can take a peek in my magical suitcase tomorrow.'

That caught their interest. 'Suitcases aren't magic,' Nicky said. Though he scoffed at her, he didn't sound too sure.

'Tell my suitcase that and see what happens,' Claire replied. She tried to smile mysteriously.

Once the children fell asleep, Kate and Nick invited Claire to come back downstairs for a glass of wine. Pleading fatigue, she declined.

Weary, she stepped into the footed tub in her bathroom, sinking into hot water scented with Kate's favorite bath salts. Claire sighed, inhaling the scent of hyacinth. The unpacking could wait until tomorrow.

A few minutes later she lay in bed. What a day. A lot had happened since she'd left her Devon apartment. There was no reason to tell Kate about the emergency at the railway station.

★　★　★

'Claire appeared a little subdued while we were talking earlier,' Nick commented to Kate in their bedroom. 'Do you think she's had second thoughts about coming home?'

'It's her first day back. Let's give her time to adjust.' Kate let down her auburn hair and began brushing it one hundred strokes, her ritual every night.

Nick took over her task as he did every evening unless he was detained at the constabulary. Those nights Kate preferred to forget since she didn't like going to bed alone.

The last few months he'd stopped waking her if she was asleep when he came home, even though she'd made it clear she didn't mind. She missed talking to him at bedtime and the comfort of falling asleep in his arms.

'You didn't answer my question yet.' He stopped brushing her hair, bent to kiss her bare shoulder.

'Nick, don't pressure me, all right?' She moved away a little and he straightened, still holding the hairbrush.

'We need to decide soon. We're not getting any younger.'

'You make it sound like we're both ready for a nursing home.' Kate stood, annoyed at the way he'd misread her. 'Just because I'm not in a big hurry to have another child doesn't mean we won't ever have another baby. Nicky and Kayla already keep me hopping all day long. Do you really want me to have a baby to tend while they're so young?'

'Detective Morris and his wife have four kids under seven and they manage, on less dough than we have.' Nick persisted, his neck starting to turn red, a sure sign he was upset.

'Let's sleep on it, love,' Kate cautioned him, tiptoeing to kiss his cheek. 'We're both tired tonight. Let's not say anything we don't mean.'

'If that's what you want.' Nick crossed the room to a chest and fumbled around in a drawer until Kate came and found him a matching pair of pajamas. He went into the adjoining bathroom to undress, a clear indication he was annoyed.

5

The next morning the weather turned colder and Claire shivered while closing a bedroom window. She'd grown accustomed to sleeping with a window open in Devon. She reminded herself she was back in Cumbria in October.

While dressing in jeans and shirt, she added a warm cardigan to her outfit before walking downstairs for breakfast.

Sipping her orange juice, Claire sat at the dining room table and skimmed the news in the morning paper. She could hear Mattie in the kitchen, cooking and talking to the children.

Kate hadn't appeared yet and neither the housekeeper nor she made a move to wake her. It wouldn't hurt Kate to get a little extra sleep. The children kept her busy all day.

The lead story in that day's Bowness Bugle covered Cumbria county politics. Since she wasn't interested in the political scene, Claire skipped that page, flipping instead to the Bowness-Windermere section to brush up on local news.

The first time she read the headline, 'Wealthy Families Not Exempt from Trouble,'

Claire didn't pay much attention. Then the name Stanhope caught her eye. 'I don't believe it,' she muttered. 'The nerve of that creep.'

Clutching the newspaper, she pushed her chair back, rushed into the kitchen and ran right into Mattie's starched apron. Claire waved the latest edition of the Bowness Bugle under the startled housekeeper's nose. 'Have you seen this?'

'No, I haven't had time,' Mattie replied, her voice calm. The older woman was seldom ruffled by the world around her. 'I'm about to give the children their breakfast. Why don't you join us?' Mattie switched off the color television in the kitchen.

'Cartoons,' protested Nicky and Kayla in unison.

'Later,' the housekeeper promised. 'Now it's time to eat breakfast.' She led the children to the kitchen table, helping them into their booster seats, tying bibs around their necks.

'It's monstrous.' Claire managed to keep her voice calm though she was quite disturbed. 'Just when people have forgotten the Stanhopes, along comes a reporter to dig it all up again.'

Mattie finished sprinkling the children's oatmeal with brown sugar. 'Pass me that bowl of raisins, please,' she asked Claire in a pleasant tone. Over Kayla and Nicky's heads, Mattie's gaze locked with Claire's. The housekeeper touched her finger to her lips. Her message was clear. Be careful what you say!

'Right, we'll talk later.' Claire stifled her anger while helping herself to some oatmeal. 'Ummmm, it's good.'

Folding the offensive section of newspaper, she slipped it into her shoulder bag. There was no reason to upset Kate.

As soon as they'd had breakfast, Claire offered to take the children for a walk. They ran across the lawn ahead of her, stopping now and then to look back and see if she was coming.

Anger still flickered inside her, yet Claire realized she couldn't do a thing that moment. Later, she promised herself.

While the children played outside with their toys, Mattie appeared in the doorway. She jingled her car keys. 'I'm going to Safeway if anyone wants to go along.' They ran to her and she helped them into their car seats.

Moments later, Mattie's Ford headed down the driveway. The children waved to Claire through the rear windows of the vehicle.

★   ★   ★

52

Alone again, Claire had time to think about the Bugle article and consider the best way to approach the newspaper. She'd always believed the direct approach was best. She'd just be polite and ask for no more stories about her family.

Leaving Kate a note she was borrowing her vehicle, Claire drove down the hill to the business district. She had no trouble locating the newspaper in a small space over a realtor's office.

Braced for a confrontation, she knocked on the Bowness Bugle's door. No one responded right away, then she heard a slight rustling inside and the door opened.

A tall dark-haired man with a neat moustache peered out at her. His gray eyes seemed to look right through her.

'Yeah?'

'I'm Claire Stanhope,' she began.

'Did you want something?'

She recognized his voice from his phone call the day she arrived. 'If you have a moment, I'd like to speak to you.'

'Come in.' He flung the door open then strode ahead of her into a small office. Gesturing to a smaller chair, he leaned on a handsome mahogany desk.

Claire sat down and got right to the point. 'The Bugle ran an article about my family, the Stanhopes. It appeared this morning in the paper,' she said.

'Pretty good, eh?' He opened a box on the desk and extracted a cigar. While she watched, he sniffed at the cigar.

Claire shrugged. 'The writing was all right. What I'm concerned about is what you said.' Faced with his rude behavior, her own good manners and patience began to slip away.

'Like what?' He shifted his attention from the cigar to her.

'You dug up a lot about the Stanhopes that was better left buried in the past.' Her temper began to flare in spite of her best intentions. 'Would you please stop writing about my family?'

'I'm sorry. That's not possible.' His tone was matter-of-fact, not apologetic. 'Let me explain. The Stanhopes are local, the family's been around here a long time so their name's well-known. People find them fascinating.'

'So what? That's no excuse to — '

He held up his hand, interrupting Claire. 'Do you realize there're seven times as many sheep in Cumbria as people?'

'Excuse me?' Claire frowned, unable to see the connection between her family and sheep.

'A lot of the local news concerns sheep. That doesn't make for stimulating reading. My poor readers are bored to death and hungry for a little scandal — '

'I resent that remark.' She could feel her cheeks flushing.

'If you'll let me finish?'

She nodded.

'Thank you. As I was saying, my readers need a little scandal to liven up their otherwise dull lives. The Stanhopes are just what I need to sell papers.'

'Watch how you use the word scandal. You happen to be talking about my family.' Feeling her temper rising, Claire paused. 'How can I convince you what you're doing is wrong?'

'You can't. Would you mind leaving? I need to attend to some business.' While talking, he'd come around the desk. Now he walked her to the door. 'Oh, before you leave, there's one other matter.' Without warning, he gathered her into his arms and began to kiss her.

Claire struggled yet she couldn't break free. She reasoned that he was no real threat to her since they were standing in the open doorway and there were other offices along the corridor.

If she couldn't escape, she'd make kissing her as unappealing as possible. To accomplish this, Claire went limp as a dust rag. No man wanted to kiss someone who didn't respond.

He'd soon get the message and let her go.

But he kept kissing her. Soon she felt herself growing warmer and warmer. At last she gave in and returned his kiss.

Claire's experience in kissing was limited to a few stolen kisses from business associates of Charles. Also, the florist shop owner in Devon, whose clothes smelled of moth balls, had kissed her once when his wife was at home ill. His slobbery kiss reminded her of a puppy she had as a child.

No one had ever kissed her like the Bowness Bugle man. Claire became so absorbed in the sheer pleasure of kissing him, she almost fell when he released her.

'Are you all right?' His voice sounded amused.

Claire blushed, too embarrassed to look him in the eye. 'Ah, I'm fine, thank you.' She smoothed her hair.

'You don't have to thank me. It was my pleasure, Miss. I always enjoy kissing a pretty girl.' When she raised her eyes and gazed in his direction, he grinned like a naughty boy caught doing God only knows what.

'I wasn't thanking you, you buffoon.' Claire didn't know when she'd been so furious.

Ignoring her rage, he patted her on the head. 'Fun's over so run along, that's a dear. I've a paper to publish.' He opened the door and stood aside.

Claire glared as she marched out of his office. If looks could kill, he'd have been a dead man that instant.

Still a little unsteady, she got in Kate's car and drove back to the hotel. Along the way, she considered her brief encounter, her thoughts unpleasant. Loathsome brute forcing himself on her. She hoped she never saw him again.

* ★ *

That afternoon Claire sat on one of the gray limestone walls defining the hotel's boundaries. The oaks' slow shedding of their golden leaves, a gray-blue Lake Windermere downhill with seagulls flying above, it was impossible not to relax in the midst of so much beauty. Her anger melted away.

She wasn't sure what had upset her most that morning, the newspaper man's words or his kiss. One thing was sure, if she was ever in his presence again, she'd stay as far away from him as possible. Other women might like being grabbed and kissed. She preferred picking the men she kissed. He'd taken advantage of her. That wouldn't happen again. Perhaps she'd take someone else with her if she ever had to visit the newspaper office again.

Meanwhile, she hoped the Bugle found more interesting topics than her family. She wanted to forget she'd ever met him.

Reminding herself that she'd come outside to relax, Claire focused on a pleasant ramble in the woods and a picnic.

When she'd announced her plans to hike around the area, Mattie insisted on packing her a lunch. A quick peek into the basket the housekeeper had given her revealed a turkey sandwich, a shiny red apple and four of Mattie's chocolate chip cookies.

These golden days wouldn't last much longer. Claire resolved to make the most of them. Soon the cold winds would howl and the first snows would appear on the higher fells.

Sliding off the wall, she explored the grounds she'd known well as a child. Today it seemed both unknown and familiar.

She walked by a gnawed hollow tree where Charles and she'd played as children. It was where they hid secret messages for each other. Resisting the urge to check the tree for messages, Claire walked on.

Down the driveway, she caught sight of the handyman raking leaves. 'Hello,' she called to Tony and waved, hoping he'd join her for a quick chat. He flashed a shy smile then turned back to his raking.

She shrugged and continued her stroll through the grounds. When she happened to look back, Tony was gone.

Later she stopped and sat on a stump of a tree in the middle of the woods, alone except for a chattering gray squirrel that appeared to watch her every move. Perhaps he imagined she was after the cache of nuts he'd buried for the winter.

On her way back to the hotel, she had caught another glimpse of Tony. This time he sat on the stone wall at the entrance to the grounds. From where she stood, he appeared engrossed in conversation with someone on a cell phone.

When she approached he looked up. Tucking the phone into his jacket, he jumped off the wall.

'Hi again,' she said. 'Isn't it time you took a break?'

'I guess so, Miss.' He stood at attention.

'My name is Claire,' she reminded him in a firm voice. 'How about a cookie? I'll share if you'll talk to me.'

'Okay.' He smiled.

She'd always been wary of too handsome men with their king-sized egos. Tony seemed to be the exception, oblivious to his appearance. If she were an artist, she'd sketch him.

Claire couldn't draw, so she did the next best thing. Acting on impulse, she pulled her camera from her pocket and snapped his picture before he realized what she was doing.

'Hey. Don't do that.' Anger flashed across his face.

'I already did,' she said, 'though it probably won't turn out. The light's not good under these trees.' That was a barefaced lie since her camera adjusted to any light.

He didn't appear happy about having his picture taken. Odd. As handsome as he was, Tony must've had his picture taken lots of times.

They sat on the low wall, sharing the cookies Mattie had included from the large wooden cookie jar in the hotel kitchen.

'Tell me about yourself,' Claire said. 'Like how old are you?' She hoped he was older than he looked.

He brushed cookie crumbs off his face. 'Twenty-two.'

Ye gads! A mere child. And yet Claire found herself studying him whenever Tony looked elsewhere. She should know better, she was twenty-six. 'I bet you have lots of brothers and sisters.'

'No, there's just my father and me,' he said.

'I just have Kate. I did have a brother — '

'You sound so sad.' He interrupted her before she could finish. 'What happened to him?'

'He died.' It still hurt to talk about Charles. 'My brother died several years ago.'

'So did mine. You're alone, except for your father. Does he live around here?'

A frown clouded Tony's face. 'No, he doesn't.'

'Do you go to see him?'

'When there's time.' Tony walked with her up the driveway, nodded and left her.

Entering the foyer, she met Kate.

'Did you enjoy your walk?'

Kate's eyes were red as if she'd been crying. 'Are you all right?' Claire wished she could help her aunt, whatever it was that troubled her.

'It'll all work out.' Kate's smile was shaky. 'Nick insists on having his own way too much.'

'I'm sorry. This may not be a good time for me to be here.' Claire was afraid to ask if her presence was causing a problem. If it was, where would she go? Back to the furnished flat in Devon? Even that was no longer hers.

That was the end of their discussion. That evening Nick entertained them all with humorous stories of people he'd met at the station. Kate on the other hand was quiet and pensive.

During the night both twins woke up, burning with fever. Claire heard them crying and hurried upstairs to help Kate. Ill, the children seemed younger. They clung to their mother.

Two days later Kayla and Nicky seemed much better. Kate and she were bone-weary from lack of sleep.

Kate and she didn't argue when Mattie shooed them both out of the house, saying, 'I'm capable of taking care of those little ones for a few hours. Go get your hair done or do some shopping. You both have been cooped up in this house long enough.'

Claire came downstairs and found Kate waiting. 'I'm ready if you are,' she said and started to follow her aunt to the car when the phone rang. Later she'd remember that time as their last moment of peace before the sky fell.

6

Constable Dennis Leary sat behind the wheel of one of Windermere Police Department's late model Fords, driving back to work after a meeting in Muncaster. He kept his eyes on the road while chatting with Pat Martin, his fellow officer and buddy.

Dennis didn't expect to remain a lowly constable forever. He viewed these interdepartmental meetings as an indication his superiors saw his potential. They were giving him the chance to grow and develop as a police officer. He'd do all he could to advance in the department, but one thing he wouldn't do, drink the miserable brew offered at the meetings. He always carried along his own thermos of fresh-perked coffee.

They were traveling east toward Windermere when the shape and color of a car parked by a rustic cabin off the main road caught his attention. Dennis slowed down, put on his turn signal then pulled off the road.

'Hey, where're you going?' Pat looked around.

'Just want to check out something,' he said. Turning off the ignition, Dennis got out and walked over to the other car. Seen up close, there was no doubt it was one of Windermere Police Department's tan vehicles.

He touched the hood of the car. It felt cold so it had been parked there for awhile. The driver was nowhere in sight.

Pat climbed from their own vehicle and followed his friend up the rough path to the cabin.

Dennis knocked on the door.

'Now what do you think you're doing?' Pat seemed bewildered at his behavior. 'There's got to be a good reason for that car being here. Maybe this cabin belongs to a Windermere Police Department employee. Come on, we'll be late getting back.'

'None of our people live way out here,' Dennis said. He wasn't going anywhere until he discovered what that vehicle was doing there.

Dennis knocked on the cabin door then stood back and waited for its occupant to respond. No answer came so he knocked a second and third time.

'There's something about this that bothers me,' he told his buddy. While waiting for someone to answer, his hand jiggled the doorknob. When the door creaked open, he jerked back. 'Come on.' Without waiting for his friend, Dennis crept into the cabin.

Inside was dim and shadowy, the sole light entered the building through one small, high window opposite the door. Dennis inhaled a musty odor. It wasn't a place that was used often.

His buddy followed him inside.

As his eyes became accustomed to the darkness, Dennis could make out a large shape resting on a bed at the back of the room. 'Careful,' he said to Pat. They both moved with caution toward the figure.

At closer range, Dennis could see a large man who appeared asleep, then his nostrils inhaled the odor of whisky. The guy wasn't asleep, he was drunk, reeked of whisky.

He put his hand on the man's shoulder. 'Hey, buddy. Wake up. Why's that police car parked out front?'

The man groaned and rolled over on his side. Dennis got a good glimpse of his face.

Superintendent Nick Connor. What the hell is he doing here?

Pat's gaping mouth and glassy-eyed stare told Dennis that his buddy was as shocked as he. In silence, they watched Nick Connor for a minute or so until the senior officer groaned.

Mobilized by the sounds Nick was making, Dennis sprung into action. 'I'll be right back.' He tossed the words over his shoulder to Pat while darting outside to their vehicle.

Opening the rear car door, Dennis snatched his thermos and hurried back inside the cabin. 'Here, help me prop him up. Maybe we can get him to drink some coffee.'

They managed to get Nick into a sitting position in spite of his protesting and trying to slide off the bed. Some of the coffee spilled on the bed covers. Some also found its way down Nick's throat.

Next, Dennis and Pat raised the drowsy superintendent to his feet so they could march him up and down.

While they walked, Dennis studied the room. It was sparsely furnished, just the king-size bed, a rustic table and two chairs. Not a room equipped for a long-term stay, more like a place someone could rest for a few hours or overnight. Did the cabin belong to their boss? Dennis wondered if it was used by people having an affair.

After walking and drinking black coffee, Nick became more alert. 'What the hell are you guys doing?' He glared at the junior officers.

Dennis glanced in Pat's direction. When his friend shrugged, Dennis took a deep breath and answered his superior. 'Sir, we found you here asleep, well not asleep, more like passed out.'

'The last thing I remember is being in my office,' Nick said. 'Where are we anyway?'

'In a cabin near Muncaster. Did someone ask you to come out here today?' Dennis tried to help the Superintendent remember.

Nick ran his hands through his hair. 'An hysterical woman called me at work this morning. She begged me to meet her here. She thought her life was in danger yet she was afraid to come to police headquarters.'

'Who was she? Somebody you know?'

Nick sat on the side of the bed, rubbing his forehead. 'I've got one lousy headache. Would you see if this dump has any water? There's a packet of aspirin in my sportscoat pocket.'

Dennis looked around. Earlier he'd been so focused on Nick, he hadn't noticed the closed door across the room. Maybe it led to a kitchen or bathroom. 'Hold on, sir,' he said. 'Let me take a look around.'

He opened the door and turned on the light. 'It's a small kitchen. Wait a minute, I'll see if the water is turned on.' Moments later he called, 'Pat, would you come in here?'

As Pat entered the kitchen, Dennis pointed.

Pat let out a short, low whistle. 'Sir,' he called to Nick, 'there's something you should see.'

Nick appeared in the doorway. 'What is it,

boys? All I wanted was a glass of water, for Pete's sake.' He stopped cold when he entered the kitchen and swore softly.

Dennis stood beside the body of a young blonde who lay like a discarded rag in a crumpled heap in a corner of the room. He knelt and took her pulse then lay her arm back on her body. 'She's dead.' His gaze fixed on Nick. 'Could this be the woman who wanted to meet you here?'

Nick glanced at the young woman's face. He paled. 'It's possible. All I can say is I've never seen her before.'

'Be careful not to touch anything in this room,' Dennis cautioned his superior. 'Why don't you go back in the other room and sit down, sir? I need to call headquarters.'

Nick swayed on his feet. 'You don't suspect me? I don't know anything about her, dammit.'

Dennis wouldn't meet his superior's angry stare.

★ ★ ★

The phone rang as Claire and Kate were leaving the hotel. Kate ran back inside to answer it.

From the porch, Claire heard Kate's voice answering the telephone. Then there was a dull thump.

'What is it?' Claire came inside. The dazed expression on her aunt's face alarmed Claire.

Kate wiped her eyes. 'Nick called from headquarters.'

'So? That's where he works,' Claire said.

'No, you don't understand.' Kate's voice became shrill. 'He's been arrested as a murder suspect. Nick asked me to find him a solicitor.'

Stunned, Claire struggled to absorb her aunt's news. She shook her head to clear it. It had been years since she'd lived in Bowness, she had no idea whom to call. The criminal solicitor who'd helped her five years ago came to mind. 'April, call Percy April. He may still have a law practice here.'

Kate opened the local telephone directory and proceeded to drop it on the floor. 'Would you mind calling him?' She bit her lip and appeared on the verge of tears.

'Katie, here, let me help you.' Claire eased Kate into a chair, got her a glass of water. 'It'll be all right. This's all a horrible mistake.'

Kate had always been there when Claire needed her. She'd vowed if she ever had the opportunity to help her aunt, she would. But she'd never expected anything like this.

It was a relief to find the solicitor's office listed in the local directory. Claire wasted no time dialing Percy's office. In less than a minute she had him on the line.

'How long have you been back?' The warm tone of his voice made it apparent he was pleased to hear from her. He must've thought she was in town on a visit since he said, 'perhaps we can have dinner while you're here.'

'Thanks. This isn't a social call.' Maybe her impression of him had been correct. During the time he was her solicitor, she'd imagined Percy found her attractive, though she'd felt nothing for him. Now wasn't the time to analyze her feelings for a man she'd never expected to see again. Claire explained her call.

'I have another appointment in a few minutes,' he responded. 'As soon as that's over, I'll visit police headquarters and see Nick. Stay home. I'll call you back.'

Claire hung up and turned to Kate.

'I'm so glad you're here.' Kate's color was returning and she managed a shaky smile. 'Please help me. Nick and I haven't been getting along too well. Still, I don't want to lose him.'

'You won't. I promise you that. We'll find out what's happened and why he's been arrested. Percy will see Nick today.'

'The children.' Kate's eyes teared. 'I can't leave them.'

Claire nodded. The shock of Nick's news had made her forget the twins momentarily. They were both still under the weather. Just yesterday she'd helped Kate take them to the pediatrician. 'You stay with Nicky and Kayla. I'll make a quick trip to headquarters and see what I can learn. If the police let anyone see Nick, it'll be Percy. I'll stay there until I can talk to him. The moment I have news, I'll call you.'

Kate handed Claire her car keys. 'You've driven my car.'

'Yes, the other day.' Her trip to the village had been the first time she'd driven a motor vehicle in five years. In the Devon village where she'd settled, she walked everywhere.

Hours later, she called Kate. 'Nick was found unconscious in a cabin near Muncaster with a dead woman. They're holding him as a murder suspect.'

Kate began to sob.

Claire could've kicked herself for being so blunt, yet no matter how she said it, Kate would've been upset. 'Hold on. We've got to be strong.'

'I don't understand. What was he doing there?'

'According to the police, he was drunk, Kate.'

'That's absurd. Nick told me that he'd only

been drunk once in his life.'

'When was that?'

'Once before we married.'

'What happened?'

'I don't know. He just said he got drunk with an old chum.' Kate paused. 'Who was the woman?'

Claire heard anger in Kate's words. 'They haven't identified her yet.' Claire hesitated. 'Was Nick having an affair?'

'Of course not.'

'Percy will get him out on bail.'

★ ★ ★

Later that evening Claire returned home. A hollow-eyed Kate waited for her downstairs in the library. She got to her feet as Claire entered the room.

'How bad is it?'

'It may be awhile before Nick can come home.'

'Why? He's only a suspect, isn't he?' Kate's voice was hoarse, a sign she'd been crying.

'He was found there in the cabin with the woman's body. And there's no evidence of anyone else being there. Also, Nick was in a drunken stupor when the two constables found him.' It didn't look good for Nick, but she wasn't about to say that to Kate.

'Who was the woman? Did he know her?'

'He swears he didn't,' she said. Claire hoped Nick was telling the truth. She knew from personal experience how one lie could lead to another and another. Before you knew it, you'd trapped yourself in a web of deceit.

'I hope he didn't.' Kate sat in silence.

'Of course he didn't.' Claire tried to sound reassuring. 'Percy will take care of things. Don't worry too much.'

She helped Kate to bed, sat by her until she fell asleep.

That night Claire slept little herself. Had Nick lied? Maybe he was afraid to tell the truth.

★ ★ ★

Next morning Claire woke to the rattling of the tea service being set down on the coffee table in the hotel library. 'What?' For a moment, she didn't know where she was.

Mattie leaned over her, an anxious expression on her wrinkled face. 'Why are you down here so early? Has something else happened?'

'I couldn't sleep.' Claire stretched. Every muscle in her body was stiff from lying curled up on the small sofa. 'I came down here to think while the house was quiet.'

73

'I just looked in on Kate and she's asleep.' Mattie wrung her hands. 'Is there anything I can do?'

'Help Kate with the children when I'm not here, try to keep her busy,' Claire said. 'I'm sure she'll want to see Nick today.' She took a close look at the housekeeper. 'Have they been having marital problems?'

Mattie gazed past Claire. 'There's been something. I don't know . . . You'd better ask Kate.'

'Ask me what?' In her gown and robe, Kate wandered into the room. Claire hadn't heard her on the stairs.

'What's been wrong between Nick and you?'

'It doesn't have anything to do with his being suspected of murder,' Kate said right away.

'We all know he's innocent. I'm just trying to understand what's going on here. If I knew, maybe I could think of some way to help Nick. Was he seeing someone else?'

Kate sank into a chair. 'Of course not.'

'Then what is it?'

'If you must know, he's been after me to have another child and I'm not ready,' Kate said.

'I see, so he's been unhappy?'

'We both have. Yesterday I gave in, told him

74

we'll try for another baby soon.'

'And there's nothing else?' Claire studied Kate.

'Not that I know.'

The morning mail slid through the slot on the front door of the hotel. It clunked, hitting the hardwood floor. Claire jerked.

Mattie stepped into the foyer, scooped up the mail and handed it to Kate.

'Oh, no. Not another one.' Kate held a plain hand-printed envelope addressed to her. She slit the envelope with a letter opener then unfolded the paper inside.

She read the letter then balled it up and started to throw it into the fire Mattie had stoked minutes ago.

'Stop.' Claire grabbed Kate's arm. 'Can I see that before you destroy it?'

'It's just another of those nasty letters,' Kate said.

'Another? You mean there're more?'

'One last week. I guess I should've shown it to Nick. I knew it'd upset him so I burned it.'

'Let me see the letter you just received.' Taking it from her aunt's hand, Claire smoothed out the paper and examined it.

She frowned after reading the letter. 'You're right. This isn't something you'd send a friend. It says Nick's been cheating on you, but it doesn't give any specifics. Do you know anyone who'd hate you or Nick enough to write such trash?'

'Well, yes,' Kate admitted with reluctance. 'But I thought she must've moved away or forgotten us by now. It's been a long time since we heard from her.'

'Who are you referring to?'

7

Kate stared into the fire for a few moments before answering. 'What do you know about Nick's first marriage?'

'Just what you've told me,' Claire said. 'He and his wife had serious problems and he filed for divorce.'

'Under the circumstances, I'm sure he won't mind our discussing it. Nick told me that he married an illusion.'

'Illusion?' Claire frowned. 'I don't understand.'

'The woman he thought he knew didn't exist. Valerie just pretended to be honest and forthright. In their first weeks of marriage, she revealed her true nature. She was a devious schemer. Nick caught her in so many lies he was forced to admit the marriage was a terrible mistake.

'There was no doubt the woman was disturbed. Much to my regret, I met her once before Nick and I married. On that occasion, Valerie almost convinced me that Nick and she were back together. Later, Nick's father-in-law informed him that a psychiatrist had diagnosed Valerie as a pathological liar.'

Kate's voice trembled. 'Her father said it appeared Valerie found lying easier than telling the truth.'

'Where is she now? Does she live around here?' Claire hoped not since just talking about Nick's ex-wife upset Kate. Was her aunt afraid of the woman?

'Still in Manchester, I expect. That's where Nick and she grew up. Her father and Nick became friends during the marriage. He still hears from his ex-father-in-law once in a while. Also, Nick paid for Valerie's psychiatric visits for years.'

'Even if Valerie sent you hate mail, she wouldn't want Nick to go to prison for someone else's crime, would she?'

'I wouldn't think so,' Kate said, thoughtfully. 'Unless she's convinced herself that he's somehow involved.'

'Percy needs to know about the letter.' Claire phoned the solicitor's office. Nick's attorney wasn't there, his aide informed her that he was still at court. She left a message.

★　★　★

Two hours later Percy got in touch with Claire. 'You called?' His tone was cool.

'We were wondering if there'd been any

78

new developments. Also, Kate wants to see Nick.'

'This afternoon, she can see him at four o'clock.'

Since he didn't say any more, Claire took the opportunity to mention Kate's letter.

'I hope she didn't destroy it,' Percy said. 'I don't suppose there was a signature or return address?'

'No, and it's hand-printed, in upper-case letters.' Claire described the letter. 'Kate has a hunch Nick's ex-wife may have sent it. Valerie and Nick were married for two years so he should be able to identify her writing.'

'It's possible, though most people sending hate mail try to conceal their identities,' Percy said. 'Where was it mailed? Maybe we can find the post office handling it.'

'It's stamped Manchester,' Claire paused. 'Anything I can do to help, please don't hesitate to ask. Kate's got her hands full right now with two sick children. I'm free.'

'Thanks. That won't be necessary.'

Did Percy reject her help because she'd refused to date him? In the past she'd never liked the man. His mood swings made her uneasy. He'd be optimistic one hour and depressed the next. She'd wondered at the time if her case had been too much for an inexperienced solicitor.

Kate visited Nick later that afternoon and returned to the hotel quiet and subdued. While telling Claire the judge had denied bail, Kate burst into tears.

Claire tried to sound positive. 'Never mind. The police are bound to find evidence soon leading to the real killer.'

That evening Percy stopped by for the letter. He slipped it into a plastic bag, at the same time issuing a word of caution. 'Don't get your hopes up.' He addressed Kate while ignoring Claire, though she stood right beside her aunt. 'Even if we find the sender, this letter might have no connection to Nick's case.'

* * *

During the next two days, the atmosphere in the hotel was tense. Claire was thankful for the children's presence. Though they had recovered from their viruses, they still needed attention.

To pass the time, Kate and Claire played rousing games of Old Maids with Nicky and Kayla on the dining room table.

'I win, I win,' Nicky cried at the conclusion of one game. He tossed his cards in the air.

Kayla didn't get excited until she won. Then she neighed and galloped around the room on her hobbyhorse.

The children's youthful exuberance cheered Claire. Kate was lucky to have the twins. They took her mind off Nick's dilemma, if only for a few minutes at a time.

The police were probably reviewing Nick's past cases. It wouldn't be the first time a former prisoner with a grudge had tried to get even with the police detective apprehending him.

Once lunch was over, she suggested Kate take a nap, offering to take the children for a walk while their mother rested. From the way Kayla and Nicky dashed to the front door, it was obvious they were ready to escape their confinement. Outside, they ran ahead of her, stopping once in a while to confirm she was coming.

Though she hadn't mentioned it to Kate, Claire was still disturbed over the Bowness Bugle article. With all that had been happening, she hadn't had time to think about it.

Tony came into view, loping across the grounds. He appeared unaware anyone was watching him, admiring him. As soon as he saw Claire, he smiled and waved.

His gesture was so natural, her frustration lessened. Such a nice boy. No, he was a man. She'd never known an adult male like him.

Stop that. Don't act like a silly adolescent.

He approached her little group and knelt to greet the children. From their giggles, it was clear Tony had no trouble communicating with four-year-olds.

Kayla and Nicky asked to play hide-and-seek and Tony agreed, volunteering to cover his eyes first.

The children found a hiding place, then Tony glanced around, pretending he couldn't imagine where they'd gone. From the excited whispers and giggles coming from behind the boxwood hedge, he'd have to be deaf, not to hear them.

He discovered them, then it was Kayla and Nicky's turn. Tony took Claire's hand and led her toward a large evergreen tree.

She didn't realize what he had in mind until he boosted her onto a branch and climbed into the tree behind her, motioning for her to climb higher. Inside the privacy of the giant old fir, they could see out, yet remain hidden from view. Below them on the lawn the children ran about, laughing and searching.

'You're a resourceful fellow.' Tony's nearness made her nervous, though he seemed oblivious to their close proximity in the little hideaway.

'I can be.'

Something flickered in his eyes and Claire realized he might be young, but he wasn't naive.

'We better let them find us before they run to the house and tell Mattie we've disappeared.' She tried to sound casual.

'Wait a moment.' He touched her arm. 'You're upset about something. I can feel it.' His dark eyes pierced her.

'There was another story in the local paper this morning,' she said. 'My family's history must fascinate the Bugle manager. This's his second article on the Stanhopes.' She shrugged. 'I shouldn't let it bother me.'

'Can I help?' He moved even closer.

His nearness made Claire uncomfortable. 'No, thanks.' As soon as she spoke, she reconsidered. People weren't standing in line to help her. 'On second thought, would you mind?'

'Let's round up those little ones first.' Tony helped her down the tree and stood aside while she called Kayla and Nicky.

Just then Mattie appeared in the doorway and the children ran to her. Car keys dangled in her hands, a sign she was going to the grocery store.

She helped the children into her car then slid into the driver's seat. Moments later, the Ford headed down the driveway, the children waving to Claire and Tony as the vehicle passed through the hotel gates.

Alone with Tony, Claire felt shy and hesitant.

'Tell me what you want me to do.'

She remembered what she'd had in mind. Maybe it wasn't such a good idea. Still, she'd asked him for help, so she owed him an explanation. 'I need to see the newspaper manager again.' She lifted her chin. 'But there's no reason for anyone else to go.'

'Wait right there.' Tony pointed to the spot where she stood. 'I'll get my jacket and come with you.' He ran into the house. In a minute or two, he returned.

Helping her into the second-hand truck he used to get around the village, he said, 'Please excuse this old wreck.'

'What?' She'd been preoccupied with what to say to the Bugle manager. She'd be firmer with the man this time. On her previous visit, she'd asked him to stop writing about the Stanhopes. This time she'd order him. 'Ah, it's fine.'

Tony turned on the ignition. Claire gave him directions then held on for dear life.

The old truck bumped and rattled down Kendal Road until she thought her teeth would be jarred loose. It was a relief when they came to a stop in front of the small shopping center by the lake. 'Why don't you wait here? I won't be long.' She glanced in his direction.

Tony shook his head. Stepping from the truck, he said, 'Let's go.' He opened the passenger door.

There wasn't time to argue so she led the way up the narrow flight of stairs to the dingy corridor and the Bowness Bugle. For the second time she knocked on the newspaper office's door.

★ ★ ★

It was like Claire's earlier experience. The man inside took his time answering the door.

'Oh, it's you,' he said, casually. 'What do you want now?'

Before she could speak, Tony stepped forward. 'Mister,' he said in a husky voice, 'Why don't you be polite and invite us into your office?'

She stared at Tony.

'Who the hell are you?' The manager straightened, his attention fixed on her companion.

Claire observed that the two men were about the same height, though the Bugle manager was broader. Tony was younger and more wiry.

85

'That doesn't matter,' Tony said. 'This lady,' he pointed to Claire, 'She wants to have a word with you.'

'All right, already. Come in.' The manager threw open the door, standing aside so they could enter.

A moment later they all stood inside. 'I found another article about my family in your paper today,' she said. The manager's gaze disturbed her. Did he remember kissing her the last time she was there? She hadn't been able to forget. Avoiding his eyes, she studied the office. There was a name plate on his desk. *Max Bronsky. That must be his name.*

'And I thought you were here to pay for a year's subscription.' Bronsky's laugh was dry.

'See here, this has to stop.'

'Excuse me?' He looked down at her.

'You must stop writing about my family.'

'Lady, gimme a break.' Bronsky's deep voice turned weary. 'Nothing happens around this place. And I can't always write about sheep. I understand they're a major source of income in this area. Even so, they're dirty, stupid animals and not newsworthy by any stretch of the imagination.'

'All right, I've tried being reasonable.' Claire had an irrational urge to punch him in the nose. Taking a deep breath, she got her emotions under control. When she spoke again, her words came out very slowly so he'd understand. 'If you persist in publishing articles on my family, I'll sue you and the paper. Do you understand?'

Bronsky nodded. 'There's one small problem.'

'What?'

'I've never printed a word that isn't documented so you wouldn't have a prayer, taking the paper or me to court.' He folded his arms and smiled.

'You smug bastard!' Having to contend with the likes of him was enough to drive a peace-loving person to violence.

Tony edged forward until he stood between Claire and Bronsky. 'See that box of cigars?' He directed the other man's attention to a container of Havanas on the desk behind them.

Bronsky glanced at the desk then back to Tony. He raised an eyebrow. 'Yeah? So what?'

'Mister, if you print another word to upset Miss Stanhope, I'll make you eat that box of cigars.' Tony's voice was cold, his Italian accent more pronounced than usual. He paused, as if in reflection. With his index finger, he reached over and jabbed Bronsky's chest. 'Then I'll cut your heart out. Capeesh?'

Claire gasped, half-expecting to see a stranger in Tony's place. She blinked hard and looked again. With his eyes narrowed, Tony looked mean and tough, tough enough to carry out his threat. She wished she were somewhere else. Anywhere.

If the Bugle manager was frightened, he didn't show it. His mouth tightened into a thin, hard line.

'All right,' he said, backing away until the desk separated him from her companion. Clearing his throat, he addressed her. 'I apologize, Miss. By the way, I don't think I ever introduced myself. My name's Max Bronsky.'

'I know.' She gestured at the name plate on his desk. 'Goodbye Mr. Bronsky. Don't bother walking us to the door, we'll let ourselves out.' Head held high, she marched from the office, followed by Tony.

In the corridor, Claire studied her companion. His facial expression was inscrutable. 'You didn't have to threaten him.' She whispered, eying the newspaper's now closed door.

'I, I don't know what came over me.' Tony said. His voice was quiet and hesitant, just like she remembered.

'Then you didn't mean what you said, about removing his, ah heart?' Just mentioning his threat made Claire queasy.

Tony's shoulders drooped. 'Do I look like a killer?'

Common sense took hold. Of course, he was just trying to be macho. All that tough talk wasn't Tony. He was a sweet, gentle man who played hide-and-seek with children. Since their first meeting, he'd treated her with respect. He'd even been reluctant to call her by her first name. 'No, of course not,' Claire reassured him. 'You're too kind to ever hurt another person.'

'Thanks. I just wanted to make an impression.'

'You definitely did that.' She patted him on the arm. 'It was sweet of you, speaking up for me like that. Please be more careful. Bronsky could've hurt you. Don't make idle threats. Someone might take you seriously.'

Tony nodded and opened the passenger door of his truck.

'Thanks.' She climbed in, tried to make herself comfortable.

They were silent on the way back to Kings Grant. As he let her off at the front of the hotel, he said, 'Maybe he won't bother you again.'

'I guess.' Though Bronsky had apologized, she doubted his sincerity. Still, it was possible he'd find other topics for his paper, topics that didn't include her family.

Tony had frightened her at the newspaper office. And judging from Bronsky's grim

89

expression, Tony had convinced him that he meant business. Of course, it was all a ruse. Tony was harmless.

Claire wished there was someone she could talk to about everything that was going on. Kate was her usual confidant but she had too much on her mind already.

8

Parking his truck behind the hotel, Tony mulled over what'd happened. Maybe he'd come on too strong in the Bugle office. Better watch out. Claire might have second thoughts about him.

He'd arrived in Bowness several days before Claire. Having already made most of his arrangements, he just had to confirm the suitability of the cabin's location. With that done, he watched the people at Kings Grant Hotel. One thing he noticed was Chris driving about the area in the hotel Rolls.

Kate Connor's partner must have many friends. Chris often stopped to visit other local business people, including the owner of a certain Italian restaurant.

Using that piece of information, Tony formed a plan. What better way to get a job in the hotel. Kate's big-hearted, good-natured business partner would rescue him.

★　★　★

The next morning Kate's thoughts wandered while she dressed the children. The solicitor was costing them a mint. Were they throwing their money away? Nick was still in jail.

She'd given the latest 'hate mail' to Percy April with the understanding he'd pass it on to the police. Without a shred of proof, Kate still believed Nick's ex-wife had sent both letters.

Now she wished she'd shown the first letter to Nick. It'd been stupid to burn it, yet part of her shied away from a confrontation with her husband. Deep inside, Kate dreaded hearing Nick's response to its accusations.

Just then Nicky looked up at his mother and Kate blinked back tears. He reminded her so much of his father. She managed a smile while helping him into his favorite sweater. 'Sometimes you look just like your Daddy.'

'And I'm like you.' Kayla said from her perch on top of the toy chest. With her crown at an angle over one eye, she reigned, wearing a pink satin and tulle princess costume.

Claire walked into the room carrying some children's books. 'Anyone want to hear a story?'

The children quickly surrounded their cousin. Kayla settled on Claire's lap and Nicky squeezed into the space beside her in the nursery armchair.

'Remember, you're going to take a nap

when we finish book number three,' she said. 'All right?'

'All right,' Kayla and Nicky said in unison.

Thirty minutes later with the children napping, or at least resting in their youth beds, Kate and Claire headed to the library on the ground floor. Claire's aunt went straight to the bar and poured herself a glass of sherry.

'Want one?' She offered a drink to Claire.

'No thanks. One-thirty's a little early for me.'

'Are you trying to give me a hard time?' Kate frowned.

'We have to talk. It's important.'

'Talk about what? My husband's stuck in jail and I'm beginning to have doubts about his solicitor. He may not have been a good choice.'

'Doubts?'

Kate nodded. 'Your Percy April keeps sending me bills for his services. If he'd do something, it wouldn't be so bad.'

'Come on. He's not 'my Percy April.' ' Claire smiled a little as if she understood how upset and worried Kate was. 'You asked me to find Nick a solicitor. I mentioned the only one I knew from personal experience. Besides, these things take time.'

'I know.' Kate felt ashamed. She took her

93

niece's hand and squeezed it. 'Please forgive me. It was a terrible shock, Nick's being arrested. He should be home with me and the children. Instead, he's in jail for a crime he didn't commit.'

'I can imagine how you feel. I'm upset, too.'

'Anyway, Percy must've given the police that nasty letter from Manchester by now. I hoped they'd find Nick's ex-wife and force her to talk. Maybe she knows something about the dead girl.' Kate paused to take a sip of sherry.

'Does Nick have any idea where she's hiding?'

'No. He's talked to Percy, told him all he can remember about Valerie,' Kate said. 'And still they can't find her.'

'Does her family live in Manchester?'

'Her father does, her mother's deceased. The police visited Mr. Doyle but he had no idea where she was.

'Nick and Mr. Doyle were close once. The old man always said he loved Nick like his own son. It figures he'd tell the police to help Nick.'

'Maybe,' Claire replied. 'But remember, Valerie's the man's daughter. Would you give me Mr. Doyle's address?'

'Why? It won't do any good.' Kate went

back to the bar. Holding up the sherry, she complained, 'look at this bottle. It's almost empty.'

'No wonder.' Claire sounded a little cross. 'I want you to promise me something.'

'What?' Kate didn't like the determined expression on her niece's face.

'I want your promise to stop drinking until Nick's free.'

'Why? This helps me unwind.' And it helped her sleep at night. Claire didn't know about the bottle in Kate's closet.

'We'll all relax when Nick's home. All right?'

'Well, all right.' Kate handed Claire the bottle. 'There's a little left. Would you like it?'

Claire shook her head. 'Why don't I pour it down the drain?'

'If you must,' Kate sighed. *What a waste of good sherry.*

★   ★   ★

That evening Claire lay in bed, trying to get involved in the plot of her latest 'cozy mystery.' Mattie had gone to bed first followed by Kate who pleaded exhaustion, retiring as soon as the children fell sleep.

A shriek pierced the quiet. Moments later there was the sound of footsteps on the stairs.

Then Kate appeared in the doorway wearing her gown and robe.

'There was an unopened bottle of sherry in my bedroom. You didn't happen to take it, did you?' Kate frowned.

'Why, yes, I did,' Claire admitted, trying to keep her voice calm and soothing. *Poor Kate.* 'Remember your promise.'

'Damn, I could've used a drink, to help me sleep.'

'Please find Nick's ex-father-in-law's address,' Claire requested. 'I want to see him.'

'He won't talk to you. The police already interviewed him.'

'Maybe he will if I pay him a visit.' Claire pointed to her stack of paperback mysteries beside the bed. 'Want a book?'

Kate shook her head. 'No, thanks. See you at breakfast.'

Though Claire's eyes remained on the page of her mystery, she listened to Kate's footsteps retreating down the hall.

Closing the book, Claire put it on the nightstand then turned off the lamp. Before she slept she relived the confrontation with Bronsky. Funny. She never got the impression he was afraid of Tony. Did he sense Tony was bluffing?

Claire fell asleep and dreamed of wandering through a maze of corridors. As soon as she found her way out of one, another loomed before her. At last she walked free. A man waited for her in the shadows. She couldn't see his face.

She woke next morning with a start. Something was tickling her foot sticking out of the bedcovers.

Opening her sleepy eyes, Claire tried to focus. A blonde wisp of a child was beside her bed, holding a feathered cap.

'I dreamed someone was tickling me. You didn't see anyone, did you?' She eyed the little girl.

'No, except . . . '

'Except what, dear?' Claire waited to see what her little cousin's vivid imagination would produce this time.

'A big pink 'lephant,' ' Kayla said solemnly. 'He left.'

'Oh.' Claire bit her lip, trying not to laugh out loud. 'Did you see which way he went?'

Kayla's blue eyes shone bright as she shook her head.

'Never mind. He may come back. Why don't we get dressed and go downstairs? Maybe he'll join us for breakfast.'

Seated across the kitchen table, Kate appeared rested. The circles under her eyes were less pronounced this morning. Maybe she had a good night's rest for a change.

While the children munched their cereal, Claire and Kate tried to carry on an adult conversation.

'I've thought about what you said, and you may be right, Kate admitted with reluctance. 'I don't suppose it'll do any harm if you want to try.' Reaching into her terry cloth robe pocket, she brought out a folded piece of paper. 'Here's Mr. Doyle's address. Nick always said he couldn't understand how a sane, rational man like that could have such a mixed-up daughter.' Kate reached over and smoothed Kayla's hair.

'I'll be careful,' Claire replied. 'Like you say, it won't hurt to try.'

★   ★   ★

After breakfast Claire hurried to dress while Kate and the children were upstairs. She wanted to leave the hotel before Kayla or Nicky saw her and begged to go along.

Charles and she'd visited Manchester a number of times for the museums or theatre, so Claire had no difficulty getting there. Along the motorway, she considered several ploys to learn where Nick's ex-wife was living. And discarded them all.

Approaching the city, she passed several older high-rise estates. When she stopped at a service station for directions, Claire found she was almost there.

From its appearance, Mr. Doyle's inner-city neighborhood was quite old. Perhaps he'd grown up there.

Claire located the estate where Mr. Doyle lived, parked Kate's car then stood by the vehicle, gazing up at the dank, drab ten-story brick building.

All was quiet this morning. The residents' children must be in school. Claire examined the address Kate had given her again. Mr. Doyle's apartment was number 1033.

She located the elevator. A maintenance crew was repairing it so she was in for a hike. Thank goodness she was wearing walking shoes.

A few minutes later Claire reached the tenth floor. Not a moment too soon since she was out of breath.

Walking down the poorly lit hall, she managed to step around an occasional bicycle parked outside an apartment door. Number 1033 was at the end of the hall. Claire pressed the doorbell.

There was no response. She waited before hitting the bell a couple more times. She was about to give up when the door pulled open and an old man peered out at her.

'Hello. Mr. Doyle?'

He nodded. 'What can I do for you, young lady?'

'I'm hoping you'll be able to help me,' she said, showing him a picture of an older woman. 'Aunt Florence has Alzheimers. Do you recall seeing her around here?'

'No, I'm sorry.' His voice creaked like a rusty old hinge. Mr. Doyle started to shut the door.

'Oh, I think I'm going to faint.' She leaned toward him.

The old man guided her inside his apartment, helping her to sit on a piece of upholstered furniture in his living room.

Lying back on the sofa, Claire closed her eyes. Her next sensation was dampness on her face. He must have brought a wet cloth to try and revive her. The old gentleman dabbed at her forehead and cheeks. Next he gave her a sip of a liquid that burned her throat, probably Scotch whiskey. She coughed.

'Thank you. All of a sudden, things began whirling around.' Claire studied the room. The place was tidy, though the furniture had seen better times and the drapes were limp.

'It's quite all right. I'm glad I could help.' His voice was gentle. 'When did you eat last?'

'I don't recall. I've been so worried about Auntie.'

'Yes, I expect you have. Your Aunt

Florence? Was that what you called her?'

'Yes, I've been going door-to-door, trying to find her.'

He turned over the photograph she'd shown him and read aloud the writing on the back, 'to Claire from her friend Agnes. September 1st, Devon.' Mr. Doyle stared at her, his eyes alert behind the thick glasses. 'Now why don't you tell me the real reason you're here.'

Sitting up, she returned his gaze. 'I'm sorry. I was afraid you'd slam the door in my face if I told you the truth,' Claire said. 'I'm trying to help Nick Connor, my aunt's husband. Nick's in bad trouble. We thought if we could find Valerie, she might have some answers.'

Mr. Doyle's stern expression changed to a smile. 'Nick? That young fellow was the best thing that ever happened to my Val.' He dug around in a cabinet drawer and located a piece of paper. 'Here, take this. It's her last-known address. I don't promise she's there now. Val moves about, skips out on paying her rent.'

'I'm so sorry.'

'Now that we've taken care of business, I was about to have lunch. Would you like to join me?' A wistful note crept into his voice. 'Please stay. It's been awhile since I had company.'

'Thank you. I'd be pleased to have lunch with you.' Claire followed Mr. Doyle into the kitchen. She watched as he removed the lid from a pan on the stove and dished out two bowls of soup.

They had the vegetable soup and hot rolls at the kitchen table. While they ate, Mr. Doyle entertained her with tales of his youth when he was a railroad conductor.

'I need to go,' she said at last. She still needed to see Valerie. Kate would be crushed if Claire returned to the hotel with no news of Nick's ex-wife.

'If you find Val, will you tell her I'd like to see her?'

His sad expression tugged at her heart. *Valerie should be ashamed of herself.* Claire nodded. 'I will, I promise. Thank you for being so kind.' On impulse, she tiptoed and kissed his cheek.

'Thank you.' He smiled and for a moment Claire could see how handsome Mr. Doyle had been as a young man.

Claire closed the door softly. She took the now repaired elevator to the ground floor then stepped out of the building.

Kate's car was parked at the curb where Claire had left it. The only difference in the scene was the figure of a man leaning against her front fender.

9

'Tony? What in the world are you doing here? Did something happen to Kate or the children?' The hotel handyman was the last person she'd expected to see in Manchester.

'Everybody's fine. Your aunt started worrying when she didn't hear from you. She asked me to see if I could find you.' He frowned. 'Are you all right?'

'See for yourself.' How odd. The Kate she used to know wouldn't have been so fretful. Maybe the strain of the last few days unnerved her.

'Mrs. Connor told me you left the hotel hours ago and she hasn't heard from you.'

'It hasn't been that long, has it?'

'Yeah. You're not wearing a wristwatch. Here, check mine.'

It was almost five o'clock. No wonder Kate was worried. 'I lost all track of the time, visiting Mr. Doyle.' Claire pulled out her cell phone and dialed the hotel's number. The line was busy. 'I'll try again later.'

'Sure you're all right?' He stared at her.

'Fine, I'm fine.'

'Did you get the daughter's address?'

'What? Oh, Kate told you. Yes, I need to see Valerie about something.'

'Good luck on that. That dame's long gone.'

His defeatist attitude made Claire all the more determined. 'Maybe. If she's still around, I intend to talk to her.'

'You're wasting your time. Why don't we go back to Bowness? I bet those little kids wonder where you are.'

'Nick's solicitor said it was just coincidence. The dead girl in the cabin and Kate's letter might not be connected. Kate and I think they are.'

'Mrs. Connor suspects this Valerie's involved?'

'Well, Kate received the letter the day after her husband was arrested. There might be a link.' Claire didn't elaborate.

'Like what?'

This was the second time Tony had tried to help her. What harm would it do to tell him? 'In the letter the writer accuses Nick of having a love nest.'

'You mean your uncle was shacking up with some dame?'

'Yes, though Nick swears he'd never been there before.'

'Of course he does.' Tony replied.

'What do you mean, of course?' Claire didn't care for the smirk on Tony's face or his smug attitude.

'Any man caught redhanded like that would swear he was innocent,' Tony said. 'Big shot like your uncle is with the police and good looking, dames must be crazy for him.'

'There're a lot of factors, lots of loose ends,' Claire said. She should've kept her big mouth shut. There was no reason for Tony to know so much.

'This time of day, traffic will be heavy,' he reminded her. 'We better get going. Your aunt's anxious to see you.'

'Now that you see I'm all right, you could head back,' she said. 'I forgot to get directions to Valerie's apartment. I'll need to find out how to get there.'

'Mrs. Connor told me not to come back without you.' Tony shook his head stubbornly. 'If you stay, so do I.'

Claire found a service station. The first man she asked either didn't know anything, or he didn't want to help a woman driving an expensive vehicle.

The second attendant was more obliging. With a tip of his hat, he gave her directions. Lacking paper to write on, she scribbled on the back page of a children's book left in the car.

She waved to Tony and he climbed into his truck, following her vehicle from the service station. Along the way, whenever she glanced in her rearview mirror, the old truck was back there. A couple of times, another car separated them, yet Tony didn't lose her once. It made her feel safe, knowing a friend was nearby, even if in another car.

Turning onto a side street, Claire located the correct address. She parked and stood at the curb, waiting for him. Tony slid from his vehicle and crossed the street to join her. 'Are you sure this's the right place?' He looked around uneasily.

Why was he so uptight? It wasn't like they were visiting someone in a tough area. It was just an older neighborhood. The shabby row houses must've been converted to apartments years ago. They leaned so much, they seemed to be holding each other up.

A drab frame, one-story house surrounded by a picket fence stood on the corner next to the make-shift apartment buildings. The color brown predominated, the house, the fence, even the dog in the yard, all were brown. The watchdog barked once, twice, then he returned to his doghouse and lay down.

The front door of the house opened and an obese woman wearing a faded green house-coat looked out at them. 'If you're selling something, I don't need it. Go on now.' Her chubby, beringed hands shooed them away.

'We're looking for someone. Does Valerie

still live here?' Claire smiled, trying to appear friendly. She prayed they'd come to the right address. Maybe this woman knew Doyle's daughter.

'Over there.' The woman pointed to the end unit.

'Her father said she lived here.'

'Her da doesn't know what he's talking about,' the woman said. Her voice warmed and she added, 'How's the old geezer?'

'You know Mr. Doyle?'

'We were neighbors years ago.'

'Do you know his daughter?'

'I'm her landlady.'

'Have you seen her today?'

'Nah.'

Claire tried to be patient. She mustn't antagonize this woman. 'Can you tell me when you saw Valerie last?'

'You with the police?'

'No.' Claire hoped the woman didn't ask who they were.

'What's it worth to you?'

This was taking them nowhere fast. Instead of answering, Claire opened her purse. One twenty pound note. She should've brought more money. She hadn't come prepared to pay bribes. 'I've got a twenty,' she volunteered.

'Go on with you.' The woman's multiple

chins shook with laughter. 'You're a fine lady, driving a Range Rover, you can do better than that.'

Tony stepped forward, opened his wallet and removed a large bill. 'Here.' He slipped the money to Claire. 'Try this.'

'But I can't let you — '

'Do it,' he said.

'How about one hundred pounds?' Claire asked the woman.

The bank note disappeared into the landlady's robe pocket. She must have been satisfied with their contribution since she invited them into her small, over-heated parlor.

Fighting down the urge to sneeze, Claire scanned the room for the reason for her distress. She found it when a motley assortment of cats started appearing from behind the furniture and drapes.

One Angora perched on Tony's lap. He straightened until his spine didn't touch the back of his chair, his hands at his sides. Claire sensed his discomfort and gave him a few points for good self-control.

The place reeked of felines. Even the air was permeated with cat hair. Claire promised herself a good scrub and shampoo when she returned to Kings Grant Hotel.

'Now,' their new friend said, 'you were

asking about my tenant?' She cuddled a large tabby cat to her ample bosom before setting him on the floor with several other felines.

'Yes,' Claire said. 'We're hoping she can help my uncle. He's been accused of a crime he didn't commit.' She didn't feel the need to elaborate.

'I'm sorry. I can't help you.'

'Would you mind telling us the last time you saw Valerie?'

The woman yawned as if bored. 'I was out in the yard yesterday. Val came out of her flat, lugging a big suitcase. She got into a nifty red sportscar and they were gone before — '

'You said they?' Claire interrupted. 'Who was with her?'

'A man, a young man. A real looker.'

'Did you get a good look at the guy?' Tony asked.

'Nah.' the woman answered, smiling at him.

'There're a lot of men like that.' Claire felt letdown.

'He was dressed like a million.' The landlady paused to look at Tony. She smiled at him again. 'He even wore one of those gold chains. A real sport, that fellow.'

Claire tried to get her questioning back on track. 'Yes, well, did she say when she'd come back?'

'Nah. From the grin on her face, I don't expect her anytime soon.' The landlady sighed and pulled her robe tighter around her obese body. 'Wish I could get me one of those boy toys.'

The black cat on the coffee table hissed and jumped onto Tony's lap, knocking the Angora off. Tony jerked.

'If you're her landlady, I wonder, would you let us into her flat, just to look around?' Claire wasn't ready to give up. She'd come so far, hated to go back to Bowness without information that would help Nick.

'Well, I might.' The woman smiled at Tony again. Claire got the impression the woman couldn't keep her eyes off him.

Tony slipped another large bill to Claire and she handed it to the landlady. Like their earlier donation, it disappeared into the deep pocket of the woman's robe. She handed Claire a key.

★   ★   ★

Valerie's apartment was filthy except for a clothes closet off the shabby bedroom that was clean and tidy. 'Look here.' Claire directed Tony's attention to several flashy sequined dresses and a shoe rack holding silver and gold high heels. 'For someone down on her luck, how could Valerie afford these? These dresses may be gaudy yet they're designer-made. And these shoes are expensive.'

'Was she working?'

'From what her father said, Valerie was lazy and not above taking handouts from him. And he lived on a pension.'

'There're other ways women can earn money for party dresses.' Tony leaned against the door jamb, watching Claire. In a voice as soft as silk, he added, 'maybe she was a whore.'

'Maybe.' His tone bothered Claire. Every time she thought she was getting to know Tony, he showed another facet of his personality. He might have the face of an angel, but from all indications, he wasn't one.

While Tony used the bathroom, Claire returned to Valerie's closet and continued digging through the musty closet. Her shoulders ached and the dust in the air irritated her sinuses. It was time to leave.

Turning, she almost ran into Tony. Startled, she jerked. The man moved like a cat. She hadn't heard him come back.

Claire gazed into his dark eyes and wondered if he'd kiss her. She was curious about him.

He backed away without speaking. Maybe she wasn't his type. Or maybe Valerie's grubby flat turned him off. His not kissing her made him even more attractive.

'Well, there's nothing here,' she said. 'Let's go.'

Valerie's landlady came to her front door, a kitty in her arms and another perched on her shoulder. 'Find anything?'

'No, thank you anyway.' Claire returned the key plus a slip of paper containing her telephone number at King's Grant. 'Please let me know when Val comes home.' With Tony right behind her, Claire headed for her vehicle.

While driving Kate's vehicle back to Bowness, Claire tried to review her day. Fatigue set in and she forced herself to concentrate solely on driving. It was dark and a long way home.

* * *

Shortly before sunset that same day, Max watched a pigeon on the rooftop outside his window while talking on his cell phone. He checked the newspaper office and his room at the bed-and-breakfast daily and had found nothing out of order. Still, he felt safer using his cell phone.

'I've found a way to get closer to our friend,' he said, talking to the person at the

112

other end of the line. Max listened for a minute or two. 'I don't know about the blonde. The fact that they came together to see me makes me wonder how long they've known each other. Well, I'll think of something. Keep in touch,' he said and turned off his phone.

Somehow Max hoped Claire wasn't involved. He had strong suspicions who Tony was and Claire didn't look like his type. What woman would be a suitable companion for a killer?

10

Claire returned to King's Grant, parking in front of the hotel next to a black Ford she didn't recognize. She hoped the vehicle didn't belong to a new guest. With Nick in jail, none of them was in the mood to be charming and gracious to strangers.

As Tony passed her in his truck, headed for the employee parking in the rear, she opened the hotel's wood-and-etched glass front door and stepped inside. 'Hello? Anyone home?'

The children ran into the foyer and hugged her. Mattie stepped out of the kitchen, addressing Claire. 'You must be starved. We saved you some dinner.' The housekeeper turned to Nicky and Kayla. 'It's bedtime, children.'

'We want a snack,' Nicky informed her.

'Is Kate upstairs?' Claire looked around.

'Down at the gatehouse with our new tenant,' Mattie said. She bent to smooth Kayla's hair and button her nightgown.

'She rented it already?' That was fast work. Chris and Diane had just moved out that morning. 'Anybody interesting?'

'An American. He has beautiful gray eyes.'

114

Max Bronsky at the Bugle had gray eyes. Claire experienced a sinking sensation inside. 'Does he have dark hair and a neat moustache?'

'Why, yes, have you met him?'

'You might say that.' It'd been a long day and Claire didn't feel up to telling Mattie about her visits to the Bugle office.

'Kate seemed pleased to rent the apartment so fast.'

'I would've called the newspaper if she asked me,' Claire said. 'I did meet the manager.' She didn't like the man, would have done her best to squelch any interest he had in the place.

'She'll tell you all about it, I'm sure.'

The front door opened and Kate walked in, holding a folded piece of paper. Her gaze meeting Claire's, she grinned and waved a check. 'I not only rented the gatehouse, he gave me this month's rent and two more months in advance.' Kate hummed while tucking the check in her purse.

'I hope he won't hang around the hotel.' The mere thought of Max's being underfoot on a daily basis was disagreeable.

'What's the matter with you?' Kate sounded annoyed. 'You should be glad we'll have a new tenant. With the solicitor's fees eating up my savings, I need some new income.'

'Your new tenant wrote unkind stories about the family,' Claire said. Sometimes her aunt was too forgiving.

'Oh? Well he probably didn't print anything but the truth,' Kate said, sitting down. The children took that as a signal to climb onto her lap. 'One at a time, please. Your mommy's tired.'

'Come along.' Mattie addressed Kayla and Nicky. 'I might be able to find a couple of sugar cookies for two good children.'

The word cookies captured their attention. The twins followed the housekeeper to the kitchen. Claire trailed along behind. While Mattie opened the warming oven and removed Claire's dinner plate, Claire poured three glasses of milk.

The moment she finished eating, Claire offered them a bribe. 'If you'll brush your teeth and get into bed, I'll read you a story. Just one, mind you. Cuz's weary tonight. I've been all the way to Manchester and back.'

Three stories later, Kayla and Nicky fell asleep. Sighing with relief, Claire tiptoed from the room, headed downstairs.

Kate waited in the library. 'Did you find Valerie?'

'No, as a matter of fact — '

Kate cut her off. 'Then where have you been?'

Hearing the stress in her aunt's voice, Claire tried to keep her patience. 'The drive to Manchester takes awhile then I had to locate Mr. Doyle's apartment. You may remember I haven't been to that city for years,' she explained.

'Go on,' Kate said, impatiently.

'Mr. Doyle gave me his daughter's address. By the way, why did you send Tony after me?' It was annoying, the way Kate sometimes treated her like a child.

'Send?' Kate raised an eyebrow. 'Tony volunteered, he seemed quite anxious to see if you were all right.'

'According to Tony, you were worried and asked him to come looking for me.'

'You must've misunderstood what he said.' Kate shrugged. 'Never mind, did you talk to Valerie?'

'No, I spent most of the time visiting her father, he even gave me lunch.' She'd enjoyed spending time with Mr. Doyle. It was a shame his daughter didn't visit him more often. Claire's throat tightened. She still missed her own father, though her memories of him were slight. He'd died when she was small.

'Claire, please tell me what you learned.'

'Her landlady told us that Valerie came back to town a few days ago then left again yesterday with a handsome younger man driving a sportscar. I asked the landlady to call me if Valerie comes home.'

'Is she reliable?'

'Who? Valerie?'

'No, goose. This landlady person.'

'If you have enough money.' Claire didn't mention that Tony lent her funds to bribe the woman. She wondered where he got that wad of pounds.

'Oh, that sort.' Kate slumped in her chair. 'I had such high hopes. It appears we've made no progress toward freeing Nick.'

'Maybe and maybe not,' Claire said. 'Mr. Doyle liked me. He may get in touch if he hears from his daughter. He's a better bet than the landlady. I think she'd sell one of her own children if the price was right.'

'What a horrible thing to say.' Kate shuddered.

'You don't understand. Her cats are her children.'

'I see.' Kate smiled slightly. 'What do we do now?'

'Get a good night's sleep. Things tend to look better in the morning.' Claire yawned. 'Oh, I almost forgot.' Grabbing her shoulder bag, she dumped the contents on the coffee

118

table then dug through the mess. She came up with a wad of papers.

'You pick the darnest times to sort out your purse.'

'I found something on the floor of Valerie's closet,' Claire said. 'Tony wasn't with me. He was using the toilet.'

'What is it?'

'Not much, just a piece or two of stationery. Look here.' She handed it to her aunt.

Kate smoothed the wrinkled paper. 'This could be a rough draft of the letter I received. Could it be used as proof Valerie sent me that hideous letter?'

'I don't know. It sure looks like she did,' Claire said. She yawned. 'Let's go to bed. Tomorrow we'll plan what to do next.'

Kate nodded, her expression tired but hopeful.

★　★　★

Down the driveway, Max glanced around his new quarters. Not bad, if a little small. The important thing was it put him where he needed to be. The man he'd come to watch was close, very close. All Max had to do was watch Tony and see whom he contacted.

His cell phone rang. Max answered, giving

his caller his new address. 'Stay away from here,' he warned. 'Come by the newspaper office if you must. Better still, meet me at the pub near the Bugle at lunchtime.'

'Okay,' the other man said. 'How about the young woman. What part does she play? Is she Tony's girl friend?'

'Your guess is as good as mine. I intend to find out.' Max couldn't figure Claire. Sometimes she seemed cool and sophisticated. On other occasions she appeared as innocent as a young girl.

'You mentioned their visiting your office the other day,' his caller said. 'She may've known him before she came home.'

'Right, or Tony could've been the only one she could think of to ask. Remember, Claire's been away for years. Chances are she's lost touch with any friends she had here.' Max rubbed his forehead, trying to put the pieces together.

The first time he'd seen Tony, Max's instincts warned him the man wasn't what he pretended to be. Tony moved too well to be a handyman. 'If he's who you people say he is, what the hell's he doing in a Lake District village off-season?'

'That's what we want you to find out.'

'Is it possible we're watching the wrong man?'

'The Yard's sources are reliable,' his contact said. 'I'll come by the bar for a game of darts if I need to see you.'

'Good,' Max replied. 'You can pass me any new information you've acquired then.'

The line went dead and Max turned off his cell phone. Was Tony really Antonio, the internationally sought assassin? Neither the FBI or its U.K. counterpart possessed a clear picture of the man, just a few blurred long distance shots of his running away from the scene of the crime, in Venice and London.

Now he'd wait and watch. Better watch the blonde, too. Max hadn't liked the glance she'd sent him at the newspaper, like he was something nasty she got on her shoes.

11

'I realize that, Mr. April,' Kate said next morning, talking to Nick's solicitor on the telephone. 'Still, there must be something you can do. My children miss their father.'

Seated next to Kate on the sofa, Claire didn't miss the stress in her aunt's voice. Unless she was mistaken, Kate seemed close to the breaking point.

Claire tapped Kate on the arm.

Glancing in her niece's direction, Kate covered the receiver. 'Wait,' she mouthed before continuing her telephone conversation. 'Well, all right. Please let me know if there're any new developments.'

Claire nudged her aunt. 'Give me the phone.'

'My niece wants to have a word with you,' Kate handed Claire the receiver.

Without wasting time on pleasantries, Claire got right to the point. 'The way things are, Valerie could come home and leave again and again and we'd never know. Why don't you hire a private detective and station him near her flat?'

'When did you get your investigator's

license?' The solicitor's soft-spoken words dripped with sarcasm.

'I did find her address,' she reminded Percy quietly.

'Thank you.' His response was slow, as if it pained him to admit a woman had succeeded after the police department failed.

'All right, I admit you're Nick's solicitor and I'm only his niece by marriage.' She attempted to sound humble. 'Even so, I love Kate and see how she's hurting. Nick's not thrilled with his present living arrangement, either.'

'Leave it to me.' Percy's voice hardened. 'When I get useful evidence, I'll turn it over to the police right away. Let them investigate. It's their job, you may recall.'

'Fair enough.' Claire hung up. Men could be so pig-headed at times. The sight of Kate at the window reminded her that she'd snatched the phone. 'I'm sorry. I didn't mean to be rude.'

When Kate turned, her cheeks were moist. A wave of pity and affection stirred inside Claire and she enveloped her aunt in a comforting hug. 'It'll be all right.'

'What was that about Percy and a detective?' Kate asked.

'Oh, I was just talking. It seemed a good idea.'

'From your end of the conversation, it sounded like Percy didn't agree.'

'You're right about that. And he didn't waste any time shooting me down, you may've noticed. Percy's content to wait for a big chunk of evidence labeled, 'proof of Nick's innocence' to fall in his lap.' Claire patted Kate's shoulder then curled up on one of the velvet antique loveseats. 'What a jerk.'

'Maybe you and I could watch for Valerie.' Kate's voice sounded positive for the first time since Nick was arrested.

'Don't even think about it. You have two four-year-old children who need their mother.' Seeing new found hope begin to fade from her aunt's face, Claire added, softly, 'I could go.'

Kate flashed a large grin. 'Did I ever tell you, you're the best person in the whole world?'

Her aunt's enthusiasm was so contagious, before she knew it, Claire found herself making plans. 'While I'm there, I'll drop by to see Valerie's dad and the landlady.'

Energized by having something she could do to help Nick, Claire went into the kitchen to pack herself a lunch. She hoped to miss the housekeeper.

She was slicing bread for a sandwich when Mattie burst into the room. Earlier Claire had no idea how upset the housekeeper was over Nick since she always kept her feelings to herself. The last few days the older woman had become more emotional.

Out of the corner of her eye, Claire caught Mattie wiping her face with a corner of her apron. 'I'm just going to sit in Kate's car and watch Valerie's apartment building,' Claire said.

'Keep your car doors locked.'

Claire waited for Mattie to make her promise not to speak to strangers. She didn't. Instead, she busied herself preparing a large thermos of hot tea then kissed Claire on the cheek. 'Remember, call if you need me. I'll be there.'

Claire began to feel like the lead character in *Mission Impossible*. She went to say goodbye to her aunt.

Kate was waiting with her own list of conditions. 'Don't get any ideas about staying overnight. I want you home by dusk. And keep your cell phone on all day, let me know you're all right.'

'Don't get your hopes up. Chances are Valerie hasn't come back to her flat.' No sooner did the words leave her mouth than Claire remembered the closet full of expensive clothes. 'On the other hand, she may want to stop by for a few things. From what

I've heard, Valerie doesn't sound like a woman who'd be happy with the bare necessities.'

★ ★ ★

Standing in the doorway to the library, Max coughed so they'd know he was there. 'Excuse me, Mrs. Connor?'

'Mr. Bronsky?' Kate started then she obviously remembered she had a tenant. 'I'm sorry, I didn't see you.' She smiled. 'How's the new apartment?'

'My oven light's burned out. Would you have a spare?'

'Of course. If you'll go to the kitchen and tell our housekeeper, she'll be glad to get you one.'

'Thanks. Nice to see you again, Miss Stanhope.' He nodded to Claire.

'Um . . . yes.'

Claire's half-hearted response seemed to indicate she found it hard to be pleasant in his presence. Max shrugged. Maybe she didn't like Americans.

He'd been a bore during Claire's two visits to his office. Being publisher of a newspaper was a new experience to Max. He didn't know how he should behave. He shouldn't have kissed her though he'd enjoyed it more

126

than he cared to admit.

Max didn't want to encourage Claire or anyone else at the hotel to stop by the Bugle when in the neighborhood. There was always the remote possibility his contact might show up.

Before he could leave, Claire addressed Max in a more civil manner. 'Are you settling in all right?'

Perhaps she'd decided it wasn't wise to be rude to Kate's only tenant. 'Fine, thanks.' He glanced from one woman to the other. Neither invited him to stay and chat, so he had no recourse but to leave. 'I'll go find the housekeeper.'

Wondering what Claire and Kate had been talking about when he appeared, Max headed down the long corridor toward the kitchen at the back of the ground floor. From the bit of conversation he'd overheard, Claire was taking a trip for her aunt. And judging by Kate's words, it wasn't a simple errand or shopping trip. Were the two women involved in a scheme with Tony? Maybe Max should follow Claire, see where she went. Tony could be sending her somewhere.

The hotel appeared quiet. Max chose to postpone seeing the housekeeper for a few minutes. Instead, he prowled the ground floor, stopping outside the workroom to observe Tony repairing a piece of furniture under Chris's supervision. From the stack of broken chairs beside him, Tony would be busy all day.

Max got the replacement light bulb from the housekeeper who was watching a kiddie program on television with the children. Then he hurried back to his flat.

Grabbing a jacket and his cell phone, he left his gatehouse flat again, locking the door behind him. Max slid down in the driver's seat of his car and waited out-of-sight.

Minutes later, Claire drove by in Kate's vehicle. Max turned on the ignition and followed her. His car's previous owner had been a Bowness teenager and it was faster than it appeared. It wouldn't be hard to keep up with Claire.

He lagged a little behind her. Once they reached the motorway, Claire drove faster and he sped up, always keeping a few cars between his vehicle and hers.

The outskirts of Manchester appeared ahead of them before long. When she slowed down, Max also reduced speed. When she turned, he did likewise. Once he almost lost her. A bread truck had broken down in the middle of a busy intersection. Max extracted his car from the snarl of traffic and looked for Claire's vehicle. She was nowhere in sight.

Now where did she go?

The traffic shifted and he heaved a sigh of relief, seeing Kate's Range Rover parked next to a tall brick apartment building named Cranley Estates.

Claire was striding down the sidewalk, entering the building as he parked his car. Max followed with caution.

By the time he stepped inside, she had disappeared and the elevator was just leaving the ground floor. With no idea where she was going, his options were limited. He could remain on the ground floor and wait for her. That wasn't a viable option since he'd have no idea which apartment she'd visited.

Max took the stairs, dashing up the first flight. He reached the next floor before the aged elevator which didn't stop, just continued its creaking ascent. Taking a deep breath, he raced up the next flight, again arriving in time to see the elevator pass by, heading upward. Soon he realized he moved faster than the antique elevator.

Again and again, he reached the next floor just before the elevator. It didn't stop, just kept going. *Damn, is she heading for the roof?*

Minutes later, Max reached the tenth floor. His heart was racing as he leaned against the wall and wiped his sweaty forehead. When the elevator arrived, he stepped around the corner to avoid being seen.

Claire got out. From his hiding place, he observed not a hair was ruffled on her head. No wonder, she hadn't dashed up ten flights of stairs.

She appeared to be reading a piece of paper in her hand then she headed down the semi-lit hall.

Muscles taut, Max followed her, prepared to change direction at any moment if she turned around.

At the end of the shadowy hall, she knocked on a door. It opened right away and she stepped inside. It appeared someone had been expecting Claire.

While Max recorded the apartment number, a soiled card tacked on the door drew his attention. He crept close enough to read the card. The name *Cyrus Doyle* was printed in firm letters. The name didn't ring any bells. Max shrugged and hid in the shadows, prepared for a long stay.

A few minutes later, the door opened and Claire stepped out. He watched as she walked back down the hall.

Max crept from his hiding place and retraced his steps down the gloomy staircase. A small dark form skittered by him in the darkness between floors. Startled, he grabbed the railing to keep from falling.

It was a relief to reach the ground floor. He must've been slower on the stairs this time since the elevator beat him for a change. It stood empty in the lobby, its doors open. Claire was out of sight.

A soft tap on his shoulder and he spun around, reaching for his gun.

Anger distorted her features.

'I'm sorry. You startled me.'

'You creep. What did you think you'd find out by following me?' Turning on her heel, she marched out of the building.

If she was Tony's girl, she'd tell her boy friend about Kate's new tenant following her. Tony wouldn't relish another man trying to get close to his woman.

Thinking fast, Max walked after Claire. 'You don't have any idea how desperate I get for a good story,' he whined. 'Wanna tell me who you were visiting?' He pulled out a pad of paper and pen then forced a leer to his face. 'If you have a boy friend here in Manchester, say so. I won't squeal to Tony.'

Her expression was stern for a moment, then she grinned. 'You sound like one of those seedy reporters in Mickey Spillane mysteries.'

Max gasped. He'd finished near the top of his class at the Academy, but nothing in his training had prepared him for her.

'You don't want to muck around with me, my lad. I read all of the old mysteries.' She cocked her head, like she was appraising him. 'Your clothes are wrong and you need to get a box of toothpicks.'

'Toothpicks? Why toothpicks?'

'You know, to hang out of your mouth. The Spillane reporters always munch on tooth-picks.'

Claire marched away. While he was standing there, chuckling at her quirky sense of humor, she got in her car and drove away.

Max ran outside. She had a head start. By the time he turned on the ignition, she was long gone.

12

Claire wasted no time driving away from Doyle's apartment building. She didn't dare look in the rearview mirror for fear she'd see Max's vehicle. Why was he following her? Was it for a story for his newspaper?

Something didn't ring true about Max. He just didn't strike her as an unscrupulous newsman.

Blocks later, he still hadn't appeared. Claire let out her breath. Good, she'd lost him. If and when she located Nick's ex-wife, she didn't want Max or any other reporter around.

She must talk to Valerie alone. The more she considered Kate's theory, the more Claire realized it was feasible. The poison pen letter had arrived the morning after Nick was found in that cabin with the dead woman. And the letter's writer alluded to Nick's 'love nest.' Also, according to Kate, Valerie had been quite upset over the divorce.

Nick's marrying Kate might've caused Valerie to become so bitter, she wanted to get even with him. Maybe she did know something about the corpse in the cabin.

Claire wondered how far Valerie'd go to hurt her ex-husband.

Parking down the block from Valerie's apartment building, Claire crossed the street, studying the neighborhood. Max's car was still nowhere in sight as she hurried to the landlady's house and hit the doorbell.

'Yeah?' A large head covered with purple hair curlers appeared at an open window. The landlady stared at Claire for a moment then her thick lips curled into a smile of recognition. 'She ain't here, sweetie.'

'Have you seen her since I visited you?'

'Nope.'

'Has she called you?'

'Nope.'

Their one-sided conversation sounded all too familiar. 'Are you sure?' Claire opened her shoulder-bag and drew out a large bank note, displaying it in the other woman's line of vision.

'Sorry, I don't know nuttin about her.' The head disappeared and the window was lowered. Seconds later, the front door opened, revealing the landlady, a curious smile on her face. 'Come on in. Least I can do is give ya a cuppa tea.'

Last time Tony had been with her. This time she was alone. It might be wise to be wary of this unscrupulous landlady who was

134

double her weight. 'No thanks. You have my card. If you'll ring me up when she returns?'

'Will do, dearie, will do.' The door shut and Claire could hear the landlady's bleating voice inside, talking babytalk to her mangy cats.

Now what? She returned to the car. Kate and she had discussed watching Valerie's apartment, and it was early yet. She'd stay around for awhile before returning to Bowness. Maybe she'd get lucky. Maybe Valerie would return.

Come home, Valerie.

★ ★ ★

Max didn't follow Claire as she no doubt feared he would. Manchester was a large city and she could've gone in any one of several directions. Instead, he took the elevator to the tenth floor, walked down the dim hall and knocked on the door where she'd visited.

'Hello?' An older gentleman answered.

Max thought fast. Sometimes the truth was the best policy. 'Sir, my name is . . . ' He showed Doyle his identification and told him the truth or part of it. Enough to convince the old man that Claire and Valerie could both be in danger.

'All right, son. I believe you.' Doyle gave

135

Max his daughter's address. 'Your friend was on her way over there.'

'I don't need to remind you that what I told you — '

'My lips are sealed.' Doyle interrupted him. 'Good luck.'

Max didn't wait for the elevator. He took the stairs instead and hit the ground floor running. He hurried to his car. Maybe she'd still be at Valerie's apartment when he got there.

★　★　★

As Claire passed the landlady's house, the lace curtain at a front window fluttered back into place. Was the landlady watching her? She drove to the next street, grabbed her purse and binoculars and slid from the vehicle.

There was a grove of trees on the vacant lot on the corner. Claire was glad she was wearing a neutral-colored sweater and slacks. They'd blend in with the browns of the autumn leaves.

She kept the binoculars fixed on the front of Valerie's apartment building until her vision blurred. Then she put them aside for a moment to rest her eyes.

The landlady's scrawny watchdog began

barking and Claire grabbed the glasses again. As she focused on the little brown house, she caught a glimpse of the landlady slipping through her side gate and closing it behind her. The dog continued barking while his owner hurried to Valerie's building and went inside.

Straining to see through the foliage, Claire wondered if it was the sun reflecting on Valerie's side windows or was there a light inside?

Aware she shouldn't go in there alone, Claire hurried to the apartment building. She had to find out if Valerie was home. As Claire entered the old building, the hallway was dark and quiet. Judging by the pungent odor, another tenant was cooking or burning meat.

Claire climbed the stairs to the second floor, then she crept down the hall to Valerie's apartment. The sound of voices attracted her and she crept closer. The door creaked and she jumped back into the shadows just in time.

Someone came out of the apartment and hurried downstairs. Moments later, Claire heard the front door slam.

Light seeped under the door as she approached Valerie's apartment. Without warning, the door opened. Claire didn't have time to run. A large hand grabbed her, yanked her inside and dumped her face down on the dusty floor.

'Well, look what we got here,' a voice said.

Claire tried to raise her head. A large boot pushed her down again. 'What ya doing, hanging around here?' A heavy hand ruffled her hair then pulled a strand so hard, Clare gasped.

'I wanted to see someone in this building.' She tried to turn. The person held her in position.

'Stay still or I'll tie you up.'

The husky voice belonged to a woman. 'Valerie?' Claire was guessing. Who else could it be?

A pause then, 'Who are you?'

'A friend of Nick's.'

'Girl friend?'

'No, a friend of his family.'

'So? What you doing here?'

'Nick's in trouble and he needs help.'

No response so she continued. 'The police think he killed someone. He didn't. I thought maybe you could help.'

'Me? God, why'd I want to help that bloke?'

'Well, you were his wife for two years. You know he wouldn't kill anybody. Don't you?'

'I guess.'

'Will you help?' Claire made the mistake of

138

raising her head and trying to see the other woman.

The woman flipped her over then lifted her off the floor. All Claire saw was an angry, pudgy face and a mop of straggly dark hair. The woman punched Claire in both eyes.

She fell back on the floor. Through a fog of pain, she heard the apartment door close then blackness.

★   ★   ★

As Max approached the apartment building a heavy-set woman ran out the front door carrying a suitcase. She would've knocked him down. At the last moment he stepped aside and let her pass.

Fearing the worst, he hurried inside. Claire's car wasn't parked outside, yet she'd been headed to this address. Max's finely tuned instincts told him she was in danger.

On the second floor, he found Valerie's apartment door ajar. He stepped inside, shutting the door behind him. A woman lay on her side on the living room's dirty hardwood floor. He recognized Claire's jacket and hurried to her.

She was out cold. No wonder, judging by the bruises on her face. She'd have a couple of shiners tomorrow.

Max knelt beside her and stroked her hair. 'Claire?'

Regaining consciousness, Claire put up her hand to protect herself before she recognized Max. 'Did you catch her?'

'The woman who just left? Was that Valerie?'

'I guess. I just got a quick glance before she slugged me.' Claire scowled. 'Ouch,' she cried and touched her injured face.

'Let me see if I can locate some ice.' In the tiny kitchen off the living room, Max searched the freezer and found it empty. A half-consumed drink with ice rested on the counter so he emptied the glass into the sink, scooping the ice cubes into his pocket handkerchief, tying it closed. He hurried back to Claire.

'Thanks.' She held the make-shift icebag against her face.

'Give me a minute to call King's Grant and tell them what's happened, then I'll take you home.'

'I can't believe you're being nice to me,' she murmured.

'Of course I am. You're hurt.' It upset Max to see her in pain. Valerie must be a brute. 'Wait until you're better. Then see how fast I change back to my usual boorish self.'

Claire shifted the icebag from one side of

her face to the other. 'I've never had a black eye before.' She winced when he bent to examine her injuries but didn't move away.

'Maybe we should find an emergency room, get your face x-rayed. You might have broken bones.'

'I just got two black eyes,' she said. 'Besides, this's no place to leave Kate's car.' Claire blinked back tears. 'What do we do now? I don't think I can drive myself home.'

'Do you want me to contact the police?'

'No, just call Chris,' she said in a shaky voice.

Max helped Claire to the sofa. While she rested, holding the makeshift ice pack over her eyes, he contacted Chris on his cell phone. When he ended the call, Max informed her, 'They'll be here as soon as they can. I'll check in with them again later.' Glancing around the apartment, he said, 'It's time we were on our way, Claire.'

'Why hurry?' She seemed confused. 'Valerie's gone.'

'I wouldn't be surprised if she came back. From the looks of this place, you interrupted her packing.' He didn't want to worry Claire yet Valerie might not be alone when she returned.

'She almost ran me off the sidewalk as I walked up to the front entrance of the building,' he said. 'I only got a fleeting glance as she rushed by me. She was lugging a suitcase. There's another by the bedroom door.' His instincts were on red alert. *Get the hell out of there.*

'Where did you leave Kate's car?' Hearing her response, Max nodded his approval then he helped her walk out of the apartment.

When Claire stumbled in the hall, he swept her into his arms and hurried down the stairs. He admitted to liking the way she rested her head on his chest while he was carrying her. At his car, he gently placed her in the passenger's seat.

Jumping into the vehicle, Max turned on the ignition. Without turning on the car's lights, he eased the Ford away from the curb, drove slowly to where Claire had parked Kate's car.

Down the block he spotted a small one-story house with a blue and white 'for sale' sign in the front yard. He nodded. That'd do. Max drove into the backyard and parked under the overhanging trees. For the first time since he found Claire, his taut muscles eased a little.

'Keep the doors locked,' he whispered, sliding out of the vehicle. 'If you need me, hit the horn twice and I'll be here fast. Understand?'

Claire nodded, her face pale in the moonlight.

Retrieving Kate's Land Rover, Max parked it in the back yard beside his own vehicle. He'd just settled himself beside Claire again when car doors slammed outside the apartment building. 'Not a moment too soon,' he said, smoothing her hair from her face.

Claire trembled and he put his arm around her. 'We're safe. I better get back to Chris. I told him to leave his phone on.'

Chris answered on the first ring. 'We're on our way.'

'Sounds like someone may be at Valerie's apartment,' Max said, his voice void of emotion. 'Stay away from there.'

'Do you expect trouble?'

'Maybe. We're parked in the backyard of a vacant white frame house down the street. Wait a minute, I'll give you the exact address.' Max slid from the car, ran to the front yard and located the house number. 'Be careful,' he warned Chris.

He returned to Claire. She appeared calm now. A curious expression was on her face.

'What is it?' Her composure surprised Max.

'Who are you?' Claire's gaze locked with his.

'Someone who'll do his best to keep you safe.'

'That sounds like a guardian angel.'

'Nobody ever called me an angel,' Max said, strangely moved. 'I don't know if I can live up to that.'

Max rolled down his car window, straining to hear any sounds coming from Valerie's apartment building. All was quiet, then a car drove past the house in front of their hiding place.

While he listened, every muscle alert, the car continued down the street. He slipped out of his vehicle and walked down the block until he could see the apartment building. There were no cars parked in front now.

In less than two hours, Kate and Chris arrived in Chris's truck. Kate took one look at Claire's face and burst into tears.

'It's not as bad as it looks,' Claire said, patting Kate.

'Let me help you to my car.' Kate looked at her niece.

'If you don't mind, I'll ride back with Max.'

Kate started to say something then she nodded. 'See you both at Kings Grant.' She got in her car and drove off, followed by Chris in his truck.

During the drive back to Bowness, Max didn't try to make conversation. From the way Claire bit her lip, it was obvious she was in pain and needed to rest. Once he looked in her direction. Her head was back, her eyes closed.

Reaching behind the driver's seat, he found an old sweater he kept there and managed to drape it over her, while keeping one hand on the steering wheel, his eyes on the road. He also checked his rearview mirror every few minutes. No one followed them.

While he drove through the darkness, Max considered his situation. Assigned to track a wanted criminal, he was close to forming an attachment for a woman he didn't know. Not smart. Still, Claire brought out all of his protective instincts. He went a step further and admitted he wanted her.

The lights of Kings Grant were a welcome sight when they drove up the driveway. Kate looked out a front window as Max parked his car. She hurried outside and opened the passenger car door, waking Claire.

'You're home, hon,' Kate said. 'Let me help you upstairs.' She might've been taking care of one of her own children, the gentle way she put her arm around Claire and led her inside.

Before going into the hotel, she looked in Max's direction. 'Thank you,' she whispered before closing the door.

Kate's tenderheartedness struck a chord

deep inside Max and he sensed she was a good mother. He moved the car down to his parking slot by the gatehouse. What a day. Before stepping into his small living room, he turned on a wall light switch. His gaze moved around the room. Best he could tell, no one had been there since he left that morning.

Pausing to pour himself a Scotch, Max then turned on his computer. Better check his email before taking a shower.

A message caught his eye. Short and to the point, it stopped him dead in his tracks. 'See enclosed photo.' No signature. There was no doubt it was from the Yard.

A color picture gradually filled the computer screen. Tony sitting in a nightclub, someone else close to him. The grainy texture of the scanned image wasn't the greatest. The woman perched on his lap was leggy, young and blonde. Though Max couldn't be dead sure, the girl looked like Claire.

And he'd found himself wanting to protect her. Fool.

13

All Claire wanted was to lie down and go to sleep. Her aunt seemed to have other ideas since she busied herself in Claire's bathroom, running a tub of warm water and putting out fluffy towels. Too weak to argue, Claire climbed in the tub.

'Want me to stick around and wash your back?'

'What? No, I'll manage.' She went through the motions of taking a bath then got out and dried herself. Kate tapped on the bathroom door before stepping back into the room.

'Here,' she said, offering a soft floral granny gown.

'Thanks.' Claire slipped it on, grateful for its warmth.

Kate wasn't done yet. She opened her hand, displaying two pink pills. 'These will help.'

Claire shook her head. 'I can't take your medicine.'

'It's just an over-the-counter medication for pain. It'll help you sleep.' Kate hesitated. 'We'll talk tomorrow.'

Trying to put herself in her aunt's place,

147

Claire fought back the fatigue and pain. 'Kate, let me tell you what happened in Manchester. First I saw Mr. Doyle. He hadn't heard from his daughter. Then I visited Valerie's apartment. I almost missed her, she was about to leave.'

'Did you try to keep her from leaving?'

'Are you kidding?' Claire grimaced. 'When she found me in the hall outside her apartment, she pulled me inside and dumped me face down on the floor.' Claire yawned, trying to focus on Kate and their conversation. Though it took all her strength, she must explain what happened. 'I turned so I could see her. That's when she yanked me up and punched me in both eyes.'

'Valerie yanked you up?' Kate's eyebrows raised.

'Yeah.' Claire yawned. All she wanted was sleep.

'I can't believe that.'

'Oh?' Things were getting hazy. She'd faint if she didn't lie down soon.

Kate must've sensed her fatigue since she helped her niece into bed. 'Someone else must know about her apartment.'

'Dunno.' Claire snuggled under the covers. 'Need to sleep.'

★ ★ ★

148

The next morning Claire's eyes were so swollen, she had trouble opening them. And her head throbbed. She brushed the hair off her face, wincing when she touched her eyes.

In a flash it all came back, Valerie attacking her then leaving her in the apartment on the floor.

The rest of the evening was a blur, though Claire recalled Max's kindness when he'd found her. He'd improvised an ice pack, even carried her to his car. Based on what she had seen of him earlier, she wouldn't have thought he could be so kind. This new side to his personality was one she definitely liked.

Finding her way to her bathroom, she splashed cold water on her face. The sight of her two shiners made Claire want to cry.

Once she'd brushed her teeth, she felt a little better so she put on her robe and slippers and went downstairs.

At the dining room table, her aunt was working on a grocery list. Kate started when she looked up and saw her. 'Good morning. I was going to bring you a tray soon.' She sent Claire a concerned glance. 'Are you sure you should be out of bed?'

'Of course. I'm not ill.' She forced a smile though it hurt.

'Sit there and I'll get you a cup of tea.' Kate hurried from the room, returning with a small

149

teapot, cup and saucer.

Before she could pour the tea, Claire spoke. 'I'd rather have coffee if there's any made.'

Moments later she was sipping the coffee Kate brought and munching on a piece of toast.

'Have you thought any more about our conversation last night?' Kate seemed anxious.

'To tell the truth, I was so tired, I don't remember much,' Claire admitted.

'You know. About Valerie, about her picking you up and slugging you.'

'Oh, right. I won't forget that anytime soon.' Claire touched one eye. It was swollen but didn't hurt as much as the previous evening. 'May I have an ice pack?'

'Of course you can, wait a minute.' Kate left the dining room. When she returned, Mattie was with her.

'Poor lamb,' the housekeeper exclaimed, bending over Claire. 'Does it hurt?'

'Only when I laugh,' Claire said, weary of so much attention. 'I'll wear dark glasses until the swelling goes down. Ice packs help.'

'We were talking about what happened last night,' Kate informed Mattie. 'Claire said Valerie picked her up. I've seen Valerie and she can't weigh one hundred pounds.'

'You've got to be kidding,' Claire exclaimed. 'Why do you keep talking about Nick's ex-wife like she's tiny? I saw her and felt her fists.'

'Dear, if the woman in Valerie's apartment was large enough to pick you up, it wasn't Valerie.' There was no doubt in Kate's words. 'Remember, before you fell asleep, I told you — .'

'All right, I get the picture,' Claire interrupted. In spite of her best intentions, she was beginning to feel irritated. 'If it wasn't Valerie who assaulted me, who was it? And what was she doing in Valerie's apartment? Where's Valerie?'

Kate nodded. 'Now we're all on the same wave length.'

'We better report this.' Claire hoped she didn't end up on the wrong side of the local authorities. Even so, she had to notify the police. Something odd was going on.

'Did you ever see the woman before?' Kate asked.

'No, but I won't forget her. She was large, heavy-set, long greasy dark hair. Most of all, I remember her expression. She looked angry and something else.' Claire closed her eyes for a moment, envisioning her assailant's features. 'Guilt was written on her face like she'd been caught somewhere she shouldn't be.'

'And you don't know anyone who looks like her?'

'No, not that I can think of, unless . . . ' Claire's voice trailed off and she lost her train of thought. Her head was throbbing. 'Where do you keep the aspirin? I'm getting a beaut of a headache.' She rubbed her forehead.

Mattie stepped into the kitchen and came back with a glass of water and two tablets. 'Here, take these.'

A few minutes later the other two women left the dining room. Claire could hear them talking in the kitchen. The low murmur of their voices reassured her.

They came back into the room and Kate felt Claire's forehead. 'You don't feel feverish, but I still think we should have our family doctor check you over.'

'Nothing doing. It's just a headache. Your head would hurt if someone gave you two shiners.'

'If that headache doesn't go away soon, I'm getting you an appointment with Dr. Nielsen.' Kate's lips set in a firm line, a clear indication her mind was made up. Claire sipped her coffee while Kate helped Mattie clear the table.

Kate called Nick's solicitor to let him know what happened. From her aunt's end of the conversation, Claire got the impression Percy

152

was anxious to talk to her. Kate was trying to put him off.

Holding out her hand for the telephone, Claire told Percy what she remembered about the woman. Before the call ended, he'd agreed to notify the police. No doubt they'd want to examine Valerie's apartment.

The bell above the entryway jangled and Max entered the hotel. His image reflected in the mirror on the dining room wall. Darn. If she'd known he'd show up so early, she'd have dressed and put on her makeup. Waiting for him, Claire smoothed her hair.

For some reason he never reached the dining room. Instead, Kate stepped into the hall to speak to him, then he left.

'What did Max want?' Perhaps he didn't realize she was downstairs. Or maybe he thought she'd be self-conscious and not want to see anyone with those black eyes.

'He wants to talk to me in his apartment.'

'Did he say why?'

'No.' Kate shrugged. 'Finish your breakfast. I'll be back.'

★   ★   ★

While waiting for Kate, Max debated the best way to handle the situation. Without revealing his true identity, he needed to see what she'd

153

tell him about Claire.

Footsteps sounded outside his door. Max stood and opened it. Kate stepped into the gatehouse.

'Thanks for coming,' he said. 'Would you like to sit down?'

Kate nodded and took a seat. 'Is there a problem with the flat?' She queried him from her perch on the edge of a chair. 'If there's something that needs repairing, I'm sure either Chris or Tony will be glad to fix it.'

'Not at all, the place's quite comfortable.' Max brushed aside her offer. All he needed was Tony snooping around. Max tried to think of the best way to begin. 'It has to do with your niece. Didn't you say she used to live in Devon?'

Kate looked mystified. 'Why, yes. She left here five years ago. Things happened that made it difficult for Claire to remain in Bowness.'

Charles's death, no doubt. Max remembered the brief news article in the Manchester Globe. 'And you didn't see her again until this month?'

'We stayed in touch.' Kate's expression became skeptical. 'What's this all about? I hope you aren't gathering material for more articles on the Stanhopes.'

'This has nothing to do with the

154

newspaper, I assure you.' He hesitated before adding, 'It's just that Claire may not be the girl she was when she left home.'

'I wouldn't think so.' Kate's smile was wry. 'Five years is a long time. Are you the same man you were five years ago?'

'No, I suppose not.' *Good point, Kate.* Max nodded. 'Back to Claire. Did she mention any friends in Devon?'

'That's none of your business,' Kate said, defending her niece's privacy.

'This isn't idle curiosity. I'm concerned about her.'

'Well, I suppose it's all right to tell you this. Claire mentioned two women she worked with in a floral shop, though not by name,' Kate said. 'I was pleased to hear she'd taken a job. It gave her the opportunity to meet people. Claire led a sheltered life here. That's the way Charles wanted it.'

'Oh?' *She and her brother must have been close.*

'I trust her.'

Max could tell Kate loved her niece, would stand in the way of anyone wanting to hurt her. 'Sorry. I didn't mean to offend you. If Claire begins to act strangely, will you tell me?'

'It's not for a story or a book, I have your word?'

'You have my word. I mean her no harm, I promise.'

'Then why are you so interested?'

'She may be in danger and if she is, you all are at risk.'

Kate stiffened. 'Who'd want to hurt Claire?'

Max shook his head. 'You have no idea.' He neglected to explain his suspicions about Claire. The computer picture was a little grainy, but the woman sure resembled Claire.

There could be several reasons why Tony had come to Bowness. He might be there to meet a member of another syndicate, to work out a deal. Or to size up local crime bosses.

A worse scenario came to mind and Max frowned. Tony might be in the Lake District as a hired assassin.

The Yard suspected Tony was Antonio, the assassin suspected of killing the president of a South American country in Venice the previous year. Also, someone meeting his description had been seen fleeing the scene of the murder of the Executive Vice President of the World Bank in London just three months ago.

If Antonio and Tony were the same person, Tony could be in the Lake District for a contract killing, though Max wasn't aware of any important dignitary being in the area.

He ran his fingers through his hair. It was up to him to find out what the man was up to and stop him. In an emergency, Scotland Yard would provide backup assistance.

Why the hell the assassin would take a job as handyman at Kate's hotel, Max didn't know. He didn't have a clue.

A muscle twitched in his cheek. He'd studied the computer picture so many times, he could close his eyes and see it. But in spite of the picture, he couldn't quite bring himself to believe the woman was Claire.

14

Tony watched Chris rubbing his eyes and yawning like he could've used a few hours more sleep. 'Bad night?'

'Yeah.' Chris said and changed the subject. 'How're the chairs coming?'

'Almost done. Do you have another project for me?' Tony wondered if he'd done anything to arouse suspicion.

'Nah, just finish those.' Chris turned and left the room.

Minutes later, Tony heard his boss talking to Mattie in the hallway between the workroom and the kitchen. Pretending to need to use the employees' washroom, Tony headed down the hall. 'Be right back,' he said, passing them.

Chris nodded and kept talking to the housekeeper.

Tony took his time walking down the hall. He strained to hear what they were saying. Claire's name was mentioned.

When he came out of the washroom, the corridor was empty. Curious as to what was going on, he returned to the workroom where he found Chris waiting for him.

'Just finish that one, all right?' Chris pointed to the last lawnchair still in need of repair. 'You're a good workman.'

Tony smiled, remembering Leo, the bodyguard/chauffeur who had befriended him when Tony first joined his father's household as a young boy. His father's employee enjoyed repairing furniture while off-duty. He must've learned something from watching Leo.

'I like working with my hands.' Tony bent to examine the chair. When he looked up, Chris was still there. 'All right?'

'What? Yeah, I guess.' Turning to leave the room, Chris stopped in the doorway. 'You've been working hard since you joined us. Take the rest of the day off when you're finished.'

'Great.' If something was going on, he better find out what it was. Tony hurried to repair the last chair then headed toward the front of the house. Maybe Mattie would tell him.

As he entered the kitchen, the housekeeper was lifting a pan of carrot-raisin bran muffins from the oven.

'Mmmmm.' He inhaled. 'You must be the best cook in Cumbria.'

His remark earned him a slight smile. 'Wait a minute,' she said. 'I'll give you one.'

'Thanks. Can I have a cup of coffee, too?'

'Sure.' The housekeeper poured him a cup.

'Mattie, is Chris upset about something?'

'Maybe.' The older lady wrinkled her brow. 'I'm sure it'll be all right.' Her unsure tone belied her words.

'Where's Chris, anyway? Did he go home?'

'No, he's at the gatehouse talking to the new tenant.'

'Oh, does the reporter have furniture that needs repairing?' Tony tried pumping her for information.

'No, he doesn't.' Taking a muffin from the pan, she placed it on a paper napkin and handed it to him. 'Here.'

Claire walked into the room and Tony couldn't help staring. Her appearance shocked him. 'What happened to your face?'

'Don't ask.' She took a pair of sunglasses from her sweater pocket and put them on.

Tony finished the muffin and tossed the paper napkin into the trash can beside the stove. 'Thanks, that was great.' He turned to go.

Following him from the kitchen, Claire spoke. 'I must look terrible.'

'I didn't mean to upset you, Miss.'

'Hey, don't start that 'Miss' stuff.' She smiled. 'What do you call me?'

'Claire.' Returning her smile, he could tell she liked him. At least she was a blonde, his preference. But Claire was too prim for his taste. He wondered if she was still a virgin. In his experience, few young women were.

Tony imagined having sex with Claire. A classy dame like her would be interesting for a change. Of course he was there on business, not pleasure. He had to find out about his brother. If that involved taking this cool Englishwoman to bed, he'd do it.

★ ★ ★

Tony seemed different now. His gaze was somehow more intimate. It made her uncomfortable, she glanced away. 'I went to Manchester again,' she said. 'And — '

'Somebody hurt you,' he interrupted. 'Tell me who the creep was. I'll make him sorry.'

'This wasn't done by a man.' Claire gestured to her face. She wondered if he meant what he said or was being macho again, like at the newspaper office. 'I was watching that apartment you and I visited. A strange woman came out and beat me up. Then she left in a hurry.'

'You didn't get a good look at her?' Tony seemed angry.

'Heck, no. It all happened too fast.' A shudder ran through Claire, recalling the experience. 'All I saw were stars.'

'Poor Claire.' He patted her arm. When she

didn't move away, Tony smiled. 'What's the matter with Chris today? Is his wife giving him a hard time?'

'Diane? Never.' Claire hastened to defend the stability of Chris and Diane's marriage. She concluded by saying, 'They're devoted to each other.'

'I just wondered.' He gazed at her curiously. 'I guess you heard about your aunt's new tenant. Does it bother you, having that guy living here?'

From Tony's unhappy expression, it was apparent he didn't care for Max. It might be wiser if she didn't mention the Bugle manager's helping her last night. She didn't want to damage her relationship with Tony. 'I don't care where the man lives as long as he minds his own business and doesn't publish any more articles about the Stanhopes.'

'Do you like him?'

'Why would you ask me that?'

Mattie called to Claire from the kitchen doorway. 'Have you visited The Folly yet?'

'Oh, rats,' Claire muttered under her breath before she answered Mattie. 'Not yet.'

'If you need help, I've finished my work,' Tony informed her. 'In fact, Chris gave me the rest of the day off. Let me get my jacket and — '

Claire cut him off. 'I've dreaded going over

162

there alone,' she confessed.

'I'll meet you out front. Do I need to bring tools?'

She shook her head. 'I just want to see how things look. The garden must've gone to weeds by now.' Claire sighed. 'I planned the flower beds and took care of them myself years ago.'

★ ★ ★

Percy April sat across from his client in the Visitors Room of the Windermere jail. His mind struggled to process what Nick had just told him.

Shaking his head, Percy said, 'I've got to stop taking my antihistamine. It's affecting my hearing. I could've sworn you just said you wanted to change your testimony.' The solicitor stared at Nick.

'That's what I said. Is it too late?'

'What happened? From the beginning, you've sworn you didn't know the dead girl. Now you tell me that you didn't just know her, you had a relationship.'

'Relationship? What are you talking about?' Nick scowled. 'Hell, we had sex once. That was a dumb mistake I admit yet — '

'Dumb?' Percy interrupted his client mid-sentence. If he had any brains in his head, he would've become a doctor. But he'd grown up addicted to reruns of the American television series Perry Mason. And convinced himself that criminal law would be exciting. 'You've just done the worst thing you could do.'

'Except one.' Nick's expression turned grim. 'I didn't kill the girl.'

'Oh, excuse me,' Percy retorted, his voice dripping with sarcasm. 'That'll help a lot. The detectives on your case are convinced you did. You're all they've got.'

'For some reason that doesn't make me feel any better.'

'Why get messed up with another woman? Good lord, man. I thought you and Kate were happy together.'

'We are. Well, most of the time. If she wasn't so pigheaded. Like I want us to have another child. Kate insists she isn't ready.'

'Maybe she isn't.' Percy sighed. 'Don't forget, if you're going to change your statement, you better tell Kate first. You wouldn't want her to hear the news second-hand.'

Nick slumped in his chair. 'That's what's so hard. The last thing I want to do is hurt her. She'll just have to understand. We'd had a fight when I attended a bachelor party the guys threw one night after work at Secrets. In

164

case you haven't heard, that's a new gentlemen's club in Kendal. I'd drunk too much and woke up in a cute little stripper's bed.'

'Who located Secrets for your group? Do you remember?'

'It must've been one of the guys in the department.' Nick frowned, concentrating. 'Art, it was Art. My younger officers call him 'Stud' behind his back. He fancies himself God's gift to women for some reason.'

Percy winced and Nick explained. 'Art's single so it doesn't matter if he cats around.'

'I presume you're referring to Arthur Walton, your second-in-command.' Percy wrote down the name on his pad.

'Yeah, for now he's Superintendent. And from what I hear, he's doing a damn good job.' Nick looked thoughtful. 'Several other DCI's applied for the Superintendent position when I did. Art was my main competition. I was lucky. The Super liked me.'

'I suggest you speak to Kate before informing the detectives assigned to your case.'

'You'll be there when I meet with them?'

'I'll be there.' Percy rose to leave.

'Hold on a minute,' Nick said. 'Did Valerie ever turn up?'

'Not yet. Since the attack happened in your ex-wife's flat, Claire assumed the woman who attacked her was Valerie, at least she did until your wife set her straight. Kate said from Claire's description of her assailant, it must have been someone else.'

Nick nodded. 'The day we met, Valerie reminded me of a porcelain doll.' A smile of remembrance flickered across his face. As he returned to the present, his usual depressed expression came back. 'Kate told me what had happened to her niece. I'm sorry Claire got hurt. Playing detective wasn't a smart thing to do. She could've been killed.'

Percy nodded. 'Your wife has Claire convinced your ex-wife's involved in the murder.'

'Val?' Nick snorted. 'No way. Valerie may have emotional problems, but she's no killer.'

'Not by herself, though Kate's theory has some merit,' Percy said. 'You've told me that your ex-wife was bitter about the divorce and your remarrying. When did you hear from her last?'

'That'd be hard to say.' Nick frowned. 'It seems like a long time ago,' he said. 'When Kate and I were first married, Valerie would call me once in a while, asking me to come back. I haven't heard from her for a couple of years.'

'Your wife has,' Percy said.

Nick stared at his solicitor. 'What did you say?'

15

The weeds growing around The Folly distressed Claire. When she'd lived there, the gardener kept the lawns and flower beds well groomed.

Gazing at the elegant pink stone mansion with its mansard roof, Claire felt her brother's presence. For a moment she imagined Charles waited for her inside, though her mind told her that was impossible. Without warning, her heart raced and her palms turned clammy.

'Hey! You all right?' Tony stared at her.

'Of course.' She couldn't say what bothered her more, having a panic attack outside The Folly or Tony's seeing it.

'You don't have to go in there today,' he said.

'Yes, I do.' Drawing a deep steadying breath, she stepped onto the porch and inserted her key into the lock.

The heavy door creaked open. 'Come on,' Claire said with more bravado than she felt.

Tony followed her into the foyer. 'Wow. This's great!'

Trying to see the familiar setting through a

stranger's eyes, Claire glanced around the foyer. 'It is nice.' Her father and mother had found the elaborate tile in Spain.

She led the way into a huge room with beamed ceilings. Sheet-protected furniture huddled around a massive stone fireplace. Bookshelves covered the opposite wall.

'It's so quiet.' She caught herself whispering.

'It won't be now that we're here. Anybody home?' He shouted.

'Thanks for coming with me. I've dreaded doing this. It's not so bad with company.'

'How about a tour?' Tony seemed eager to see The Folly.

'All right.' Leading him from room to room, she commented on those features she considered noteworthy.

Once they'd seen the rooms downstairs, Claire led Tony up the winding staircase to the next floor. In the master bedroom, she rediscovered several family treasures. Observing a disinterested look on Tony's face, she asked, 'Am I boring you?'

He shook his head.

On one side of the large room, she uncovered a little rosewood table coated with a layer of dust. 'This was my mother's,' she explained. 'It's from the Isle of Capri. Her father bought it for her on her sixteenth birthday. Her name was Rosanna Fiquisteri.'

Surprised, Tony stared at her. 'Your mother was Italian? You could've fooled me. You're so English.'

'Like the Stanhopes,' she said. 'But I'm half Italian.'

'Do you ever go back?'

'Where? To Milan? No, my grandparents are dead.'

'My ancestors came from Ravenna on the east coast of Italy.'

'I don't know much about you.'

'You know all that matters.' Tony stepped closer.

She backed away. 'Let's move along. There's more to see.'

As they walked down the corridor, her feet sank into plush Berber carpet. She stopped and opened a door. 'Here.'

Claire preceded him into a large shadowy bedroom. The sight of her favorite pastel print still hanging on the wall over the canopied bed pleased her. She admitted she'd missed her own home.

'Like it?' She gazed around. 'It's supposed to be an underwater scene. Notice the shades of green and blue, the draped windows. This is where I came when I wanted to get away.'

'It's okay,' Tony said. 'The bed looks comfortable.' Without asking her permission, he took off his loafers and lay across the wide mattress. 'Join me?' He grinned, patting the covers.

Feeling threatened, Claire quickly moved away. 'Ah, let's get out of here. It's so dusty, my allergies are having a fit.' She walked across the room and waited for him by the door.

He rolled off the bed and followed her, shoes in hand.

* * *

That same morning Kate sat at her desk in the hotel office. She'd never felt so alone. It seemed an eternity since Nick had been with her.

The phone's ring interrupted her thoughts.

'Kate, I need to talk to you.' Nick's voice sounded more strained than usual. 'Are you alone?'

'Mattie and the children are taking a walk and Claire has gone over to The Folly.' She was surprised to hear from him. Nick usually called her evenings. 'I'm paying bills. That can drive you crazy.'

'Yeah, I know. Well, Kate, I, I mean I . . . ' He paused.

'What is it?' His hesitation unnerved her.

'I'm changing my statement to the police.'

171

'I don't understand.' Fear rippled through her.

'I lied. I did know the girl in the cabin.'

'You knew her?' She felt breathless with anticipation.

'I met her, in fact I . . . ' Nick hesitated. 'I love you.'

'And I love you.' What had he done?

'And you believe I'm innocent?'

'You knew the girl?' She evaded his question by repeating hers. Remembering the poison-pen letter's mention of Nick's love nest, Kate wasn't sure she wanted to hear his answer.

Guilt overcame her fear. She should've told him about the letters. They'd never kept secrets from each other in the past. What would his response be when he found out?

'I slept with her one night when you and I weren't getting along,' he told her. 'That's all.'

Kate's world shattered like delicate crystal. 'That's all?' She shook with emotion. More than husband, Nick was her friend, trusted confidant and lover. Their relationship had always been special, untouched, until now.

'Are you there? Kate? Katie?'

Tears clouded her vision as Kate eased the phone into its cradle, too upset to answer. Nick had betrayed her.

*   ★   ★

Answering his cell phone, Max settled back on the sofa in the gatehouse, propped his feet on the coffee table, and prepared to listen to an investigator at the Yard.

The officer ran through the information he'd requested. 'You asked about the Grambellos. Your assignment doesn't involve Tony's missing brother, Francisco Grambello. Even so, you might be interested in this. He was last seen in Bowness.'

'I know. Can you tell me the circumstances?'

'The night he vanished, Franciso left his suite key at the hotel's front desk before going to an engagement. The assistant concierge remembered wishing him a good evening. Grambello commented he wouldn't be late. To our knowledge, that was the last time anyone saw him.'

'Did the hotel have any idea where he was going?'

'No.'

'It sounds like a dead end.' Or maybe not, Max thought.

'He never returned to the hotel.'

'He could've been with the Stanhopes,' Max said.

'His father contacted the authorities when

173

he didn't hear from Francisco. The police investigated and found no trace of him. Sometime later, a Bowness resident told a local policeman he'd seen Franciso with Miss Stanhope the week he vanished, so we visited them.'

'Was Charles Stanhope helpful?' Max had his doubts.

'Not really. Charles denied seeing Francisco that evening.'

'What about Miss Stanhope?'

'She gave the same story as her brother.'

'What about that other matter?' Max kept querying the Yard agent. 'I'm referring to Charles Stanhope.'

'Yes, a sad business. From what we can piece together, Charles lost over a million pounds, investing. That included a trust fund their father had set up for him and his sister. Later Charles seems to have suffered a nervous breakdown. Perhaps the strain of losing a fortune would be too much for a man to bear.'

'Who knows.' Max commented dryly. 'Go on.'

'Sorry, old man. I didn't mean to get off the track. Where was I?'

'Charles had a breakdown?' *Get on with it.*

'Ah, yes. Then he kidnapped his aunt.'

'That'd be Kate Stanhope.'

'Correct. Charles didn't hurt Mrs. Stanhope, he used her as a hostage while trying to elude the local police and escape across Morecambe Bay at low tide.'

'Kate Stanhope survived. I wonder why Charles didn't.'

'It's believed he hit a patch of quicksand and drowned. The police never recovered his body.'

'Is that all?'

'Well, almost. There was a hearing. Under oath, Miss Stanhope testified her brother forced her to join him in a scheme to ruin their aunt's new hotel business.'

'How the hell were they going to do that?' That didn't sound like the Claire that Max knew.

'Well, Miss Stanhope liked to garden, knew a lot about plants and rare herbs — '

'Poison?' Max cut him off in mid-sentence. He'd never pick Claire for a poisoner. Had she deceived him?

'It seems a poisonous herb was involved. Miss Stanhope swore that was accidental. According to her testimony, Charles reasoned that if the hotel business failed, Kate Stanhope would become so discouraged she'd give him the hotel and return to the States.

'Before Kate and Stanhope met, Stephen

175

Stanhope had promised to leave the property to his nephew and niece, Charles and Clarissa. He changed his will in favor of Kate after they married.'

'I see.' And now Claire could be involved with a criminal, Antonio Gambello. It appeared she wasn't a good judge of men. 'Thanks for the information.' Max turned off his phone.

The closer he came to Claire, the less he knew her.

★ ★ ★

Returning to King's Grant from The Folly, Claire pried Tony's fingers off her knee. 'You can let me out here,' she told him in front of the hotel. His roving fingers had made her nervous during the drive. 'Thanks for going with me,' she said. She opened the passenger door and slid out of the truck before he could make further advances.

Tony drove away to park the truck.

As she entered the hotel, Claire reviewed her day. Tony's behavior in her childhood bedroom was a definite sign he'd changed. She wasn't sure she liked his new persona.

Claire met Kate in the doorway. 'The place doesn't look bad inside. The gardens are a disaster.'

'Tony's a handyman,' her aunt reminded her. 'You don't want to become too friendly with him.'

'That's my business, not yours,' Claire snapped and went upstairs. In the privacy of her room, she reconsidered. Kate was right. What had she been thinking?

Crossing the room to her window, Claire gazed outside.

Tony came into sight.

He walked by under her window. As she watched, his mouth twisted into an unfamiliar cruel smile. And his swagger resembled a jungle predator on the prowl.

Tony continued on, moving out of sight and Claire wondered if she'd misinterpreted what she'd just seen. Or perhaps she didn't really know the man.

Since her return to Bowness, life was different. In Devon there'd been no one special. Except for a clumsy, half-hearted pass or two from her employer at the florist shop, she'd been as cloistered as a nun, living alone and working with two older women. Then she returned home and met two interesting men.

With an apology on her lips, Claire descended to the ground floor. Finding her aunt in the library, she said, 'I'm sorry.'

'It's all right.' Kate patted the sofa beside her. 'Come sit with me for a few minutes.'

'It's been wonderful, staying here with you all,' Claire began, taking a seat beside Kate. 'Still, it's not like I don't have my own home. I went over there to see how the house looks. I may sell it.'

'Are you sure you won't regret doing that?'

Claire thought a few moments. 'Maybe,' she admitted. 'A lot of my memories center around The Folly. And they're not all bad. It's just that I don't know if I can live there again.'

'Why don't you do a little housecleaning and have the yards groomed? Then you might try staying for short periods of time, like overnight. Give yourself a chance to find out what you really want to do. Don't rush into a decision.'

'Good idea.' She took Kate's hand. 'You've always been here when I needed you. I wish I could help you now.'

'You have. Just by coming home.' Kate let out a deep sigh. 'Nick lied about the dead girl. They had an affair.'

'I'm so sorry. Is there anything I can do?' And she'd envied Kate and Nick's perfect marriage. Claire felt disillusioned.

'No, unless you can promise me that lie is the only one he's told,' Kate replied.

'What do you mean?' Claire frowned. 'You don't think he killed the girl? Nick was

178

unconscious when they found him.'

'For how long?' Kate's eyes filled with tears.

★ ★ ★

During the night Tony slipped downstairs. The ground floor was in shadows. Since Nick's arrest, Kate left night lights on through the hotel.

Stepping outside on the front lawn, Tony studied the windows above. The upper floors were dark. They should be since it was two o'clock in the morning. He crept down the driveway and peered into the newspaperman's windows. All was dark.

Having made sure no one would notice his leaving, Tony headed downhill to the village.

★ ★ ★

Not everyone at the hotel slumbered. Max hadn't been able to sleep and had come outside to inhale the fresh country air. While Tony glanced around, Max was standing in the shadows. Curious as to what the handyman was doing, Max didn't move a muscle. The moment Tony left the hotel grounds, Max trailed him.

As he followed his suspect toward the

179

village, Max wondered where they were headed and the reason for this late night stroll.

Tony stopped in front of a convenience store. It was now almost two-thirty. All of the businesses in Bowness were shuttered and locked, including this store.

The shop owner had taken all of the grocery carts inside. Nothing remained outside except a trio of pay phones.

The stop now made more sense. Tony's cell phone must be unreliable, or he'd come down the fell to find a place to talk without fear of others overhearing.

Tony deposited change in one of the pay phones while behind a tree Max waited. Straining to hear, he edged closer.

Tony raised his voice. 'You heard me. You have your orders. Do what I tell ya. Don't give me any lip.' He paused. 'Just keep her quiet.'

Max didn't draw a breath. If Tony knew he had an audience, he would never have made that call.

Walking fast on the shoulder of the road, Tony returned to the hotel with Max trailing along behind. Once a stick cracked under Max's foot. Tony stopped and stood motionless, listening.

Not bad. Max gave the other man reluctant

praise. But he was an old hand at this game. Tony wouldn't catch him.

In his function as unseen escort, Max saw Tony to the hotel, waiting until the handyman eased open the door and slipped inside. Then Max returned to his flat.

Sitting erect in his narrow bed, he puzzled over what he'd heard. He'd read the Yard's file on Antonio and recalled the assassin's penchant for blondes.

The phrase, 'cat and mouse' came to mind. Antonio liked to play with the young women he dated. He was the cat and the woman was the mouse. That instant Max had a hunch where Valerie was.

16

The next morning Kate answered the telephone. She listened to the caller then handed the receiver to Claire. 'You talk to Percy.' She whispered so the solicitor wouldn't hear. 'I don't want to hear anything else about Nick right now.'

'Kate? Are you there?' The solicitor's voice inquired.

'It's me, Claire. Can I help? Kate's indisposed right now.'

'I guess. I'm calling to see if she's all right.' Percy hesitated. 'Nick told Kate about the dead woman. How is she?'

'Not very well. Was that all?' *What did he expect?*

'Nick says Kate hangs up the phone whenever he calls.'

'She'll come around. Why don't you both leave her alone for awhile? It must've been a terrible shock, hearing about Nick and that woman.'

Before Nick's solicitor could hang up, Claire asked, 'What's going on? Do the police have any leads?'

'Not as far as I know. We met with the

detectives on Nick's case this morning. They don't believe a word he says.'

'Kate told me Nick's changed his statement.'

'Yes, he did. Fleming, the lead detective sneered.' Percy said. 'If we can't find proof of his innocence, Nick doesn't stand a chance when we go to trial.'

'I'm sorry.' Claire wished she could help. 'I guess Valerie never turned up?'

'Not yet. I even drove to Manchester, hoping to find someone who knows her. You mentioned meeting her landlady?'

'Yes. That was an interesting experience.' *And expensive.*

'She wasn't home when I arrived. Her younger sister told me they have no idea where Valerie is. The sister was hurrying out the front door when I drove up. She was taking some groceries and fresh laundry to a sick friend.'

'Good for her. Does she resemble her sister?'

'From what you told me, I'd say so. She's a large woman with a mop of dark hair. I only saw her for a couple of minutes.'

His description reminded Claire of her assailant at Valerie's apartment. No doubt there were thousands of large brunettes in the area. 'I'll tell Kate that Nick misses her. And you let him know she'll be all right.' A thought hit Claire and she caught her breath. 'Percy, do you think Nick was set up?'

'At the cabin? No doubt he was.'

'Right. How about at the stag party? Who arranged it anyway?' Claire wished she could do something to end Nick and Kate's nightmare.

'I looked into that. It was Nick's second-in-command, Arthur Walton. When I talked to him, Arthur said that was the last stag party he'd ever arrange.'

★ ★ ★

Max strolled into the lobby of the hotel. The place appeared deserted. 'Hello?'

At the rear of the ground floor a door opened. Then steps hurried in his direction.

'Did you need something?' Kate appeared, her eyes appeared red and swollen. Had she been crying?

'Sorry, I'll come back later.' He turned to leave.

'Mr. Bronsky, what can I do for you?'

'The light over my kitchen sink's burned out and I wondered if . . . ' He didn't mean to stare yet he'd never seen anyone looking so miserable. 'Is it Claire?'

'What? Oh, no. Do you have a few

minutes? I need to talk to you about something.'

Max followed Kate into the library. 'Remember I asked you to let me know if she did anything troubling?' He wondered what had happened and if it involved Claire.

'This isn't about my niece.' Kate inhaled deeply. 'I've learned my husband lied about knowing the dead woman.'

'That's enough to upset anyone,' Max said, trying to be diplomatic. He didn't know Nick.

'The day the police picked him up, Nick gave a statement, saying he had never seen the dead woman before,' Kate said. 'Now he admits that he not only knew the girl, he had sex with her on a previous occasion.'

'So the police think they've got their killer?'

'I'm afraid so.'

'How do you feel about all of this?' Max inquired.

'Me? I'm hurt and angry. But — '

'You don't think he killed her.' Max interrupted.

'I don't know, I hope he didn't.'

'What evidence do they have?' Though it wasn't his case, Max liked Kate. At the moment he wasn't sure about Claire.

'I believe Percy said the police found no other fingerprints in the cabin, only Nick's and the woman's. Oh, I take that back, there was one set of prints they haven't been able to identify.'

'Was the woman . . . ' He hesitated.

'Raped?' Kate's laugh was bitter. 'You don't need to be delicate around me. Remember, I'm a police officer's wife.'

'All right. Was she?'

'No, though Percy found out she'd had sexual intercourse shortly before her death.'

'I'm sure you know that DNA can determine if she had sex with your husband,' Max said. 'Are the labs running tests?'

'I believe so. That takes time.'

'They'll find out the truth.' Max tried to sound encouraging. 'Hold on to your faith in your husband. Right now he needs you more than ever.'

'I guess so.'

'I better be going. That light bulb can wait.'

'Please stay a little longer. I would like to talk to you about my niece.'

He nodded, wondering what Claire had done.

'I think she's spending too much time with Tony, the handyman,' Kate said.

'Oh?' Max recalled seeing Claire and Tony together around the hotel. And on her second visit to Max's office, Claire had brought the hotel's handyman with her.

Under other circumstances, Max would've

186

considered Tony's words no more than youthful bravado, a younger man showing off in front of the woman he wanted to impress. But the Yard suspected Tony might be Antonio, the assassin. So what he'd said must be taken seriously.

Max had reported the incident to the Yard and asked them to run a check on Tony. No indication of criminal activity turned up though his father was in Dartmouth Prison for life.

There was also Tony's walk to the village the other night and his conversation on a pay-phone.

'Claire's life hasn't been easy,' Kate said. 'For that reason, I haven't nagged her about her family home, though she does need to make a decision about the property. Today she at least visited The Folly. Tony went with her.'

'And that worries you?' Max found himself in a quandary between the Yard's position that Claire could be a link to Antonio and his own personal feelings. The more he saw her, the more he doubted she'd be involved with a criminal.

'She's led a sheltered life,' her aunt said. 'I don't believe she's dated anyone except for a couple business associates of her brother's.'

'I can see why you'd be concerned.'

'You're very understanding.'

'If you like, I'll keep an eye on Claire. Tony did appear out of the blue. We don't know a thing about him.' Was the handyman really the international assassin in disguise? Max's jaw muscle tensed.

★　★　★

Claire started down the stairs. She stopped at the sound of Max's deep voice. Bits and pieces of the conversation drifted up to her. Her aunt's voice seemed to change from troubled to appreciative. Was Kate flirting with her American tenant? A small spark of envy ignited inside Claire.

Creeping downstairs, she stood in the hall outside the library. Claire became so absorbed in the others' conversation, she forgot she was eavesdropping.

Max stepped out of the library unexpectedly and bumped into her in the darkened hall. 'What the hell? Sorry, I didn't see you there.' He smiled as if he knew she'd been listening.

'I'm looking for my aunt. Is she in the library?'

Putting his head inside the doorway, Max called to Kate. 'Here's someone to keep you company.' He gave Claire a gentle shove into the room.

188

'What was that all about?' Kate asked as Claire walked into the room.

'What?' Claire tried to act like Max hadn't caught her listening. 'Oh, him. You know Americans.' She flushed, realizing too late that Kate had been born in Philadelphia.

'What did you decide about The Folly? Will you sell it?'

'No.' She hated to leave Kate though they were starting to get on each other's nerves. It was time she moved back home. 'I'm going to give it a good cleaning and move back in.'

'That's great,' Kate said. 'If there's anything I can do, just ask.'

'Thanks.' Taking Kate's hand, she offered words of encouragement. 'The police could find evidence any day proving someone else killed the dead woman.'

'Don't hold your breath.' Kate didn't sound optimistic.

'Anyway, I'm not gone yet.' Claire tried to think of some way to cheer up her despondent aunt. 'Let's go out to dinner. And there's a new romantic comedy at the Lakeside Theatre. Maybe Mattie wouldn't mind putting the children to bed when we come back from the restaurant. You and I could go to the movie.'

'That sounds like fun.' Kate rallied. The smile she flashed made her look more like her old self. 'I'll ask her.' She headed toward the kitchen.

Waiting for her aunt to return, Claire caught a glimpse of Max through the library's mullioned windows. Why was he wandering around the grounds holding a book? Curious, she ran outside and caught up with him. Claire recognized the book he carried. 'I didn't know you were a birder,' she said.

'I'm not though I'd like to identify the pretty black bird with white wings that I keep seeing.'

'That's a magpie.' She stood smiling at him a moment. On impulse she offered an invitation. 'It looks like we may all go out to dinner tonight. Would you like to join us?'

'That sounds like a family outing. Are you sure I wouldn't be intruding?' Max sounded pleased.

Recalling his kindness the night she was assaulted, Claire saw this as an opportunity. She could show her appreciation for his help by taking him to dinner. Also, he was Kate's tenant and a stranger in town. It wouldn't hurt for her to be hospitable.

'You're more than welcome. Please come, if you're free.' She smiled to show she really wanted him to join them.

'All right. Just give me a few minutes to change into something more presentable.' He gestured at his jeans and slip-over sweater.

'You're fine the way you are. This's a family restaurant. You might want to leave your Audubon guide in the car, though.' Claire grinned. 'There won't be any birds in the restaurant.'

The library window opened and Kate leaned out. 'Mattie said some other time.' Kate smiled at them. 'Maybe Max would go.'

'If you stay home, I do, too.' Claire wasn't about to abandon her aunt. It'd been her idea to get Kate out of the hotel. Besides, Claire wasn't sure she wanted to be alone with Max. She felt a little embarrassed around him since he found her listening to his conversation with her aunt.

Kate closed the window. A couple of minutes later, she appeared around the corner of the building. 'Mattie and the children are involved in a game of Old Maids. And their favorite supper, beef pot pie, is baking in the oven. If you don't mind, I think I will join you after all.'

'All right, ladies.' Max smiled. 'I'm ready when you are.'

Max drove down the hill and along the lake for a mile before reaching the restaurant. Walking up to the entrance, Claire and he flanked Kate.

As they approached, Claire took a deep

191

breath. 'What a wonderful aroma. I wonder what it is.'

Max smiled. 'Maybe a little pepperoni, some garlic — '

'Stop, you're making me hungry,' she cried. She flashed a smile at the Italian host who led them to a table.

Kate looked around. 'Some things never change. I like this restaurant. Nick and I've been here so many times.' Her face changed to pensive and she studied the tablecloth.

Claire patted Kate's hand. 'And you will, again. I promise.'

A waiter appeared to hand them the menus.

Directing her attention to the menu, Claire spoke to the waiter. 'You used to have a sampler plate, you know, lasagna, manicotti, spaghetti.'

'There it is.' He pointed to an item.

They all chose the sampler. When their dinners came, a collective sigh rose from their mouths.

That evening Claire tried to keep the conversation light. She got the impression Max was doing his best to help her.

'It's all right,' Kate said at last. 'We can talk about Nick. In fact, I'd like to hear what Max thinks about the situation.' She turned to him.

He raised an eyebrow. 'Hey, Kate. I'm no expert on police work. I'm a free-lance journalist.'

'We know that,' Claire said.

Kate nodded in agreement. 'Just tell us what you think, Max. Where do the police go from here?'

'Well, this is only my opinion, all right?'

They both nodded.

'You've told me the local police think Nick's guilty. That may be due to their not having any other suspects. He was found alone in the cabin with the dead woman. Still, they need to follow up on Nick's ex-wife. Claire mentioned that Valerie has been bitter about his divorcing her and remarrying.' He shook his head. 'I'd say that makes her a possible candidate. At least they should make more effort to find her, interrogate her.' He turned to Kate. 'Did the police ever get the DNA results from the lab?'

Kate looked at Claire. Both shrugged. 'We never heard,' Claire said.

She gazed in her aunt's direction. 'There was also that set of fingerprints they couldn't identify. The police need to follow up on that.'

'There's something else.' Max paused to take a drink of water. 'The cabin, whose is it?'

'Have you ever been told you should be in

law enforcement?' Claire seemed impressed.

He smiled. 'Once or twice.'

Kate had written down the points they covered. 'I'll give Nick's solicitor a call in the morning. Maybe he knows something he hasn't told me.'

Claire turned the conversation to Max and he told them about growing up in Brooklyn. By the time they left the restaurant, she felt she knew him better. She liked what she saw.

Back at the hotel, Kate yawned. 'Morning comes early when you have two youngsters. I believe I'll excuse myself now.' She smiled and left the room.

17

While Claire and Max relaxed in the hotel library, he noticed a few logs stacked in the fireplace. 'Are you chilly?'

'Now that you mention it, it's a little cool in here. Would you light the fire?'

He struck a match and the wood soon began to burn. They both sat watching its bright flames.

Claire smiled. 'When I was a child, my brother and I'd look at the fire and try to identify what the flames resembled.'

'I did the same thing in Brooklyn,' he said. 'I guess this far north, we can expect winter soon.'

Tony burst into the room. 'Claire, I . . . ' He frowned at Max. 'I'm sorry, I didn't mean to intrude.'

From Claire's bewildered expression, Max could tell she didn't know how to handle the situation. An earlier conversation came to mind. Kate wasn't happy about her niece socializing with the help.

'You're not,' Claire said. 'Is anything wrong?'

'No, Claire.' Tony left as abruptly as he'd entered.

'I'm sorry,' she said, leaning toward Max. 'Tony's become a little possessive and I don't know how to — '

'How to what?' Max interrupted. 'Put him in his place?'

'That's not quite what I meant.' Claire bit her lip. 'Tony's been a friend, though he's changed the last day or two. He's not the shy, reserved guy I met when I first came home.'

It looked like Tony was moving in on Claire. Clearing his throat, Max made a suggestion. 'If you have any problems with him, let me know. I could talk to him. Or you might ask Chris. He is Tony's boss.'

'He's become aggressive the last day or so, I don't know what happened.' Claire sounded perplexed.

'Let me know if he becomes a problem.'

'I will.'

'Thanks for letting me tag along tonight. Please let me treat you both next time.' He'd find excuses to stay close to Claire until he determined just who Tony was. Max again thought of Antonio the assassin. Were Antonio and Tony the same man?

While Max and Claire talked by the fire, they found they shared several interests.

'I don't suppose you like old movies?' He inquired.

'I certainly do,' she said. 'One of my

favorites is *To Kill A Mockingbird*. I'm a big fan of Gregory Peck's.'

'So am I,' Max replied. 'Did you see *Cape Fear?*

'Yes. I prefer the original. Peck was excellent.'

They went on, comparing movies and actors they'd liked and why. They also found they both liked rainy days. She confessed to loving licorice, they both liked gardening.

Claire enchanted Max, she seemed so natural and untouched. He admitted that she resembled his dream girl.

Max recalled the walk down the hill to the village the previous night and Tony's mysterious telephone call. He'd heard Tony telling the person on the other end of the line to take care of her. Was he referring to Valerie? She was still missing.

Saying good night to Claire, Max strolled down the driveway to the gatehouse. Thoughts of her made him smile.

Unlocking the door, he turned on the light switch in the sitting room. He jerked. 'Damn.'

Overturned chairs were the first indication that someone had been in his flat. Max ran upstairs to his small neat bedroom and found the bedcovers dumped on the floor and the pillows slashed.

Goose feathers coated the carpet and

furniture in the small bedroom and the bureau drawers were turned upside down on the floor. Lamp shades had been removed and thrown in the corners.

Max headed for the study. His lap top was missing from the now overturned desk, books and magazines were strewn across the room. It was lucky he kept his case notes in his head.

Max wished he could call the police. It didn't take him long to discard that notion. No sense in having the local authorities dig into his life. All it'd take was one nosy reporter and his cover went up in smoke.

Working at a steady pace, Max tidied the flat. Tomorrow, he'd replace the goosedown pillows. And the broken lamp was no problem. He'd tell Kate he'd broken it himself and offer to pay for a replacement.

Having done all he could to restore order, Max lay down. He had a good idea who'd trashed his apartment.

★ ★ ★

Tony undressed, preparing to take a shower. When a lone goose feather floated out of his shirt, he snickered. He wondered how the reporter had liked his little surprise. There'd be more if the dumb jerk didn't stay away from Claire.

What got into the broad? Earlier she'd made it clear she couldn't stand the American and Tony encouraged her dislike for Max every chance he got.

Something must've changed because tonight the reporter, Claire and Kate had driven off in the guy's car. Later they returned. Tony bet they had dinner together.

If his plans progressed according to schedule, Claire would soon be living in her own place a mile away. He'd walked around The Folly and was pleased to find she had no neighbors.

The mansion was set on the rim of another fell, surrounded by dense forest. It'd be the perfect setting for him to seduce her. Afterwards, he'd get her to tell him about Francisco.

Tony frowned. Kate might be a problem. He hadn't missed her disapproving glances whenever she found Claire and him together.

Claire's aunt didn't seem to mind his offering to help clean up The Folly. That was the way she saw him, an employee, good enough to do the dirty work, yet not good enough for her precious niece. It was a pity he couldn't tell Kate who he really was.

He moved on to the business at hand. Valerie's keeper had complained he wasn't paying her enough. If she had half a brain, she'd keep her mouth shut.

Picking up his cell phone, Tony was pleased when the call went through. 'Are things under control?' He queried Valerie's keeper. Then he lay on his bed and let her rant for a few moments. 'All right, I'll be there tonight. Tell your companion I have a job for her.'

It was time to move things along. Tony switched off the cell phone then pulled on his shoes, all the while planning ahead.

Again he slipped from the hotel, unobserved. En route he pulled his jacket around him, shivering in the unheated truck.

In fifteen minutes he arrived at the motel. Still announcing 'No Vacancies,' the faded sign overhead creaked in the autumn wind. The motel had been abandoned years ago.

Tony knocked twice on the door of the manager's quarters, a two-bedroom unit a little larger than the others. A young woman wearing a hooded sweatshirt and jeans appeared. He took one quick glance around before slipping inside. 'Where is she?'

'Asleep. I keep her drugged most of the time. She's less trouble that way.' The woman's voice was flat, emotionless.

'Good.' Once he finished with Valerie, her keeper would also have to go, she knew too much. For now, he'd put up with her. 'You've done well. Here's your pay.'

He threw her a wad of bills and she caught it. Her dull eyes brightened, opening the package.

'Gee. You gave me more than I expected. Thanks.'

He nodded. 'Get her.' He sat on a rickedy chair.

The keeper returned with a young woman who stumbled and almost fell before slumping into another chair.

'I've got a job for you, Valerie.' He studied her glazed eyes and dirty hair. What a beast. She didn't respond so he slid a piece of paper and a ballpoint pen across the coffee table between them. 'You're going to write a letter to the police. I'll tell you what to say.'

'Then you'll let me go?' Her dull gaze begged him.

'Sure, honey. Just write the letter so I can take you back to Manchester.' When she wasn't looking, he winked at her keeper.

Without warning Valerie collapsed, her head hit the table.

'Damn,' Tony cried. 'How much did you give her?'

Valerie's guard turned pale. 'Just what you told me.'

'I bet. Get her a glass of water.'

The guard ran out of the room. Moments

later Tony could hear dishes rattling down the hall.

Walking into the tiny kitchen, Tony curled his lip in disgust. 'What a pig sty.' Not a clean dish in the place. He fished a dirty glass out of the sink and rinsed it out.

When he reentered the living room with the glass of water, the room was empty.

'She's gone! The broad tricked us.' Tony threw open the front door, looked outside. 'You check in here, I'll search the yard.'

Running outside, Tony cursed. things weren't going like he planned. Then he calmed, licking his lips. He'd find her.

Minutes later, he returned inside. Valerie's keeper was wringing her hands. 'She hasn't gone far. Stay here,' he ordered. Climbing into the truck, he backed out of the parking slot.

Driving down the road, he scanned the shadows. Soon he saw a figure staggering ahead. As he approached, she fell in the mud.

'Bitch, it's a good thing I need you. Otherwise, you'd be dead right now.' Tony stopped his vehicle, got out and picked her up, held her limp body in his arms. 'Good girl. Now we go home and you can write that letter.'

Back at the motel, he slapped her until she revived. She promptly burst into tears.

Putting the pen in her hand, he pushed the pad of paper in front of her. 'Write what I say.'

This time she obeyed. When the letter was finished, Valerie looked up at him.

'Sign it,' he ordered.

She signed her name then sat back.

Tony picked up the letter and folded it. 'Take her to her room and let her rest. I'll get her later.' He fanned the air with the letter. 'Get her some clean clothes. She smells like she fell in a sewer.'

'She doesn't have anything else to wear,' the guard whined.

'Then put one of your hooded sweatshirts on her. And find her some jeans.'

The woman took hold of Valerie and led her away.

When he returned to the motel driving his own car that had been hidden nearby, the rooms were freezing. The keeper had her hood on so not much of her face was visible. 'Where is she?'

She motioned to the broken-down bed in the next room.

Entering the poorly lit room, Tony nudged Valerie but she was out cold. 'Did you give her some more medicine?'

Valerie's guard nodded.

'That's all right. She can sleep in the

trunk.' Picking up the unconscious Valerie, he carried her to his car, placed her in the trunk and slammed the lid. All the while, the other woman stood watching. 'I'll settle with you as soon as I get back.'

She nodded again before going inside and closing the door.

Dumb broad. He turned his truck around and headed for Manchester.

★ ★ ★

Next morning, the janitor of Manchester's tallest office building had a terrible surprise when he arrived at work. In the atrium at the center of the building, what he'd first thought was a pile of debris turned out to be something much more serious. Grim-faced, he dialed the emergency number for the city police.

When the woman's body was examined, a crumpled note was found in the pocket of her hooded sweatshirt. A call was made to the party to whom the envelope was addressed.

18

Percy April sat at his desk. As a rule, he enjoyed the seasonal changes. Today his mood didn't allow him that pleasure or any other.

Why the hell did he take Nick's case in the first place? Percy had earned the reputation of winning most cases, even when things looked bad at the start. He'd never win this one.

The detectives assigned to the case agreed on Nick's guilt. The sole evidence of someone else having been in the cabin consisted of two yet unidentified fingerprints. They could have been there for a long time. Also, Nick had motive if the woman was threatening to blackmail him.

While Percy considered the possibility of a mid-life career change, the phone on his desk buzzed. Hearing his secretary's chirpy greeting, he winced. 'Put him through,' he ordered and straightened in his desk chair. 'Good morning.' He hated the lead detective on Nick's case but it wouldn't be wise to be rude. 'What is it?'

Listening to his caller, Percy snapped to

attention at the phrase 'pertinent to your client's defense.' 'May I see it?' He held his breath. 'I'll be right there.'

A short walk later, he entered the police headquarters.

A departmental secretary beamed and announced his arrival. 'He's waiting for you,' she said, gesturing for Percy to enter her boss's office. He walked into a large room where the detective sat staring at a sheet of paper on his overloaded desk.

Percy resisted the urge to run over to the desk and examine whatever it was. Instead, he took a seat.

'You wanted to see it,' the detective said. 'Come take a look.' He motioned for Percy to come closer.

Percy approached the desk. 'What is it anyway?'

'The Manchester Police are sending the original by special courier,' the detective explained. 'It'll be here in a couple of hours. When they read the message to me over the phone, I asked for a fax.' Removing his glasses, he took his time wiping them as if he didn't have anything more pressing to do.

Percy knew the man well and didn't miss the slight tremble of his hands. That was a dead giveaway that he was excited.

'Well, since I'm here, I might as well read it,' he said, trying not to show his own agitation. He put his reading glasses on and studied the fax. The first thing he noticed was the handwriting. The letters were irregular, like the writer had been in a hurry or unwell. He read the text.

Nick Connor Case Detectives-Bowness Constabulary:

'I helped Nick Connor kill a girl to save his career.

When Nick reneged on his promise we'd be together again, I drugged him and left him for the police to find.

Nick Connor is guilty as I am. May God forgive us.

Valerie Connor.'

'You haven't asked how we got hold of this.' The Chief raised his head and studied Percy.

'All right. Where?' *Nick won't get out of this.*

'In Valerie Connor's pocket. She committed suicide by jumping off a Manchester office building last night. The custodian found her body in the atrium this morning.'

'Has the body been identified yet?'

'Not yet. It's possible it's another woman, though I have my doubts with this signed confession by Valerie Connor. The Manchester police have been looking for her, as you know.'

'Please inform me when you have positive identification.' Percy shook his head. 'What a hell of a way to die.'

19

The next day Claire stood on a stepladder in the hotel's supply closet, stretching to reach a bottle of window cleaner on an upper shelf. Something touched her left leg. She jerked and almost fell. Looking down she found Tony.

Climbing down the ladder, she frowned. 'Do you have to creep up on people?' The handyman was starting to get on her nerves.

'Sorry. Mattie told me you were in here.' He examined a mop and pail. 'Chris still doesn't have any work for me so I can go over to The Folly with you.' Tony smiled. 'That's a funny name for a house.'

'It's a long story,' she replied. 'Are you sure Chris won't need you?' Claire was growing weary. Everywhere she went, he followed her. She'd tried being cool yet he didn't take the hint.

'No. I'm all yours.' Tony winked at her.

She could use another pair of hands, Claire rationalized. And if Tony got out of line, she'd send him back to the hotel. 'Well, all right if Chris approves.' She noticed a bandage on the handyman's cheek. 'Did you hurt yourself?'

'I scratched myself in my sleep.' Shrugging, Tony trailed her to Kate's vehicle. 'We could take the truck.'

'No, this'll work better,' Claire said. 'I'll drive this car and you follow me. That way if one of us wants to leave before the other, he won't be stuck over there.' She remembered the other time they'd visited her home. Today she wanted to be able to leave if Tony became too friendly.

'Okay.' From the irritated tone of his voice, he wasn't overjoyed with her suggestion.

'See you there.' She loaded the cleaning supplies in the back of Kate's car, got in and headed down the driveway. In her haste, Claire almost ran over Max standing outside the gatehouse. He held up his hand like a school crossing guard.

Braking, she rolled down the car window. 'Be careful. I could've hit you.'

'Where are you going in such a hurry?'

'Tony and I are off to The Folly. I'm going to mop the kitchen floor while he cleans windows.' Max was holding her up. Part of her wanted him to move out of the way. The other remembered his protecting her in Manchester and wished he were going along.

'Unlock the car door,' Max ordered. 'I'm going with you.'

'If I were suspicious, I'd think Tony and

you were conspiring against me.' Claire smiled to show she was joking.

Max didn't return her smile. 'What do you mean?'

'First he insists on helping me, now you.' Men were a nuisance sometimes.

'Open the passenger door, Claire.'

From his tone, Max wouldn't take no for an answer. She sighed and let him into the vehicle.

'I'll keep you company today.' He fastened the seat belt.

'If you want to go along, that's fine, though it isn't necessary. I'm a big girl, in case you haven't noticed. I even stay out after dark.' Men could be a pain sometimes.

'Okay, maybe I wanted to spend some time with you,' he admitted. 'I haven't seen much of you since the night the three of us went out to dinner.' Max frowned. 'Are you all right?'

'Sure.' Claire tried to sound carefree. 'I don't have any problems.' Except the bad dreams almost every night since she'd made up her mind to move back home. She needed to redo Charles's study and bedroom. There were too many reminders of her brother at her family home.

At a narrow lane almost hidden in the woods, Claire turned and followed the private road to The Folly. The sight of the elegant mansion at the end of the road made her sigh. 'I hope I haven't made a mistake.'

'What's wrong? Is it too much for you?'

'What?'

'You know what I mean.' Max's keen eyes studied her. 'You must have a lot of memories associated with this place. Wasn't it your family home until you moved to Devon?'

Her head swirled about. 'How did you know about Devon?'

'Kate told me you moved down there after your brother died.'

'My dear aunt has a big mouth.'

'Maybe, yet she cares about you.'

Claire bit her lip to keep from saying, 'mind your own business.'

Tony's truck rattled up behind them. As Max climbed from the car, Tony looked annoyed. 'I didn't know you were coming.'

Max smiled. 'The more the merrier.'

Tony didn't reply, just scowled. Gathering up some of the cleaning supplies, he left the mops and pails behind. 'If you want to help, Bronsky, you can carry those.' Tony walked ahead of them to the front of the house. 'Hurry up,' he said. 'Let's get to work.'

Claire studied the second floor windows. 'I could swear I saw something moving up there.'

'The sunlight's reflecting on the glass,' Max suggested.

An hour later, the kitchen floor shone. While they waited for it to dry, Max started cleaning windows in the other ground floor rooms. 'Here,' he handed Tony a roll of paper towels and a bottle of window cleaner. 'You clean the outside panes and I'll do the inside while Claire polishes the paneling.'

Glaring at Max, Tony went outside.

'I don't like the way he looks at you,' Max said.

The idea of two attractive men vying for her attention amused Claire until she gazed in his direction. Her stomach knotted. Max wasn't flirting, he was dead serious. A muscle twitched in his jaw and his posture was stiff, like he was ready for trouble. 'Don't talk like that. You're scaring me.'

'Am I?' He moved closer. 'Good, you ought to be scared to death. I'm not kidding, Claire. You're in danger right now.'

'Why in the world?' She stepped back. 'You don't think that Tony . . . ' She let her words trail off, not knowing what to say.

'You got it. Don't be alone with him,' Max said, his voice terse. 'Keep your distance, he's up to something.'

With the kitchen floor dry, they moved back into that room. Max picked up the cleaner and sprayed the panes over the sink just as Tony appeared at the window. The handyman frowned at Max through the glass.

'I promise you, this's for real.' Max spoke in an undertone with his head turned away from Tony.

'Oh, come on.' Claire tried to laugh. 'Even if Tony is a little possessive, that doesn't make him a threat.'

'He says he was just passing through the county, picking up odd jobs when he came to work at the hotel.'

'Right and he was.' As she gazed into Max's cool gray eyes, she saw danger. And it was headed straight at her. Fear spiked through her like an electrical current. 'Wasn't he?'

'He wants to get you alone,' Max said, his head turned away from the windows. 'Watch him. He'll insist on staying with you while I drive his truck back to the hotel. When he discovers I won't leave you, he won't like it.'

'Why do you keep doing that?' Max baffled her. She wondered if he was playing a game with her. 'You act like you think he's reading our lips.'

'I'm not giving him the chance.'

'This's silly. Maybe I should ask him if he's a criminal.' Trying to relieve the tension, Claire teased Max.

He took hold of her wrist. 'Don't be a fool. That'll put him on guard. He may be suspicious of me already.'

'You're too much. First you say he's not a handyman, drifting from job to job. Next I suppose you'll tell me that you aren't a free-lance journalist.' She laughed, expecting him to grin and laugh with her. He didn't.

Tony came back inside.

'Well, the place's looking a lot better.' Claire tried to appear calm for Tony's benefit. 'And you two have been a big help. Let's stop for today.'

The handyman moved forward. 'Good idea.' Tony stared at Max standing close to Claire. 'Tell you what, I'll stay here and load our mops and pails and all that other stuff in my truck. Max can drive your aunt's car back to the hotel. He must have things he needs to do. He's been here working for hours.' He smiled.

Max smiled back. 'I don't have other plans for today. On the other hand, your boss may've found you another chore, so I suggest you run along,' he said, dismissing the handyman. 'We'll be there soon.'

Claire held her breath. Moments passed as the two men stared each other down. At last Tony nodded. 'If that's the way you want it. See you back at the hotel.' He drove off in his truck.

'You told me he'd insist on staying. How did you know?'

215

'He's up to no good. And you're involved.' Max hesitated. 'Did you know him before he came to Bowness?' The way he asked her seemed to indicate it was important to him.

'You mean in Devon? No, of course not. I never laid eyes on him until he delivered the trunk to my room the day I got back.' Where did Max ever get such a harebrained idea?

His glance locked with hers. 'You're sure about that?'

'Yes, what is this about? You say I'm in danger? Why?'

'If it were up to me, I'd tell you. But it's not. You'll have to take my word for it. I promise I won't let him hurt you or your family.'

'All right. We'll talk more about this later.' She looked around. The more they worked on it, the more the place felt like home again. 'Wait a moment.' She started up the stairs.

'Where're you going?'

'Just upstairs for a minute. I noticed a small picture of my mother the other day. I want to get it reframed.' She turned, took a step toward him. 'Wipe that worried expression off your face, you can come with me.'

Max followed her upstairs, leaning in the doorway of her parents' old bedroom while she located the picture. 'You thought you noticed something moving in a front window on this floor while we were outside,' he said. 'Which room would that be?'

'Charles's study or his bedroom, I suppose.' Claire's attention was focused on the picture. 'Both are on the front side of the house. His study is to the left down the hall, second door. But I'm sure you were right, it must've been the sun shining on the window panes.'

'If you don't mind, I'll check it out.'

'Oh, all right.' Claire blew a strand of hair off her face. 'Go ahead, I'll be there in a moment.'

Max left her. She was about to follow when he called to her.

'Claire? Would you come here?'

20

As Claire entered the paneled study her brother had once used for a dressing room, Max was reaching out his hand to a small figure in jeans and hooded sweatshirt.

'Don't hurt me, please,' said a woman's lilting voice.

'Who're you?' It was a shock to find a stranger in her home. Before the other woman could reply, Claire turned to Max. 'I could've sworn the doors and windows were locked.'

'Someone left the kitchen door open,' the intruder said. Removing her hood, a woman pushed matted hair that might've been blonde off her cheek. 'I planned to sleep here tonight then see Kate in the morning.'

'Kate Stanhope?' Max studied the woman. 'You know her?'

'She's married to my . . . to Nick Connor. I'm Valerie.'

'Valerie? For pity's sake, woman. Where have you been? Everyone's been searching for you,' Claire said sharply. Then she looked closer and noticed the other woman's bruised cheek. She didn't need to be browbeaten as well.

218

Ashamed of her rude behavior, she softened her tone, trying to speak more pleasantly. 'Kate and the children have gone to Carlisle for a couple of days. I'm Claire Stanhope, her niece. Can I help you?'

'I need to get away. If I stay in this area, he'll find me.' Valerie's anxious gaze slid from Max to Claire. 'He was going to kill me until I tricked him.'

'Who tried to kill you?' Claire stared in amazement. According to Valerie's landlady, Nick's ex-wife had left her flat in the company of a new boy friend. 'Do you know his name?'

'He told me that he was to be 'Lover' to me.' Valerie's attempt at a shrug ended in a wince of pain. 'He said every woman he's ever known loved him and I would, too. He's a horrible man. He likes to hurt women.'

'And where were you when you escaped from him?' Max asked, his voice deadly calm.

'An abandoned motor court, I don't know the name of the place. It can't be very far from here. In that direction.' She pointed toward the rear of Claire's mansion.

'You came that way?' Claire stared at her unexpected guest. She hastened to explain to Max. 'My property's similar to Kate's. The Folly and King's Grant are both built on the ridges of fells though The Folly has a much sharper decline. The King's Grant property gradually slopes down to dense forest that continues for a mile before you come to a road.'

'So?' Max wrinkled his brow.

'There's a rough path running through the woods. My brother and I often used it as a shortcut to King's Grant. Valerie's a stranger here. I'm surprised she didn't get lost.'

'I did until an older climber showed me the way,' Valerie said. 'I don't know where he came from. He appeared out of nowhere. After he pointed me to your house, he vanished.'

When Valerie stopped to wipe her nose on a dirty handkerchief, Claire got a good look at the other woman's hands. They were scratched and bleeding. She sucked in her breath. 'Max, she needs a doctor.'

'I know. We better take her to the hospital.'

Valerie shook her head. 'I'm not going to any hospital. He'd find me. Please, just let me rest awhile. There's something I need to tell Kate, then she'll help me get away.'

'No one's going to hurt you.' Max knelt and patted Valerie's arm. 'Claire, did we drink all of the soft drinks?'

'No, I'll get her one.' Before she'd met Valerie, Claire had hated the woman for the grief she'd caused her father. Now pity stirred deep inside. Valerie was suffering now and needed their help. 'Are you hungry?'

'Yes.' She wiped a tear off her cheek. 'Thanks for being so kind. If you'll let me rest a little, I'll find somewhere else to hide until Kate gets home. I don't want to bring you trouble.'

Claire helped the other woman shower and lent her an old pair of slacks and a knit shirt that she found hanging in her closet. She also found some clean underwear, socks and an old pair of tennis shoes. Once Valerie washed her hair, she looked better, though fear remained in her eyes.

'You mentioned talking to Kate.' Max sat near Valerie while she finished a second ham-and-cheese sandwich, a remnant of the food Claire had brought from King's Grant that day. 'Why don't you tell us why you want to see her? Maybe we can help.'

'No thanks.' Valerie shook her head again. 'What I have to say is for Kate.'

'Lover.' Max said the name aloud. 'I can't imagine a man kidding about a name like that. The guy must have an ego as big as a house. Can you describe him?'

'Can't that wait awhile?' Claire glanced at Max. 'She needs to rest.' What was the hurry? The creep must be far away by now.

From where he knelt beside Valerie, Max

turned and stared in Claire's direction. 'And she will rest. Just give me a moment.' Addressing Valerie, he said, 'Go on. I need to know his description. Like how old is he?'

'I don't know. He has a sweet, boyish face.' Valerie frowned. 'Mid-twenties?'

'Height?'

'Your height, six feet or more, he's slimmer than you.'

'Hair and eye color?'

'Black hair and his eyes are dark. He looked Italian to me.'

Claire's gaze locked with Max's. An unexpected chill hit her body and she shivered, pulling her sweater closer. 'If I didn't know better, I'd say Valerie's described Tony.' Claire forced a weak smile. Thoughts whirled inside her brain.

Valerie stared first at Claire then Max. 'Who the heck is this Tony character?'

'The handyman Kate's business partner hired to help around the hotel,' Claire explained.

'If you'll excuse us for a minute?' Max escorted Claire from the room, closing the door behind them. 'I agree with you. The man who held Valerie prisoner sounds like the person you and I know as Tony. I've been watching him since he came to Bowness, in fact, he's the reason I'm here.'

'Watching him?' Bewildered, Claire frowned. 'Why would you do that? Are you a bounty hunter?'

'No, I'm not.'

'What then? Some kind of detective?' Was that the reason Max had stayed so close? She'd thought he liked her. Was he just doing his job? Disappointment stung her.

He nodded. 'Please keep my secret.' He led Claire back into the study where Valerie was now reclining on the day bed. Max addressed her. 'You should be safe here for awhile.'

Walking across the room to the windows, he pulled back a sheer curtain and peered outside. Apparently satisfied that no one was there, Max continued. 'The local police would be interested in Tony. Other law enforcement groups would like to talk to him, also.'

Max's words seemed to reassure Valerie. 'I'm so tired.' She lay back on the day bed pillows, closing her eyes. 'Can I rest for a few minutes?'

'Of course.' Claire navigated Max out of the room, half-closing the study's door. 'Leave her alone. She's been through a terrible ordeal.'

As they descended to the ground floor, Claire was glad she hadn't said anything to Max about her feelings for him. Thank goodness. He might have laughed at her. Or worse still, used her to further his investigation. 'I need to let Mattie and Chris know we've been detained.' She dialed Kings Grant Hotel. The housekeeper answered right away.

'I never cared for the girl,' Mattie blurted out before Claire could tell her why she called. 'Still, I'm sorry for her.'

What was she talking about? 'Just a moment, please.' She beckoned to Max and he took his place behind her, sharing the receiver. His hard body pressed against her back and she began to feel aroused. Not now, she told her body, however she still felt warm where their bodies touched. His woodsy cologne bothered her.

'What were you saying, Mattie?'

'Percy April, Nick's solicitor, told Nick the Manchester police coroner's examining a body of a young woman who committed suicide in Manchester last night,' Mattie began.

'That's too bad but what does it have to do with Nick?'

'Lord, child. You're so impatient.' Mattie responded. 'Papers on the body indicate it's Nick's ex-wife Valerie. The coroner hasn't made definite identification yet.'

'I see.' Impossible. At that moment, Valerie was upstairs resting in the study. Claire's hand gripped the cell phone so hard, her fingers numbed.

If Max hadn't taken her into his confidence, she might have been able to convince herself that Tony's resemblance to Valerie's assailant was coincidence. Claire's instincts told her that Max was an honest man. She believed him. 'Is Tony there?'

'He's already gone.'

'Gone?' Claire found herself staring dumbly at the telephone. 'Gone where? He was just over here awhile ago, cleaning windows.'

'I thought you knew . . . ' Mattie's voice trailed off.

'Knew what?' Please God, no more surprises. She'd had enough of those today.

'Haven't you been listening to Chris? For days he's said he was running out of odd jobs around the hotel. Tony has completed all of the work Chris needed done. When Tony returned to the hotel this afternoon, Chris paid him and sent him on his way.'

'That was fast. Did he tell Tony he could keep his room until he found another job?'

'No. I think Chris decided it'd be better this way.'

'I see.' Max believed Tony was a criminal who called himself 'Lover.' 'Was he upset?'

'No, in fact I was surprised at how eager he was to leave,' Mattie said. 'Can we expect you for supper?'

'Go ahead and eat. We have a few more

things to do here. And would you — .'

Max bumped her arm so hard, Claire dropped the phone on the floor. Surprised, she stared at him.

Picking up the phone, he covered the speaker. 'Shhhh,' he whispered. 'Don't tell Mattie about our guest. Tell her you dropped the phone. Tell her we'll be there soon.'

Claire glared at him then decided he must have good reason. 'I'm sorry, I dropped the phone. We'll be there as soon as we can. Go ahead with your meal.' Turning off her cell phone, she spoke to Max. 'Now you can explain.'

'Think a moment,' he said. 'If Tony's the man who kept Valerie hostage, he'll be looking for her. Don't you realize he'd watch the hotel to see if she comes there for help?' Max's face was solemn, his lips a thin, hard line.

'Oh, I see what you mean.' *This isn't one of the mysteries I read in bed at night, it's the real thing.* Her heart thudded faster.

Claire gazed at Max, remembering her earliest impression of him. The first Bugle article had set her off, she'd hated him before they met. The day she visited his office, he made matters worse by grabbing her and kissing her. Claire smiled, recalling. No one else had ever kissed her like that. Then Max spoiled the mood and she'd left furious.

The last few days she'd changed her opinion of him. If she ever hated him, Claire didn't now. In fact, it wouldn't be hard to fall in love with Max. Be careful, a small inner voice warned. You thought you knew Tony and see what happened. Max hasn't told you that he cares. Wait and see.

'Have you ever met Valerie?'

'Not until today.' Claire chewed her lip, a habit since childhood when she was upset or uncertain. 'There's something else we must consider now.'

'What is it?' He raised an eyebrow.

'You heard Mattie. It's possible the woman upstairs is an imposter. Valerie may be lying on a slab in the morgue.'

'That's true.' Max agreed.

Claire thought for a moment. 'Even so, the woman couldn't fake being hurt. We saw her scrapes and bruises.'

Max nodded. 'And she described a man who looks like Tony.'

'As I see it, we have two possibilities,' she said. 'First, maybe Valerie did kill herself and we have an imposter in Charles' old study.'

'Right.' Max nodded. 'Or the dead woman's not Valerie since she's sleeping upstairs. Which do you believe?'

'I don't know.'

'Well, there's no time like the present to find out.' Max grabbed her hand and rushed toward the stairs.

Claire dragged her feet until he stopped.

He frowned down at her. 'What now?'

'We can't just barge in there and wake her,' she said. 'You'll scare her to death.'

'All right.' Max folded his arms and looked in her direction. 'When is Nick's birthday?'

'Oh, April ninth, I believe.'

'If this woman's Valerie, she'd know her ex-husband's birthday.' Max headed for the stairs. 'Coming?'

'Coming.' With reluctance, Claire followed him.

Max reached the next floor first. From the study, his voice drifted down to her. 'We're too late. She's gone.'

Climbing the stairs, Claire stood face-to-face with him in the shadowy hall. 'Are you sure? Let's search the house.' She ran downstairs and looked through the rooms. From the bottom of the stairway, she called to him. 'She's not down here.'

'Not on this floor either.' His deep voice answered.

'I don't guess we can go outside and call for her,' Claire said as Max returned to the ground floor.

'No. If Tony's out there, we don't want to

228

tip him off that Valerie's been here.'

'It's getting dark and she's alone.'

'And that creep's hunting for her,' Max replied.

His tone was quiet and matter-of-fact. Nevertheless, his words chilled Claire. She envisioned a lone woman fleeing through the night, pursued by a man with murder on his mind.

'Whoever she is, he's looking for her,' Max said. 'I can feel it.'

'What do we do now?' Claire fought down panic.

21

Valerie stumbled and fell to her knees. The bandage on her right hand had come undone so she reattached it. 'Got to find a place to hide,' she muttered, getting to her feet. It was almost dark and a cold night wind was blowing over the fell. In the dim light, the evergreens in the woods appeared sinister, like twisted giants towering over her.

A noise nearby sent her heart racing. She left the path and sheltered behind a tree stump, bracing herself for whatever was following her down the crude path. If she'd been religious, she'd have prayed but the days when she attended the small Anglican church in Manchester were only a faint memory.

★   ★   ★

Tony grew impatient. By now he should've found Valerie. She'd left a trail through the woods. This time she wouldn't trick him. This time he'd kill her. He turned up his jacket collar and walked on, his flashlight casting a narrow beam on the path ahead.

★ ★ ★

'Sit down for a minute.' Max gestured to a chair. 'We need to decide what to do.'

'From your tone, you've already made up your mind.' Claire stood her ground. She didn't like 'take charge' type men. Charles had tried to control her every thought, every movement.

'All right.' Max sounded impatient. 'What do you think we should do?'

She guessed he was humoring her, for the moment at least. 'Call the police, of course. They have the manpower to search these woods,' she said. Claire paused. When Max didn't respond, she went on. 'They can find Valerie and Tony faster than we can.'

'And the first roadblock or uniformed officer Tony sees, he'll take off,' Max replied. 'They'll never catch him.'

'At least Valerie would be safe.'

'For the moment, yes.'

An idea came to mind and Claire put her hand on Max's arm, eager to help. Afraid he wouldn't let her. 'How about this? Let's trap him ourselves. We can do it.'

'You're not suggesting you want to get involved.' A muscle in his jaw tightened.

'In case you haven't noticed, I'm involved already.' She glared at Max. 'I'm not afraid.'

Maybe she was though she wouldn't let him see her fear.

'You're a fool if you aren't.'

'Thanks a lot.' Claire's scowl was as fierce as his. 'Look at it this way. We don't want him to escape. If he's the monster you say he is, there's only one place for Tony. In prison.'

'Right, but — '

'Let's try.' Claire cut Max off.

'All right, if you're sure. We'll give it twelve hours, no more. If he hasn't come back by morning, we call the police.'

'Okay.' Trying to appear confident, she drew a deep breath.

'Tell me what you think of this.' Max lowered his voice though they were alone in the mansion.

★ ★ ★

A mile away in the woods, Tony continued tracking Valerie. He hoped she didn't head for The Folly. He didn't want Claire to see Valerie or hear what she'd say about him. If she did, he'd have to kill both women. Of course, he could have some fun with them before he ended their lives. Excitement surged through his body. Killing was a real turn-on.

While lurking in the middle of a thicket of

spruces, he heard a car leave The Folly. Tony moved cautiously through the woods toward Claire's home.

★ ★ ★

Claire locked the front door and leaned against it. The sound of Max's starting the Land Rover made her want to run after him before he got away. She could tell him she'd changed her mind. Claire rejected that idea immediately, she didn't want Max to know she was afraid. With her back pressed against the massive wooden door, she listened. The car's sounds faded away.

Would Tony come back tonight? Max had described the man he believed Tony was as 'cruel, cold-blooded and unswerving once he made up his mind.' He'd be back.

Claire walked through the house, locking the doors and closing the shutters in the large living room. The image of people barricading a fortress, preparing for an attack by hostile forces came to mind. She ascended to the next floor and walked quickly down the quiet hall past Charles's old study, pausing long enough to look into the room. The daybed was unmade, the blue sheets rumpled just as Valerie had left them.

The situation bore down on Claire until

she had a sense of being closed-in, trapped.

Her stomach rumbled at that point and she descended to the ground floor in search of food. In the kitchen Claire found cookies they'd brought from Kings Grant and nibbled on one. How did she ever get in this predicament?

Life had seemed much simpler in Devon while she'd planned her trip home. She had given up her apartment, thinking she would never need it again. Maybe she should have kept it. At least she would've had somewhere to go if she needed to leave.

Claire straightened her shoulders. She couldn't keep running away. This time she was going to stay.

At the moment, she found herself waiting for a killer. What in the world did he want with her?

If only she could talk to someone. Though Kate wouldn't be back until tomorrow, Mattie was at the hotel. Claire picked up her cell phone and punched in the number.

Mattie answered. 'Are you all right?' The housekeeper asked.

The older woman's caring tone made Claire want to weep. For a moment she weakened, wishing she was a child again so she could climb into Mattie's lap and be safe. 'I just wanted to tell you that I've decided to spend the night here.' She didn't know how much her friend had heard and didn't want to alarm her needlessly. 'I've some clothes, a little food and the place isn't in bad shape. I'll come back to the hotel in time for us to meet Kate at the station. What time does her train arrive?'

'About eleven,' a deeper voice answered.

'Chris?' Was he on another phone?

'Are you sure you're all right?' Concern rang in his voice.

He knew, she could tell. 'Fine. Ah, have you seen Max?'

'Here,' Max answered on an extension. 'Keep your cell phone on so we can listen. When you need me, you speak up. Agreed?'

'Yes.' She looked around. From where she stood, she could look into the darkened dining room and the hall. Only one light was on and that was in the kitchen. 'This place sure is quiet.'

'In the car, I can be there in a couple of minutes,' Max reminded her.

'I think I'll straighten up the kitchen, have a cup of tea and find a book to read.' That's it. No need to let them know she was a bundle of nerves.

'Good idea. Is your phone battery good for awhile?'

'I charged it before we came over here today.'

'Keep your phone on. We'll talk again later.'

Claire placed the cellphone on the counter and busied herself picking up trash and wiping the counters. Every now and then, she stopped and listened. Once she thought she heard a faint tapping noise. It stopped.

There it was again. Then she thought she heard her name being called. That couldn't be her imagination.

Claire picked up the phone. 'I'm going to open the kitchen door,' she told her listeners. 'I heard something right outside the back door and I'm going to investigate. I'll let you know when I'm inside again.'

Max and Chris yelled in unison, 'No, don't . . . ' She tucked the cell phone into her pocket before unlocking the door and stepping onto the back porch. The light by the door was dim. Claire made a mental note to replace the bulb.

The night was still and dark. From deep in the woods, she heard a rustling, like a bird settling in for the night. Far down the fell, a small animal cried out.

An involuntary shudder shook Claire. On such a night, she'd prefer the warmth and comfort of a roaring fire.

Something cold touched her leg and she

swallowed a scream. 'What? Who is it?'

'Help me. Please help me.'

Claire felt around her. There was a form to the left of the door. Kneeling, she came in contact with a soft shape, long hair. Realizing who it was, she whispered, 'Valerie. Hold on, I'll get you inside. We need to be quiet. Someone might hear.' There was no need to explain who that someone might be. She helped Valerie inside, depositing her cold, limp body into a kitchen chair.

'Wait,' Claire ordered as she closed and locked the back door. She pulled the cell phone from her pocket and spoke to her friends at the hotel. 'It's Valerie. I think she's all right. She's in the kitchen with me now.'

In the dimmed kitchen light, Claire studied Nick's ex-wife. Valerie was paler than she'd been earlier that day, her bandages had come loose, her clothes were torn and soiled.

'Why did you run away? We just wanted to help you.' Without waiting for an answer, Claire took a clean dish towel out of a drawer, moistened it and wiped the other woman's face. 'I'll make you a hot drink. Is coffee all right?'

Valerie managed a wan smile. She nodded. 'I'm sorry. I tried to get away, then someone else was in the woods. I had to come back. I hope it's not Lover. If he finds me, he'll kill me.'

'How far away was he? Did you see him?' This wasn't what Max and she had planned. Valerie complicated what would have been a far simpler scheme. If this woman was Valerie. Claire decided to worry about that later.

'I don't know.' Valerie shuddered. 'I kept trying to convince myself that it was an animal.'

'We may not have much time.' Claire gazed around the kitchen. If Tony was Valerie's assailant, he might kill them both on the spot if he came back and found Valerie with her.

Conflicting emotions quaked inside Claire. Anger over his treatment of Valerie proved stronger than her fear.

Opening the pantry door, Claire pushed aside canned goods on the floor, making a place for the other woman to hide. 'Max and I believe this Lover who held you hostage is Tony, the handyman at Kate's hotel. If he comes here, you must hide in the pantry and keep quiet. I've got my cell phone turned on and Max is on the line, listening at the hotel. He can get here fast if necessary.'

Big-eyed, Valerie nodded.

Claire hugged her. If Tony returned, she must hide her fear.

Valerie sat slumped at the table while Claire stood, locked in thought, leaning against the kitchen counter. If she was wrong, they might spend the whole night there, waiting for something that wasn't going to happen.

The hall clock chimed nine o'clock. Valerie yawned and stretched, calmer now that she wasn't alone. 'It doesn't look like he's coming. If you don't mind, I'm going to lie down on the sofa in the living room.' She rose from her chair.

'Shhh.' Claire pointed toward the back door. She could've sworn she heard something outside.

The loud knock confirmed her fears. Tony? If he was tracking Valerie, there was a chance he didn't realize she had managed to get back to the mansion.

When Claire gestured, Valerie scurried into the pantry. Claire quietly shut the door. A quick glimpse around the kitchen told her Valerie hadn't left any personal items behind.

On her way to the back door, Claire's gaze landed on her cell phone in plain sight. Scooping it up, she hid it behind a box of cleaning products on the kitchen counter. With that done, she hurried to let him in.

Claire pasted a welcoming smile on her face, displaying an emotion she didn't feel.

She opened the door and found him waiting.

'Tony? You surprised me. Why did you come to the back of the house?' She let him in.

'That damn piece of junk I've been driving died on me as I turned off the main road,' he muttered, walking into the kitchen. 'I had to walk the rest of the way.' He looked around.

'You must be frozen. Here, let me help you.' Claire bustled around, taking his jacket. She lifted innocent, concerned eyes to his. 'Want a cup of coffee?'

'Did the jerk go home?'

'Who? Oh, him.' Claire shrugged. 'To tell the truth, he was getting to be a bore. I'm glad to see you. It's lonely out here.'

Tony moved closer to her, making her nervous. She said, 'Good. It's perking.' Turning to the stove, she picked up the coffee pot and poured him a cup. As she handed him his coffee, she asked, 'Did you have dinner yet?'

'No, I'm hungry as a bear.'

'Sit down and I'll find you something.' She looked around. 'How about a ham-and-cheese sandwich? There's two left.'

'How about some hot soup?' He stood and headed in the direction of the pantry.

'I'm afraid not. I need to go to the grocery store tomorrow. Tonight we'll have to make do with sandwiches, coffee and some cookies. We can eat in the family room. How about making a fire while I get the food?'

He left the room and she put the sandwiches on paper plates then found a clean bowl for the cookies and poured them each another cup of coffee. All the while, her ear was attuned to the sounds coming from the next room.

Tony crept up behind her and hugged her. 'Oh,' she gasped. 'You startled me.'

'You're sure uptight. What's the matter?'

'Nothing. Did you make the fire?'

'I'm working on it.' He left the room again.

Max and the others needed to know Tony had returned. Claire waited a minute or two. 'Tony,' she raised her voice. That should do it, if they were still listening.

'What?' He came back into the room.

'Nothing. I just wondered if you'd be able to get a fire going. That fireplace hasn't been used in years.' She gestured to the tray. 'Here's our supper.'

'Let me carry it for you.' Lifting the tray, Tony followed Claire into the next room. 'Just a sec.' He went back to the kitchen and returned, carrying the bottle of ketchup she'd brought from the hotel.

They sat on the sofa near the hearth while the fire sputtered from the draft down the chimney then caught on. In a few minutes the room began to grow warmer.

Even the heat from the burning logs didn't warm Claire. One false move and the game was over. He seemed to be watching every move she made. She mustn't do anything to make him suspicious.

Tony wiped his mouth with a paper napkin, crumpled it and threw it on the table. 'Got any booze around here?'

'No, sorry.'

'If you don't want to be alone, I can spend the night.'

'Don't you have to work tomorrow?' She pretended she didn't know Chris had dismissed him.

'Nope. The boss ran out of odd jobs.' Tony got up and stretched then he removed his shoes and unfastened the top buttons of his shirt. 'This room's good and warm now. Why don't you get comfortable? You're over-dressed.'

Claire glanced at her wool sweater, shirt and slacks, not knowing what to do. If she refused, he might sense a trap. On the other hand, she didn't want to appear too easy. That might tip him off as well. Maybe she'd act interested but a little timid, draw him out. If she was careful, she might be able to talk her way out of this. God, what was she thinking when she'd sent Max away?

'I feel a draft.' Claire rose from the sofa and walked into the kitchen. She eyed the counter where she'd hidden her cell phone. 'It's not coming from here,' she said in a loud voice before returning to the living room.

'Sit down, will ya? You're as nervous as a cat.' Tony patted the sofa.

She took a seat by him again. 'Is there anything to watch on television?'

'I don't know.' He got up, turned on the television and got nothing but static. 'You need a new set. That's an antique.'

'They're expensive. I'll get this one fixed.'

'Maybe I could get you one.' He patted her knee then got up and stoked the fire. 'It's okay for awhile. Why don't we go upstairs? I'd like to try out that fluffy bed in your room.' He smiled as if he had just thought of it.

Ignoring his remark, Claire rubbed her back. 'I get these nasty muscle spasms in my shoulders.'

'I'll give you a massage.'

She wanted to refuse but went along with him. 'All right though I don't think it'll do any good.'

'If it doesn't, I know something else we can try.' He massaged her shoulders, stopping long enough to kiss her cheek.

She managed not to shudder while he

rubbed her back. A few minutes later, she got up. 'That does help. How about some hot tea? I'll get us some if you'll tend the fire. It looks like it's about to go out.'

Claire walked into the kitchen and filled the tea kettle, putting it on the stove. She busied herself, getting mugs and the remainder of the cookies. Claire listened until she could hear Tony stirring the fire, then she reached behind the plates on the counter and picked up the cell phone to alert Max.

A muscular arm encircled her. An angry hand knocked the phone out of her reach. 'Who the hell are you calling?'

'Settle down. I was just turning off my cell phone.' Taking the offensive, Claire glared at Tony. Fear knotted her stomach. She was lost if he realized what she was doing.

Retrieving the phone, she turned it off. When she glanced in his direction, Claire was relieved to see a flicker of uncertainty in his eyes. 'I'm always leaving it on.'

'You on the level?'

'Come on now. Would I lie to you? I've waited all evening for you to come back.' Her nerves quaking with dread, Claire did her best to sound convincing. Taking his hand, she led him back to the living room sofa and the fire now blazing on the hearth.

'Now that I think of it, I bet I can find us a

bottle or two. My father kept a wine cellar. There must be something left.'

'Oh, yeah?' Tony seemed to believe her for the moment.

'Yeah.' She gave his chest a playful punch. 'You want to go down and get us a bottle? This may be a long night.' She winked.

Tony seemed to be reappraising her. 'Good girl, I thought there was more to you than that prim Jane act you put on.' He followed her to the cellar door. 'Come and help me?'

'You want me to break a leg?' Claire motioned at her high-heeled boots. 'I'll wait for you here. Go on. It's over on your right around the corner.'

He went downstairs, turning on the lights as he descended.

At the bottom of the stairs, he called to her. 'Where did you say it was?'

'Just around the corner. You'll see it.' While he was occupied in the cellar, Claire retrieved her phone and turned it on. Thank God he hadn't broken it. She punched in the hotel's number. Someone picked it up on the first ring and she whispered, 'Max, he's here. Stand by. I'm going to try and find out what he's doing in Bowness.'

Tony came back up the cellar stairs a few minutes later, carrying several dusty bottles. 'This enough?'

'That's great.' Claire wiped off the bottles then found a cork screw.

Tony opened two bottles. 'Get us a couple of glasses and we'll have a snort,' he called, carrying the bottles to the living room.

'Wonderful.' She followed him. Claire had devised a plan. She hoped it would work.

22

Claire watched Tony.

He eyed the open bottle. 'It looks okay.'

'Of course it does.' As he poured them each a glass, she spoke up. 'Do you know the proper way for drinking wine?'

'Nope. Why don't you educate me,' he said playfully.

Was he planning to get her so drunk, she'd do anything he wanted? Claire set down her glass. 'First you sniff the cork then you take a small sip and swish it around in your mouth. If it appears to be all right, you let the steward serve you a glass.'

'Ah, hell. How did I ever find such a classy broad?' Tony laughed. 'Can't we just drink it?'

'No, just do as I say. You'll enjoy it more.'

He humored her, going through the procedure then picking up his glass and holding it. 'We should have a toast.' He motioned to her so Claire picked up her glass. 'Down the hatch.' Tony tilted his head and drank the wine.

She followed suit. 'Give me another.'

'Atta girl.' He laughed out loud. He didn't waste any time pouring her a second glass.

It had been a long time since she'd had a drink. Again Claire drank the whole glass.

Tony also had a second glass. He set his empty glass on the coffee table and turned to her.

Her first instinct was to push him away. Instead, she sat motionless and let him touch her breasts and start unbuttoning her shirt. Just before he finished, her stomach convulsed. She didn't fight the nausea. In fact, she welcomed it.

As soon as Claire put her glass down, Tony pulled her to her feet and leaned over to kiss her. Without warning, she threw up.

He jumped back but not fast enough. The vomit hit his shirt. From the look of disgust on his face, it was clear he was repulsed. 'What happened?'

Claire wiped her lips on a paper napkin. 'Gee, I don't know. I was fine a minute ago.' Lifting her face, she asked, 'Want to try again? Maybe I won't throw up any more.'

Tony shook his head. 'Yuck. I never could stand that smell.' He looked pale. 'No broad's ever barfed on me before.'

'I'm sorry, Tony.' She bit her lip to keep from laughing. That was why she never drank. She was allergic to alcohol.

He touched his wet shirt. 'If you don't mind, I'll use the washroom. Where is it?'

'In the hall. Go ahead. I think I'll get a glass of water.' She waited until he'd closed the bathroom door before darting into the kitchen and picking up the phone. 'It shouldn't be long now, Max. Keep listening.' She put the phone aside then rinsed out her mouth with water and dabbed at her sweater and buttoned her shirt. Fortunately, most of the contents of her stomach had landed on Tony's clothing.

He returned, wearing his undershirt and jeans. He draped his wet shirt over a chair. 'Maybe we should just sit and watch television until you feel better?' He eyed her uneasily.

'Fine.' That might give her a chance to find out what he was up to and how she was involved.

Tony fooled with the television until he found an old American western. For a few minutes he seemed content to watch John Wayne chasing Indians across the desert. While he watched, he finished off the first bottle and started on the second. His speech gradually became slurred. 'Tell me something, Claire?'

'What is it?'

'A good-looking chick usually has a lotta men hanging around. I haven't seen any around you.' He paused as if he were reconsidering what he'd just said. 'Unless you count that Max character and I know you can't stand him.'

It wouldn't hurt to tell Tony the truth, at least part of the truth. 'My brother Charles didn't like men hanging around. He discouraged men who wanted to date me.' Claire watched for Tony's reaction.

'That's terrible. Did you date at all?'

'A few of my brother's business associates.'

'Anybody special?'

'There was one guy . . . ' She recalled Frankie.

'See.' Tony hit the table with the empty bottle. 'I knew there was one.' He slouched on the sofa, cradling the bottle in his arms. 'Tell me all about him.'

'I met him when I was twenty-one. He asked me to be his wife the week we met,' she said wistfully. She'd fancied herself in love the way young, impressionable girls do. What she felt for Frankie paled in comparison to her feelings for Max.

'What was his name?' Tony appeared more interested than she would've expected.

'Frankie and I would've married him if my brother hadn't refused.' It seemed strange to sit there, telling Tony what she'd never revealed to Max. Claire admitted that she might be fooling herself. Max hadn't told her that he loved her yet.

'What happened to him?'

'I wish I knew.' She'd often wondered about that.

Tony sent her a look she couldn't interpret. 'For your information, his name was Francisco. Frankie was just a nickname used by family and close friends.'

'How would you know somehing like that?' Bewildered, she stared at him.

"Cause he was my brother.' Tony looked sad and angry at the same time.

'You're his younger brother?' As she recovered from the initial shock, Claire could see a resemblance.

'That's right.' Tony put his hands on her shoulders. 'Did you really care for him? Tell me the truth.'

Claire sat very still. It would be a waste of time, trying to get away from him. He was much stronger than she was.

'I loved him, I swear I loved him. My heart was broken when he went away.' She drew a deep breath. 'If you're really his brother, tell me where he is.'

'That's why I'm here. My father needs to know what happened to Frankie. The last we heard, he was up here in the Lake District visiting a business associate. That could've been your brother. What did you and Charles do to him?'

'Nothing, Charles just sent him away. He told me what he'd done the next morning. My brother was very possessive. He wanted to keep me with him.' *Charles, what did you do?*

'I don't believe a word you've said,' he responded, scowling at her. 'Dames are all alike. None of you can be trusted. The way I figure it, your brother killed Frankie then you helped him get rid of the body.' Tony stared at her. 'I'm going to stay here until you tell me the truth, even if it takes all night.' He took another drink from the second wine bottle. Then he lay his head on the back of the sofa, watching her.

'I can't tell you what I don't know,' she insisted. 'Frankie kissed me goodnight before sending me upstairs. He was going to talk to Charles about our getting married.' Claire was becoming more afraid of Tony drunk than she had been when he was sober. If he kept drinking, she wouldn't be able to reason with him. A sob caught in her throat. *I need you, Max.*

Tony went to the bathroom again. When he returned to the living room, he ordered, 'Make me some coffee.'

She went into the kitchen and filled the kettle.

Roaming the kitchen, Tony muttered to himself, opening and closing the cabinet drawers. Something seemed to catch his eye. It wasn't until he lunged at her that Claire realized he'd found a butcher knife.

She moved away, trying not to appear frightened. When she backed into the living room, he followed her, a drunken haze in his dark eyes.

'You don't want to hurt me.' She tried to keep her voice calm. 'Look, why don't you sit down? We'll have some coffee then we can try to figure what happened to Frankie, I mean Francisco. I'd like to know, too. Your brother was a special man and I loved him.' At least she thought she did at the time. Since meeting Max, she realized she hadn't known a thing about love.

Tony followed her. Trying to evade him, she managed to put the sofa between them. 'Stop, Tony. I know you're just playing a game but it isn't funny.'

'You scared, Claire?' He mocked her. 'Tell me, how did Charles kill him?' He came on, no matter where she went. If she got behind a chair, he pushed it aside. Once she slipped and he almost caught her.

'Stop.' Claire tripped again and this time Tony caught hold of her and raised the knife over her head. Her heart seemed to stop for one long breathless moment.

The front window exploded, then two shots rang out. Claire covered her face with her hands. A moment later, strong arms were holding her in a tight embrace.

Fearful that it was Tony, she struggled then the room spun around and she fainted.

When she regained consciousness, she was lying on the sofa. The sound of a man's low voice came to her from across the room.

Tears of gratitude filled her eyes as she realized who it was. Max was talking on his cell phone. She heard him say, ' . . . at The Folly, the Charles Stanhope residence. Please send the coroner and a police officer.'

She tried to get up. Max returned and held her.

'It's over, Claire. You're all right now.'

She noticed a mound covered by a coat on the floor. 'What? What happened? Did you . . . '

'He was going to kill you. I had no choice.' Max's voice was calm, devoid of emotion. His face was expressionless.

A car pulled up outside and Chris and Mattie ran inside. 'Claire, are you all right?' The housekeeper hugged her.

Once Chris determined she wasn't hurt, he took Max aside. The two men conferred in a corner, talking in low tones.

Max went into the dining room to make another call. When he came back, he told her friends to sit down. Mattie and Chris flanked her on the sofa while Max talked.

'I've been tracking Tony since I arrived in Bowness,' he said. 'Preston, my contact from Scotland Yard is outside waiting for the police. He'll show you his own identification and verify that I'm an FBI Special Agent. We're both part of an international Task Force of agents from the Yard, the FBI and other law enforcement groups.

'Tony was a hired assassin known as Antonio, and sought in several countries. He was also the only surviving son of an international crime boss now in Dartmouth Prison. Tony's older brother vanished five years ago, and their father suspected that Charles and Claire had killed him. Tony struck up a friendship with Claire to find the truth.'

'Claire?' Mattie looked at Kate's niece. 'You don't know anything about what happened to this Francisco, do you?'

'Nothing except what Charles told me.' Claire put her head in her hands and wept. 'Charles could've killed Francisco. You know how possessive my brother was.'

'Max, is there any reason we can't take Claire back to the hotel? She's had a nasty shock.' Mattie kept her arm around Claire while she was talking.

'In a while. The local police will want to question her when they get here. And someone from the Yard will interrogate her.'

'That can wait until the morning, can't it?'

Claire began to laugh and the others stared at her. 'It's all right. I'm not hysterical. I just remembered something. Max, would you please go and tell Valerie it's all right to come out of the pantry now?'

Max hurried into the kitchen. Claire could hear voices then Max reappeared. Valerie hesitantly followed him into the room.

Glancing around, she asked, 'Is he really dead?'

Two crime scene investigators walked into the room and Max led them to the far corner where Tony's body was. The investigator raised the blanket covering Tony and took pictures.

Returning, Max asked, 'Claire, is there another room nearby that we can use? We don't want to be in the way.'

She led the group to a sitting room near the front door. 'Is this all right?'

'Fine,' he said. 'To answer your question, Valerie. Yes, Tony's dead. You don't have to be afraid any more.'

'Thank God, he would've killed both of us.'

Taking a seat, Valerie wiped her eyes.

'If Claire doesn't mind, I think I'll go back to Kings Grant now. It's almost two o'clock.' Mattie got to her feet. 'Can I take Valerie?'

Max shook his head. 'We need to talk with her, also.'

Valerie looked at Max. His stern face must have frightened her since she began sobbing.

Claire sat down by Valerie and took her hand. 'Don't be alarmed. Just tell them the truth and you'll be all right. Would you like someone to call your father?'

'Yes, please.' Valerie murmured.

'I'll call him if you'll give me the number.' Max's voice was firm, yet not unkind.

Valerie responded with a faint smile. 'Thank you.'

Before the housekeeper left, Claire spoke to Max. 'Could I see you for a moment?'

He nodded and followed her to the kitchen, closing the door.

Claire shook her head. 'What can I say? You saved my life.'

'I was afraid I'd lost you.' He held out his arms and she walked into his embrace.

'When we found out who you really were, I was afraid you'd just been staying close to me because of your assignment.'

'That's how it started. Claire, look at me.' He held her in his arms until she raised her eyes. Their gazes locked. 'An FBI agent didn't fire that shot. That was the man who . . . ' His voice faltered. 'the man who loves to be with you.'

Claire couldn't help noticing Max shied away from the three little words she yearned to hear. Though she was disappointed, she told herself it was a start. Maybe he'd had a bad experience in the past. This time his kiss was different, more tender, almost gentle.

A knock sounded on the kitchen door. The door opened and a distinguished older man with silver hair gazed at them. 'Excuse me, Max,' he said. 'I just wanted to let you know the police have arrived.'

'You're the professor from the train.' Claire cried in surprise. She looked from Max to the older man.

'This is Robert Preston in our Task Force. He's been helping me track Tony and keep you safe,' Max explained.

'Thank you.' Claire shook his hand.

'Miss, the pleasure was all mine.' Preston had dropped his Western twang and now spoke with a British accent.

Mattie looked in. 'The police want to speak to you, Claire.'

The detectives were kind, especially the older one. He asked Claire to tell him what happened. Once she'd done that, he smiled. 'It's late, Miss Stanhope. If you'll promise to be at the constabulary at ten a.m. tomorrow, you can go home now.'

Mattie and Claire left soon after that.

★ ★ ★

Max stared after them.

Chris got to his feet. 'If it's all right, I'll be going, too. My wife will have a thousand questions. Even if it's the middle of the night, she'll be waiting up for me.'

Max shook Chris's hand. 'Thanks for everything you've done. If you ever tire of hotel work, the Agency could use a man who thinks and moves fast.'

Chris laughed and went out the front door.

Max and Preston stood alone. The sound of the police officers' voices drifted to them from the living room.

'You sure made a mess of that glass,' Preston said. He'd come through the window right after Max. 'That was a close one.'

'That bastard almost cut her throat.' Max shivered. 'Damn him to Hell.'

'You don't have to say that,' Preston responded.

'What do you mean?'

'If there's any justice in the world, he's there already.'

259

Max's laugh was hollow. Would he ever rid himself of the image of Claire on the floor and Tony leaning over her with that butcher knife?

23

Claire fled from Tony through a labyrinth of dimly lit rooms. No matter how fast she ran, he came closer and closer. Her heart raced so hard she thought it would burst. With one last surge of energy, he grabbed her. She screamed.

She jolted back to consciousness, sitting upright in her bed. Claire blinked hard, trying to adjust her vision to the morning light. As her pulse rate slowed, her tense muscles relaxed.

Through the windows to her right, she glimpsed the remaining leaves on the oaks fluttering in the autumn winds. Her wary gaze traveled around the yellow floral room she'd used since returning to Bowness. All was in order.

She was quite alone in the room, yet it had seemed so real. Claire realized she'd been reliving the horrors of the previous evening in an all-too-realistic nightmare.

The lock tumbled in the door to her room and Claire's stomach knotted. Before she could climb out of bed, Mattie rushed into the room, holding a set of the hotel keys.

'What happened? I was tidying up the nursery when you screamed like a banshee.'

Claire managed a faint smile, not wanting to worry the housekeeper. Now that she was fully conscious, the nightmare faded away. 'I guess last night was too much for me. I must have been dreaming about Tony and . . . you know.' Claire reached for her friend's hand. 'I'm fine now.'

Mattie took her hand. 'You're as cold as ice.' Worry crept into her voice and she patted Claire's arm. 'Are you sure you're all right? I could call Kate and Nick's family doctor.'

'Thanks. It was only a bad dream.' Claire pushed the hair off her face. A vague recollection of childhood slid into her mind. When she'd been the twins' age, she had been convinced there was a witch in her closet at night after her nanny turned off the nursery lights. 'I'm glad Kayla and Nicky are with their mother in Carlisle. If they were home, I might have frightened them.'

'Are you kidding?' The housekeeper chuckled. 'They hear lots of bloodcurdling screams on television. Besides, they wouldn't have heard you if they were downstairs watching those noisy cartoon programs. If I didn't know better, I'd swear Nicky turns up the volume on the television whenever I leave the kitchen.'

'Did Max call?' Claire blurted out what she'd been dying to ask. She wanted, no, she needed to see him again. If Tony's attack seemed a nightmare, Max's tenderness last evening had been a beautiful dream. He'd come so close to saying he loved her. Maybe he would today.

'No, he hasn't.' Mattie cocked her head, watching her.

'Oh, I see.'

The housekeeper's eyes twinkled as if she'd heard the disappointment in Claire's words. 'He didn't need to call. Max's been downstairs for hours. From his red eyes, I don't believe the poor man slept a wink last night. Goodness knows what time he finished with the police. I told him to go back to his flat and take a nap. I'd call when you woke up. Then he could come back and have breakfast with us. He insisted on waiting downstairs. That's one determined young man.' Mattie slapped her forehead. 'Whoops. I almost forgot. Wait a moment.'

With that, she stepped into the corridor and returned carrying a large vase of red roses. 'These came for you.'

'Oh, how lovely.' Claire flung her covers back and climbed from bed. She padded across the room, watching as the housekeeper set the large glass vase of flowers on a dresser.

Burying her face in the arrangement, Claire inhaled the sweet fragrance of the long-stemmed roses. The blossoms were just opening and drops of water clung like diamonds to the dark green leaves. 'That was so dear of him.'

'Him? Who?'

Claire stared at her friend. 'That's a good question. I assumed they're from Max. Who else would send me red roses?'

'Is there an enclosure card?'

She plucked a small envelope off the arrangement, opened it and read the short message. 'They're from Nick.' Claire smiled, trying to hide her disappointment. She'd been so sure the flowers were from Max.

'Nick? But why?'

Claire shrugged. 'I guess they're his way of thanking me for helping with his case.' As if he needed to thank her after all he'd done after Charles's death. Remembering Nick's kindness, Claire handed the note to Mattie. 'Here, you can read what he wrote. I need to take a quick shower.'

Stepping into her bathroom, Claire turned on the shower. Moments later the hot water was beating down on her body, relaxing her tense muscles and clearing her head. Hurry, she told herself. Max was waiting.

By the time she returned to her bedroom,

the housekeeper was sitting in a chair by the fireplace.

Claire smiled. 'From his note, it sounds like Nick hopes to be released today.'

Mattie's usual composure vanished and she frowned. 'Kate and Nick are both coming home today and look at this place.' She flicked an invisible flake of dust off a table with the corner of her apron. 'Also, what am I going to fix for dinner? It's got to be something special tonight.'

Claire placed her arms around her friend. 'Slow down. We haven't been notified yet.'

'I know. Still . . . '

From Mattie's fretful expression, Claire could tell the housekeeper's mind was made up. Barring evidence to the contrary, Nick was coming home that day. Or so Mattie believed. 'Nick's solicitor hasn't contacted us yet,' Claire told her old friend. 'I'm sure he would've been in touch if Nick were being freed.'

'I feel it in my bones, like when a storm's brewing,' Mattie said. 'Today's the day.'

'You'll be ready. Meanwhile, let's have breakfast.'

Mattie nodded and hurried from the room.

Claire's heart beat faster thinking of Max. Hurrying to get dressed, she slipped into a pair of dark green wool slacks and a white

265

turtleneck sweater and hurried downstairs.

As she walked into the sunny room, he sat at the dining room table reading the paper.

He looked up and saw her watching him.

Feeling shy, she greeted him. 'Good morning. Isn't it a glorious day?'

He glanced outside. 'When I left my flat it was dark and cold.' He smiled at her. 'But you're right. The sun's out now.'

'I guess you'll be leaving now that the case is closed.' Claire eased into a chair near his. She mustn't make him think she was asking him to stay, to make a commitment. Yet she dreaded his going away.

A lot had happened the last few days. And last night Max had kissed her tenderly. His eyes seemed to say 'I love you' even if his lips didn't tell her. Inexperienced with men, Claire wondered if Max loved her.

Other than last night, he'd never said or done anything to lead her to believe he cared. Claire shook her head. He'd kissed her the day they met. If she concentrated, she could almost feel his lips on hers.

'I've got to get back to the Yard to be debriefed. Antonio was just one of a lot of criminals who . . . ' Max's voice trailed off. Maybe he didn't think it wise to say too much about the man they had both known as Tony.

'Will we see you again?' She hoped he'd be back.

'For a little while. I have a few days off between my assignments.'

'Then perhaps you'll let me show you the Lake District I know,' Claire said, striving for a light touch. She mustn't sound demanding. She had no claims on the man. At that instance there was no doubt in her mind she loved him. The realization made her feel lightheaded, but she managed to finish what she'd been saying. 'So far you've either been stuck away in the Bugle's office or watching Tony.'

'You're right. And I'd like to see more of this beautiful area of England while I'm here.' He reached over and took her hand, holding it for a minute or two until the housekeeper burst into the room.

Nerves seemed to drive Mattie as she bustled about straightening the dining room.

'Did you spend the whole night with the Windermere police?' Claire queried Max. Anxious for news of her uncle, she wondered if Max had heard anything about Nick's release.

'It was almost dawn when I left the constabulary so there wasn't much sense in going to bed,' he admitted, yawning.

Looking closer, Claire noticed Max's eyes

were heavy with fatigue. And he had a five o'clock shadow. That was a first. As long as she'd known him, he'd been clean-shaven and well groomed. 'What about Valerie?'

'She's being held for questioning. I expect there'll be a hearing today or tomorrow. She should have legal counsel by now.'

Mattie spoke up. 'We had a note from Nick this morning. Is he really going to be released?'

'Today, I believe. Why don't you check with his solicitor? Who is he?'

'Percy April.' The housekeeper replied, headed for the hall.

'Now where are you going?' Claire stared after her friend.

'Go ahead with your breakfast. I won't be able to eat a bite until I know if Nick's coming home today. I'll call Percy. He should've notified us if Nick's being released.'

Max moved his chair closer to Claire's. 'While we're alone, I want to thank you for helping us apprehend Antonio.' His gaze became curious. 'What convinced you to offer to help?'

'I don't know. Maybe it was seeing Valerie's bruises, learning how he mistreated her. He didn't like women very much, did he?'

'No, except as toys. Tony was a user. I don't

think the man had an ounce of kindness in him.'

'Could that be at least partly due to the way he was raised?' She flushed. 'I'm sorry. I guess I'm still trying to learn why he became a criminal.'

'If anyone has the right to inquire about Tony, it's one of his intended victims. Scotland Yard found out a little about his family. His mother and father were divorced in the States, then his father brought Tony and his older brother to England and enrolled them in military school.'

There had been something lost and sad about the man. 'Was he really just twenty-two?'

'As far as I know. That baby-face was a killer, Claire. Don't feel sorry for him. He was suspected of killing several high ranking officials. Valerie is very fortunate to have escaped him. She owes you a debt of gratitude for hiding her last night. She wouldn't have stood a chance in the woods if he'd caught up with her. Valerie fooled him once. She wouldn't have done it a second time.'

Claire shivered. 'I was lucky, too. If you hadn't turned up when you did, he would've cut my throat.'

Max gave her hand a quick squeeze before

releasing it. 'Enough of that. He won't bother you or anyone else again.' With one quick movement, he tilted his coffee cup and drained it.

Getting to his feet, Max said, 'I have to get cleaned up and take the noon train to London. The debriefing shouldn't take more than a day or so. Chances are I'll be free after that. Then I'll remind you of your offer to give me an escorted tour of this area. Okay?'

'That's fine. I'll look forward to it.' She kept her seat, watching him leave the dining room. As the hotel's front door opened and closed, she wished he'd kissed her goodbye. Did he care for her? Uncertainty made her sad.

Mattie came back into the room. Her worried expression had been replaced by a smiling countenance. 'It's true, Nick will be here this afternoon.' She paused. 'Hmmm . . . I wonder if Kate would like us to take the children somewhere later today so Nick and she can have some time to themselves.'

'That's a good idea,' Claire replied. 'I imagine Kayla and Nicky would enjoy that new kiddie movie playing at the Lakeside Theatre down in the village. We could go to the early show.'

The housekeeper went into the kitchen. When she didn't return in a few minutes,

Claire went upstairs for a warm jacket and left the house for a walk. Maybe some fresh air would help.

★   ★   ★

Max stepped into the gatehouse to prepare for the trip to London. When he returned, Claire had promised him a short tour of the area before he left for good.

A frown crossed his face as he remembered the previous night. Relieved to reach The Folly in time, he'd almost slipped and told Claire he loved her. Fortunately, he'd caught himself. In the cold light of day, he wasn't sure how he felt.

Since his parents' death, he'd played it safe, not allowing himself to become attached to anyone. Loving meant being vulnerable.

Max didn't dare love Claire as she deserved to be loved. Suppose he did and something horrific happened to her? He'd be left alone again. Ten years ago he'd had a family. Because of a drunken driver, Max had lost both of his parents. By now he was almost used to the solitary life.

Oh well. He yawned and looked longingly at his unmade bed. There was no time for a nap. He had to get cleaned up then take the shuttle to Oxenholme and make a connection to British Rail. He was due at the Yard for a debriefing first thing in the morning. His job was most important in his life. Hell, who was he fooling? It was his life.

24

'Would you take the muffins out of the oven?' Mattie called to Claire from the top of the stairs.

'Sure.' She went into the kitchen while the housekeeper finished dressing upstairs. Kate's train from Carlisle was due at the Windermere station in thirty minutes.

Claire had just leaned over the lower oven to remove the muffins when the bell outside the hotel's front door jangled.

'Max?' Maybe he'd come back to say goodbye before going to the train station. No one replied. The silence bothered her.

The hair on the back of her head prickled. She was almost afraid to move, so strong was the feeling that someone was there. At last Claire took hold of the muffin tins with the oven mitts and lifted the pans out of the oven. She turned slowly and took a quick look around.

At first nothing appeared out of the ordinary. Then a familiar voice spoke and her head swiveled to the right.

He was leaning in the doorway.

'Nick?' She could hardly speak. 'We didn't

know when you were coming. I didn't hear a car.'

He beamed. 'Well, give your uncle a hug.' He opened his arms and she flew into them.

'It's wonderful to see you. We've all waited so long. Did Percy bring you home?' Claire glanced out the front windows. 'I don't see his car. Where did he park?'

'He dropped me at the end of the driveway. I wanted to walk home from the village. Percy insisted on bringing me up the hill.' Nick walked around the kitchen, touching the dishes, picking up a toy soldier. 'It seems a million years since I've been here. You have no idea how good everything looks.' He stood back, studying her. 'You look tired. Did the flowers come?'

'Yes and the lovely note. Thank you. I'm not sure I deserve roses. I didn't do much.'

'You certainly did. Because you were there to take Valerie in and hide her, she lived to tell the police the truth, clearing me.' He looked concerned. 'I heard about that woman beating you up. Who was she anyway?'

'I don't know. You'll have to ask the police.'

'Percy's been keeping me up-to-date with the family. I can hardly wait to see Kayla and Nicky . . . and Kate.' Nick prowled around a bit more. 'Can I have one?' He eyed the muffins.

'I bet you didn't have any breakfast.' Claire handed him two muffins on a plate. 'How about coffee?'

'Great.' He glanced around. 'Where's Mattie?'

'Upstairs getting dressed to go to the station. Why don't you surprise her?'

Nodding, he put his finger over his lips.

Nick left the kitchen and Claire listened expectantly for several minutes. There was a shriek then Nick and Mattie came downstairs together.

'Why didn't you warn me?' The house-keeper looked in Claire's direction. Mattie's eyes were moist.

'You both make me feel very welcome. It's great to be home.' When he smiled, he looked more like the Nick they knew and loved. 'Maybe I should go away more often.'

'Heaven forbid.' There was a lump in Claire's throat. If she wasn't careful, she'd get weepy herself. She glanced at the wall clock. 'Goodness, look at the time. If we don't leave soon, Kate and the children will arrive with nobody there to greet them.' Claire found her jacket and put it on, picked up her purse.

'If you don't mind,' Nick began, looking at his shoes. He hesitated then continued. 'I think I'll stay here and see Kate when you bring her home. In fact, I think it might be better if I were upstairs in our room when she arrived.'

Was he afraid Kate was still angry? 'All right, if that's what you prefer.' Claire wanted to reassure Nick about his wife yet she wasn't sure Kate would greet him with open arms. 'We won't tell Kate you're home. You can surprise her.'

While Claire drove Kate's car down the hill to the village, Mattie sat in the passenger seat, looking back over her shoulder.

'Don't worry.' Claire tried to reassure her friend. 'He'll still be there when we get back.'

'I know. It's just that I didn't realize how much Nick meant to me until he was arrested. He's a good man, Claire.'

'I agree. He just made one mistake and it cost him dearly.' Claire gazed anxiously at the clock on the dashboard. 'I hope we get to the station before the train.'

'I've been in Bowness a lot longer than you, dear,' Mattie reminded her. 'And one thing's sure. That shuttle has never been on schedule.'

'There's always a first time.' Claire pushed the speed limit, driving down to the village and into the train station parking lot.

The train was just pulling into the Windermere station as they parked the car. 'Hurry.' Though she knew Mattie didn't like to be rushed, Claire took the housekeeper by the arm and hurried her through the small, limestone building and out the other side to the platform.

'There they are.' Mattie pointed to an open window in the last coach where Kayla and Nicky were waving. Kate stood behind them. When she saw them, she waved. Though she smiled, she didn't look too happy.

Claire wished she could tell Kate who was waiting for her at the hotel. Nick didn't want his wife to know he was back until he greeted her in person, so Claire said nothing.

All the way home, the children chattered away about riding on the train and swimming in the hotel's heated pool.

'You're glad to be home, aren't you?' The anxious expression on Mattie's wrinkled face indicated the housekeeper was a little concerned. 'I bet you didn't miss old Mattie one bit.'

'Of course we did.' Kayla put her little arms around the older lady, the closest thing they had to a grandmother. Not to be left out, Nicky hugged them both.

At last they drove up the driveway. As soon as the car stopped, the children jumped out and ran around the yard.

'They're like wild things,' Kate exclaimed. 'I didn't realize how much they disliked being confined until we came back on the train.'

'Let them run and get some fresh air.' Mattie smiled as Kayla and Nicky chased each other. 'It's a beautiful day. I'll stay out with them for a few minutes.'

'I'll join you.' Claire wanted to give her aunt time to go upstairs and find Nick. She prayed Kate had forgiven her husband. Kate had been quite upset yet time had passed since she heard her husband had been unfaithful.

As Kate went indoors, she turned and called them from the porch. 'If you two don't mind, I'm going to go upstairs and rest for a few minutes.'

'You do that. We'll keep an eye on the children.' Mattie nodded, the picture of encouragement.

Claire sat with the housekeeper on the patio, watching the children and listening. No sound came from the house. Then Claire noticed something of interest and nudged her friend.

Someone was drawing the drapes in Kate's room. She must have seen Nick by now, so that was probably a good sign. Claire smiled at Mattie and the housekeeper returned her smile. They sat together, watching the children run and play in the sunshine.

25

The next morning Max exited the London Holiday Inn where he'd spent the night. One glance at the snarls of rush-hour traffic outside convinced him to refuse the taxi the uniformed doorman offered. It was just a few blocks to his destination so he opted to walk.

Before starting out, he studied the overcast sky, inhaling the mixed odor of vehicle exhaust fumes and the smell of rain. A cold wind blew uncollected scraps of trash down the street. Max pulled his trenchcoat closer.

Within a few minutes he arrived at his destination. Silver metallic letters on the revolving sign in front announced, 'New Scotland Yard.' The gray buildings exuded solemn authority. Stepping inside the main entrance, he approached the Information Desk. While personnel looked him up in the Yard's online directory, Max removed his trenchcoat, folding it over the arm that also held his briefcase. He pinned a badge on the lapel of his suit, asking for directions to the meeting.

As he walked down the long corridor, he could have been invisible for all the attention he received from the crowds of people hurrying by. Each person who passed him seemed preoccupied with his own business.

At the meeting room, Max showed his identification badge to gain admission. Several men had gathered around a conference table when he entered. 'Good morning Special Agent Bronsky.' The man at the head of the table greeted him. 'It's good to see you. Why don't you take a seat over there.' The leader pointed toward an empty chair.

Max sat down and took a folder from his briefcase. His notes were ample considering he'd written most of them last night. He liked to keep the information on a case in his head as much as possible. It was safer.

'I hear congratulations are in order.' The leader began to clap his hands and the other men followed his lead, applauding Max's successful mission.

Max flushed, not accustomed to so much praise. Like New Scotland Yard, The Federal Bureau of Investigation expected excellence from its personnel.

Following the display of approval, the leader said, 'I know you'll turn in copious notes on your investigation, however today we'd be interested in a brief summary of your findings.'

'Yes sir.' Max stood, gazing at the curious

faces turned toward him. The only familiar person was Preston, who'd been his Yard counterpart. 'I appreciate your approval. Before discussing the case, I'd like to commend someone else.

'From the first, Robert Preston proved invaluable on the assignment. Posing as a fellow traveler, he observed Miss Stanhope en route to Bowness. Later he watched over her when she left her aunt's hotel. And he also helped Superintendent Connor's ex-wife reach Miss Stanhope's home the night the subject was killed. If Antonio had found her in the woods, she wouldn't have stood a chance.' Max smiled across the table at his fellow agent.

'I'm glad to hear Preston was helpful.' The head of the Task Force beamed. 'Now if you'll give us your summary.'

Max spent the next few minutes describing his surveillance of the suspect, his concern about Miss Stanhope's safety and the events leading up to Antonio's death.

'So Miss Stanhope knew nothing about the older brother's disappearance?' Another member of the Task Force queried Max.

'She has no idea what happened to Francisco,' Max said.

The Task Force leader looked up from a communiqué he'd received while Max was speaking. 'I've just heard from the Warden at Dartmouth Prison where the subject's father is serving a life sentence.' Concern covered the leader's features. 'The prisoner became violent on hearing of Antonio's death.'

Max's muscles tightened. 'Antonio was his father's last surviving son.'

The Task Force leader nodded in agreement. 'In fact he had to be restrained. He kept screaming about getting even until the doctor sedated him. He blames Miss Stanhope for Antonio's death.'

'Wasn't he told an FBI agent shot Antonio before he could kill Miss Stanhope?' Another group member asked.

'Something like that, I'm sure.' The leader frowned. 'Before he was sedated, the last thing Tony's father said was, 'That dame's going to pay.''

'It's a good thing he's in for life,' Max responded. An icy fist squeezed his heart and he was afraid for Claire.

'Yes, he is, though he must have friends on the outside. It may be an idle threat. We'll check with the warden in a day or so and see if the father has calmed down.'

'And if he hasn't, what can we do?' Max asked.

'You must realize we can't post a guard because Miss Stanhope's life might be in danger,' the Project Head responded. 'I don't suppose she'd consider relocating to another part of England or going abroad for awhile?' He asked Max.

'I doubt it.' Max shook his head. 'She just returned to Bowness a few weeks ago to be with her family.'

'Well, you know the woman so maybe you could talk to her, at least tell her to be careful. This may not come to anything. Convicts shoot off their mouths all the time.'

'I'll warn her and advise her to notify the police in the event of threatening letters or phone calls. You're aware of who her uncle is. Now that the charges against Nick Connor have been dropped and he's been reinstated as Cumbria Superintendent of Police, I'm sure he'll do all he can to protect his niece. She should be safer in Bowness than anywhere else.'

Max had thought it was over when he killed Tony. Maybe it wasn't after all. He dreaded telling Claire she could be in danger, and then having to leave her. It would only be a few days before the Task Force gave him another assignment. God only knew where it would be next time.

He had a sinking feeling inside. For a moment he wished he could stay in Bowness and keep Claire safe. Then his pragmatic nature took over. That was utter foolishness. He had to go where his assignments took him. They were tracking down and capturing a list of international criminals. It was a difficult assignment yet he must do his best like the rest of the team.

'Take a few days' leave, Bronsky. You've earned it.'

'Thank you, sir.'

With those words, the Task Force leader closed his portfolio and stood. Briefcases were slammed shut and chairs shoved back from the conference table as the members of the group followed his example. Max gathered his notes, stuck them in his briefcase and prepared to follow the others from the room.

Preston took his time so he and Max were the last ones leaving the room. 'Bronsky?'

'It doesn't sound good for her, does it?'

'It's just as well you don't really know the woman. You'd worry yourself to death.' The older man grimaced. 'That's why I never married. When you have family, you're always afraid they may become victims.'

Max nodded. Though the idea of Claire's being in danger disturbed him, he should resist loving her. It was too risky.

★ ★ ★

Kate sensed something different, approaching her bedroom. When she found Nick asleep on the bed, her heart pounded so hard, she thought she'd faint. Instead, she clung to the four-poster bed in silence, looking down on the only man she'd ever loved.

A stranger would find that hard to believe since she'd been a thirty-year-old widow when she'd met Nick. The truth was she and Stephen Stanhope had both married for the wrong reasons. He'd come into her life at a time when she was lonely. Saddened by her mother's death, Kate had been flattered by the debonair banker's lavish attentions. Later she discovered Stephen had married her because he couldn't have her mother. He had been so cold and cruel, Kate soon changed from an innocent romantic to a disillusioned wife.

As she watched Nick, she felt a warm feeling in the direction of the heart she'd thought frozen. A tear rolled down her cheek and she knelt beside him, willing him to wake up.

'What?' Nick opened his eyes. 'Kate? I wanted to surprise you. I guess I dozed off while I waited.'

'It's good to see you.' She kicked off her shoes and sat on the bed beside him. Wanting to embrace Nick, she held back. First she needed to know how he felt about her. They had been apart for weeks. People did change.

'I need a shave. Are my things . . . ' He motioned toward the bathroom they'd shared before he went to jail.

'Everything's just as you left it,' she murmured. She could've added including your wife. He looked good to her though he'd lost his tan. His skin was too pale.

'Give me a few minutes to get cleaned up, then we'll talk. There's so much I want to tell you. I've had a lot of time to think in jail.'

'There's no rush. I'll unpack.'

Minutes later, she heard the water running in the bathroom. On impulse, Kate began removing her clothes.

Nick was washing his hair when she opened the shower door. 'What is it?' he said.

'Would you like me to wash your back?'

'I'd love it.' Nick made room in the shower stall for her.

After Kate washed his back, Nick turned. 'I don't suppose you'd be interested . . . ,' he began.

She could see he was aroused. 'Yes, I would,' she said, smiling at the man she adored. After all that had happened, they were together again.

Nick found a towel and insisted on carrying her to their bed like he had the morning after they made love for the first time. 'Kate, I was a terrible fool. Can you ever forgive me?'

'Of course I can.' She kissed him and he tightened his arms around her. There was a discrete knock on the door then Mattie called out, 'Are you decent? The children heard your voices and know their father is home. Claire and I want to take them out for supper and a movie. They won't budge until they see Nick, know he's all right.'

'Wait a moment.' Kate jumped out of bed, found their robes and slipped into hers while Nick did the same. When they were both clothed, he opened the door.

Kayla threw herself into her father's arms.

'Daddy.' Kayla kissed his cheek again and again until Nicky grew impatient and gave her a gentle shove out of the way. Though the boy wasn't much into kissing, he let his father give him a quick hug then he showed Nick his new baseball and bat.

'That's really something.' Nick admired Nicky's new equipment. 'If the weather's good tomorrow, let's go outside and practice on the lawn.'

'Mattie offered to throw me some balls,' the little boy said. 'I told her I'd wait until my Dad came home.' Nicky hugged his father once more before leaving the room.

'Thanks for doing this for us.' Kate wanted to cry. She blinked back the tears.

'Is everything all right now?' Claire asked.

'Oh, yes.' Kate couldn't remember ever being so filled with happiness. 'We're as right as rain. See you all in the morning.'

'There's some vegetable soup, rolls and cake in the kitchen when you're hungry,' Mattie called over her shoulder as she followed the children downstairs.

The door closed and Nick got up and locked it.

'You're home at last,' Kate said.

'Home at last,' he said, echoing her words. Nick hugged her.

'Let's make a baby,' she suggested without warning. With their troubles behind them, she wanted to add to their family.

'Are you sure?' Nick seemed to study her.

'Yes, I want our child to come from this night. And years from now, when we look at him, we'll remember.'

Nick smiled and nodded. Though he didn't say anything, Kate sensed he was deeply moved. A sense of thanksgiving filled her. They were together again. She couldn't ask for more.

26

That evening Claire sat in the nursery, reading the children a bedtime story. 'And the Prince kissed Sleeping Beauty and woke her and they were married and lived happily ever after.'

Kayla sighed and kissed her dolly. Nicky snuggled down in his twin bed. 'How about one more, Cuz?' He looked hopeful.

'You two wanted just one more a half-hour ago,' Claire said, ruefully. 'It's time to go to sleep now.' She kissed them both and smoothed their covers.

Nick came in to kiss the children. Passing Claire in the doorway, he spoke to her. 'Max's on the line.'

Claire took the call in the kitchen, sitting on a bar stool. First Max reassured her that he'd be there the next day. His voice became tense as he continued.

'During the Task Force meeting this morning your name came up.'

'I would imagine it did under the circumstances,' she said dryly. Claire tried not to think about the evening she'd almost lost her life. If Max and his fellow agent hadn't burst into the house, she doubted she'd have survived.

'Antonio's father is very upset over his son's death and he blames you.'

'That doesn't make sense,' she wailed. 'I was his victim.'

'Criminals don't see things like normal people,' Max told her. 'In his twisted way of thinking, you're responsible for his last surviving son's death. He may also blame you for whatever happened to his older son.'

'Did the police tell him that two Task Force agents shot Antonio to save my life?'

'I'm sure they did. Anyway, the bottom line is the father has threatened your life. So be careful. It was probably just a lot of talk. Still . . . '

'Maybe I should stick around the hotel for awhile?'

'That's a good idea,' Max responded quickly as if relieved she was taking his news so well. 'At least, don't go anywhere by yourself. We can still go on your tour. I can protect you.'

She heard a smile in his voice. 'I know.'

'From what I hear, Tony's father has heart trouble,' Max commented. 'He may not be around much longer.'

Then they'd turned to more pleasant topics, like where Claire planned to take him on their excursion.

Now she waited impatiently for him to come back from London. Max hadn't told her which train he'd take.

Starting after lunch, Claire waited. As the hours passed, Max didn't appear and she grew more and more uneasy. At last she put on a warm coat and walked about the front lawns then stationed herself on the knoll of a hill. It was an ideal spot from which to watch the cars passing below on Kendal Road. Before dusk, the west wind turned colder and Claire retreated indoors. She found Mattie in the kitchen.

'He'll never come if you just sit there and stare at the traffic,' the housekeeper warned her. 'Find something to do and the time will pass faster.'

'That's easier said than done. I wish he'd get here.'

'Did he say when he expected to arrive?'

'He didn't know. And I didn't want to seem too eager.' Claire gazed at her friend. 'What would you do?'

'Wait, he'll be back. He has to, doesn't he? I mean, his clothes and things are still in the gatehouse.'

'I'd like to think he's coming back because of me as well,' Claire murmured, growing more unsure by the minute.

'Of course he is.' Mattie put a pie in the oven then washed her hands. She turned her head in the direction of the wall clock. 'There's another shuttle due in about five minutes.'

'I'm going outside one more time. If he doesn't show up in fifteen minutes, I'll come in and help you get supper on the table.' Claire rebuttoned her wool coat and went outside again.

The autumn sun was sinking in the west, leaving the air crisp and cold. Winter was on its way.

From the front lawn, Claire watched the cars down on Lendal Road. It was dusk now and drivers were switching on their headlights. All of the vehicles whisked by King's Grant, none turned onto the hotel entrance.

The wind became stronger and she was about to give up when a dark vehicle appeared over the hill and turned onto the private roadway belonging to the hotel. It stopped at the gatehouse, the lights were turned off then someone opened the car door.

Max! Her heart thumped with excitement. For a moment Claire hesitated. Maybe she should go back inside. Her heart told her otherwise. Before she knew what she was doing, she was running down the lawn, waving and calling his name.

He turned and she could feel his pleasure to see her before she saw his smile. They converged halfway up the drive.

'Hello. Have you been waiting for me?' His grin told her that he knew she'd been doing exactly that.

'Oh, for a little,' Claire tried to sound nonchalant though it was difficult. 'I had a feeling you'd be on the last train.'

'I almost didn't make it. We had to stop at a station along the way when the engineer became ill and had to leave us. Getting a replacement must've taken over an hour.'

'Mattie says the shuttle's never on time.'

'Today I'm glad. Otherwise, I would've had to get a cab and it's thirty miles from Oxenholme to Bowness.' He paused for a moment before asking, 'Do you suppose I can have supper at the hotel tonight? My cupboard's bare.'

'We planned for you to eat with us. It'll be a few minutes. Mattie's cooking stew and biscuits. And her famous Lemon Meringue Pie.' Claire laughed, her spirits high now that he'd arrived. She hoped he didn't mind her chatter, she was so glad to see him. 'Around these parts, people can't get enough of it.'

'Then let's not keep her waiting.' Max took her hand and held it for a minute. 'I'll miss you when I leave.' His expression became serious. 'It's been good to be with you.'

She waited for him to say more. Anything would have been better than the way his gaze slid away from hers.

'You're not gone yet. Beat you to the door.' Trying to lighten the mood, she took off with Max at her heels. At the hotel entrance, they both stopped, out of breath.

'Is our tour still on for tomorrow?' Max asked.

'If it doesn't rain.' Claire glanced overhead. Now that the sun had set, the evening stars were beginning to twinkle in the darkened sky. 'I think it'll be a perfect day. Come up here for breakfast. That way we can make an early start. There's a lot I want to show you.'

'I can imagine.' His mischievous grin made her flush.

At the table, Max and she talked more than anyone else. Nick and Kate sat close together and Claire got the distinct impression that whatever their problems had been, everything was as it should be now. The children finished first then squirmed in their chairs until Kate released them to play in the next room. 'No fighting and no Indian wrestling,' she ordered.

They agreed and galloped away, obviously delighted to have some free time away from their elders.

After dinner, Claire helped Kate clear the table. 'You sit and talk to Nick and Max while we clean up the kitchen and serve the pie, Mattie,' Kate said. The housekeeper had cooked dinner while Nick and Kate were upstairs in their room and Claire waited outside for Max.

Kate rinsed the dishes and Claire loaded them in the dishwasher. 'It's good to have Max with us tonight,' Kate said in a low voice.

'We're spending the day together tomorrow.'

'Has he . . . ?' Kate prompted Claire.

'No, we're just friends.' That didn't mean she couldn't dream of more. If only Max would stay longer. Long enough for him to decide he needed her in his life.

'Come on, I've seen the way he looks at you.'

'I'm hoping he'll write.' Doubt weighed heavy on Claire's shoulders. Did he plan to walk out of her life? 'So far he hasn't said he would.'

'It's time you settled down and from what I've seen of him, Max would be a good choice. He's bright and handsome and a darn nice guy. You deserve someone special after all of that trouble with Charles.'

The door opened and Max stuck his head

into the kitchen. Claire wondered if he'd overheard their conversation.

'Excuse me. I just wanted to see how much longer you'll be. The two of you've been out here awhile.'

'We're finished.' Kate sliced the pie into individual servings, putting each piece on a dessert plate. Next Claire transported the plates to a tray and carried it into the living room where Mattie and Nick were chatting. Kate followed with a carafe of steaming coffee and fresh cups and saucers.

The time passed quickly and soon Nick yawned.

'Poor man, he didn't sleep well in jail,' Kate explained. 'He needs to get some rest.' Gathering the children, she and Nick said good night and went upstairs.

Next Mattie retired, leaving Claire and Max alone.

'I guess I should be going, too.' Max stood and headed toward the door.

Claire followed him. 'Come for breakfast around eight. That way we can make an early start. And don't forget to wear comfortable walking shoes.'

Nodding, he gave Claire a peck on the cheek. 'You know what I said about Antonio's father? Don't worry too much. He's in Dartmouth for life.'

'I know.'

'Still, it wouldn't hurt to be careful,' he added, easing out of the door.

Standing in the foyer, Claire felt lonely. Didn't Max want her? Earlier she'd imagined he did. Maybe she'd been wrong. She wished she weren't so inexperienced with men.

Claire turned off the lights and went upstairs to her room. She caught herself checking under the bed and in the closet before retiring.

★　★　★

Walking down the driveway to his flat, Max was confused. Part of him wanted to stay with Claire. The others had retired for the evening, so if she had encouraged him, he might have invited her down to his apartment for a drink. There they would have had complete privacy. His imagination ran rampant as he imagined what they might have done if they hadn't had to worry about her family walking in on them.

Since he returned that evening, Claire's behavior had bothered him. There weren't but a few years between them but she'd acted younger this time. Puzzled by her behavior, he'd only kissed her cheek when saying good night.

Tomorrow they'd be on their own, away from the hotel. Max admitted he wanted Claire yet wouldn't lead her on. That wouldn't be fair since he couldn't make her any promises. Heck, he didn't know what he should do.

Packing, he wished he could stay. Well, they'd have tomorrow and part of the following day. Then he must get back to London to be briefed on his next assignment.

Usually he felt excited at the prospect of a new case. Tonight there was no surge of enthusiasm, just dull resignation.

If he went away for months, would Claire wait for him? Like lightning, it struck Max. Claire was the girl he'd dreamed about for years, the girl who'd waited for him to find her.

Since losing his parents, he had shied away from a serious commitment. There was always the chance he'd lose the woman he loved. Claire was worth the risk.

Max's jaw tightened. Tomorrow he'd tell her how he felt and hope she felt the same way.

27

Next morning Claire woke early. A sleepy glance around her bedroom proved disappointing. No beams of sunlight reflected in the crystal vases on the mantel. On the other hand, she didn't hear the patter of rain on the roof. Glancing at the bedside clock, she was relieved to find it was just seven o'clock. This late in the year, the best she could hope for that day was brisk temperatures and cloudy skies.

If it just didn't rain. Claire peered anxiously out her bedroom window before turning to make her bed. From a bureau drawer she retrieved a new set of lacy lingerie she'd bought in a local store and tucked away, saving it for a special occasion. Maybe today would be a good time to wear the abbreviated creamy silk bra and matching bikinis. She rubbed the material against her cheek and wondered if Max would approve.

After taking a bath, Claire put on her new purchases then a blue wool sweater and matching slacks. She pulled on warm wool socks and stepped into sleek black leather boots. Now she was ready for whatever the day brought.

Downstairs was still dark and quiet. Claire eased open the front door to get the morning newspaper. Her heart beat fast at the sight of Max walking up the driveway. 'Good morning.'

'I'm not too early, am I?' He seemed a little nervous.

'Not at all. I'll start the coffee. There's a breakfast cake Mattie made yesterday.' A thought occurred. Maybe Max would like a heartier breakfast. Just because she preferred to start her day with coffee, cereal and juice didn't mean everyone did. 'Maybe you'd like more, maybe a bowl of oatmeal or eggs and ham?'

He shook his head. 'No, the cake and some coffee would be great. We'll find a good place for lunch later.'

She nodded. It was nice to discover the two of them were alike in little ways. Claire imagined they could be great companions as well as lovers. Thinking of Max in bed with her, she felt her cheeks growing warmer.

'There's a lot to see and we have only one day. I'll give you a choice,' she said. 'We can drive north to Carlisle on the Scottish border or west to the Irish Sea. Muncaster Castle's out that way. And you mustn't miss a ride on one of our steamboats. Lake Windermere is the longest lake in England, ten miles from north to south and it's a nice ride, most days. The Lakeside Hotel on the far end of the lake serves an excellent lunch.'

'Let's go west to the sea, tour the castle then come back and ride the steamboat,' he suggested. 'And lunch at the hotel on Lake Windermere sounds good.'

With that settled, they had breakfast and left before the others came downstairs.

The sun was rising behind them while they rode along in quiet companionship. Claire wished they could continue for ever.

At the Irish Sea, they stopped and walked along the coarse gravel for a few minutes. Max peered across the choppy waters. In the distance fishing boats could be seen. 'I wouldn't want to be out there this morning, not in a small craft,' he said.

'Do you ever get seasick?' She inquired.

'You might say that.' He grimaced. 'I'll take a fast car chase, even parachuting out of a plane anytime to being on the sea during a storm.'

During their drive, Claire had thought about what happened on her way home from Devon. She found herself wanting to tell Max. 'A friend of mine had an interesting experience a few weeks ago. She was waiting for a train when a young boy jumped or fell off the station platform.' She talked about it like it had happened to someone else. 'She jumped off after him. Seconds later, an express train came through. If she hadn't reacted so quickly, the little boy might have been killed.'

'That was a courageous thing for you to do. Have you told your aunt yet?'

'No, I mean, how did you know I was the woman?' She hadn't mentioned it to anyone else.

'Remember Robert Preston, the Scotland Yard agent?'

'My professor from the train? I'll never forget him. The two of you saved my life.'

'He heard some of the British Rail employees talking about it on your train.' He smiled at her.

'I'm just glad I was there to help,' she said. 'Now that you know, I better tell Kate or her feelings will be hurt. She and I have always been close.'

Soon they could see Muncaster Castle through the trees. They were the first party to visit that day so the sweet white-haired docent gave them a special tour. As they left, she commented she hadn't met such charming newlyweds in a long time. Claire was secretly pleased when Max made no effort to correct her.

Mid-morning they reached the Winder-mere slip and Max bought their tickets, round-trip. 'Can we return anytime?'

The ship's captain nodded. 'That's right. Stay down at Lakeside all day if you want. I don't know if there's enough down there for you to see. There's the hotel, of course.' He went inside his cabin.

Max stood by her while the boat moved out of the slip. As they got underway, the gulls flew over the ship, begging for handouts.

The wind became cold and damp so Claire took Max's hand and led him inside to seats below deck. There was so much she wanted to tell him yet she was afraid.

'I meant what I said,' he said after they sat in silence for a few minutes. 'I will miss you.'

'Well, you could drop me a line.'

'Claire, I think we could have something special if we let ourselves.'

'Is that why you grabbed me the day we met and kissed me?'

'No. I just got tired of your ranting. By the way, you're lovely when you're angry. Your eyes sparkle and . . . '

'Why have you waited so long to tell me how you feel? I mean, you're going away tomorrow.'

'We have today.' He reached over and kissed her on the lips.

A wave of longing rose inside her. Claire

took his hand and they sat gazing at each other.

Time passed and other passengers began gathering their possessions, a sign the trip would soon end. The sky had grown dark by the time Lakeside appeared and Max led her onto the deck. They watched the captain ease the steamboat into the slip.

A lovely old Victorian hotel loomed on the horizon a block or two from the water. 'Is that the hotel you mentioned?'

'Yes, and they have great lunches. Shall we get something to eat there?' After a brisk walk, they entered the hotel.

Max escorted her into the restaurant. When she'd taken a seat at one of the tables, he said, 'Wait a minute.' He left the room for a few minutes and she could see him in the lobby, talking to the maitre d'. He came back, smiling.

'Would you like to have lunch in one of their guest rooms?

'Or we could wait and have lunch later,' she suggested. Breathless, Claire could scarcely believe what she had said.

They took the small, creaking elevator to the second floor and a large guest room overlooking the bay where rain was now falling. A four-poster bed had place of honor in the large airy room full of antiques.

'Is this all right?' Now that they were there, he seemed unsure, as if he was afraid he had misunderstood her.

'It's lovely, Max.' She kissed him softly and was rewarded when his arms tightened around her.

They eased out of their clothes, helping each other undress. While he was still in his briefs, Max had the presence of mind to close the front drapes. Claire had to smile. As high as they were in the hotel, there was no one outside to see them unless it was the seagulls and they didn't matter.

Max kissed her from the top of her head to the tips of her toes and she thought she'd faint with pleasure. His hard, lean body fit with hers.

He nuzzled her neck, wrapped himself around her. 'Now you can't get away.'

She wanted to tell him she had no desire to escape. She was right where she'd wanted to be for weeks.

They kissed, fondled each other until their bodies were damp with perspiration. Finally they came together while a storm thundered over the hotel.

Afterward, they rested, snug under the goosedown covers. Max smiled. 'It's a good thing we're not out there on the mountain. This rain could last for hours.'

And while it did, they talked. 'The first time we met, I had an inkling. It was only later that I realized.'

'Realized what, Max?'

'I've had a dream of a perfect girl, someone who's never been in love with anyone else.'

And she hadn't. Charles had forced her into an incestuous relationship when she was thirteen years old. Later, she was wary of men and avoided close relationships. *Charles, you ruined your life. I hope what you did doesn't ruin mine too.*

The ride back to Windermere was uneventful. Claire's thoughts were unsettled. Questions kept darting about in her mind. What should she do? If she didn't tell Max and later he found out, would he ever forgive her?

Feeling like a coward, she put off the inevitable. She'd tell him later.

They returned to King's Grant, windblown and tired. Mattie stuck her head out of the kitchen as they walked into the dining room. 'Well, hello. Did you have a good day?' Her bright eyes looked them over and she nodded, like she approved what she saw.

'Yes, we did.' Max spoke when Claire didn't respond.

They again had dinner with the family and again Kate and Nick excused themselves early followed by Mattie.

'Why don't you come down to my flat?' He invited her as soon as they were alone. 'You could help me pack.' Max hugged her.

'All right.' She had to tell him and what better place than the gatehouse. No one would be able to hear them.

They walked together down the driveway, surrounded by the ancient boxwood hedges bordering the road. Claire inhaled a delightful blend of the smell of rain and the woodsy fragrance of the cedars and spruce on the property. If she weren't steeling herself to disclose a hideous secret to the man she loved, she'd be content.

All the while, Max kept hold of her arm protectively, as if she'd stumble if he didn't guide her. She didn't have the heart to tell him she could find her way around the property with eyes closed. Somewhere between them and the now invisible lake, a bird cried out in the darkness. Claire shivered.

Max led her down to the stone gatehouse, a miniature of the hotel with its slanting roofs and weathervane on top.

Inserting his key in the door, he stood aside so she could enter. As soon as they were both inside, he closed the door and locked it.

From his slight frown, she wondered if Max sensed something different. On edge herself, she knew what was going to happen, at least her part.

Claire prowled the lower level of the flat with its small sitting room and Pullman kitchen. She glanced upward. 'I guess you sleep upstairs?'

'Sure. Want to see?'

She preceded him up the narrow stairs. 'It's not very big, is it?' She looked around, trying to put off the inevitable, or at least find the best way to tell him.

'What's the matter?' He appeared concerned. 'You seem tense. Did I do something to upset you?'

'It wasn't what you did, just something you said.' She pointed to two armchairs by a tiny fireplace. 'Can we sit down?'

He sat, worry riveting wrinkles in his brow.

'You said I'm your dream girl.' She began. Dear God, let him love her enough to understand.

'And you are.' He took her hand and kissed it.

She retrieved her hand then stood before him. 'If you want a girl who's waited for you, I'm the one. I've dreamed of a man like you for years.'

He seemed to relax. 'Thanks.'

'In my heart I've waited for you. But I was with another man for years.'

A frown crossed his face. 'You told me that you'd never been in love before.'

Claire nodded. 'That's right. But I didn't say I hadn't had a sexual relationship. It was with my brother.'

'You're kidding.' There was a catch in his voice and a muscle jumped in his jaw. 'Brother and sister . . . ' He shook his head. 'That's not something people do.'

'Sometimes they do. Charles and I were intimate for years. You weren't the first man in my bed. In my heart, yes. In my bed, no.' Seeing the bewilderment and raw anguish on his face, Claire wanted to weep.

'You should've told me.'

'When, Max? When's the best time to tell the man you love you lost your innocence with a member of your own family?' She bit her lip.

'An incestuous relationship with your brother, that's disgusting.' His voice was shaky. He stood and looked at his watch. 'It's getting late. I'll walk you back to the hotel.'

'Just like that? Won't you let me explain?' She couldn't believe he was being so unfair.

'There's nothing to say. Let's go.' Max led her outside. Though they walked together, this time he made no effort to touch her. She'd never felt so alone. At the door of the hotel, he gazed at her as if she were someone he'd just met and didn't care to know better.

'I'll be busy tomorrow, getting ready to leave, so let's say our goodbyes now.' He held out his hand.

Was that all she meant to him, a handshake? She ignored his outstretched hand and ran inside. Moisture welled in her eyes as she climbed the stairs to the next floor and her room.

Locking the door, Claire managed to reach the bed and throw herself across it before the dam of tears she'd been holding back broke. If he'd loved her, he would've let her explain. He didn't ask what happened. Max didn't love her, he was in love with a foolish dream. Damn the man, she never wanted to see him again.

28

Max walked back down the driveway to the gatehouse. Once inside, he slumped in the armchair in the tiny sitting room, sick at heart. What happened? They'd been so happy. She'd been everything he dreamed, warm, sweet and generous. Why did he shoot off his mouth, talking about his perfect woman?

It was apparent his comments made Claire feel guilty and compelled to tell him the truth. If only she hadn't waited until he'd fallen in love with her.

He'd learned his lesson. Never again would he fantasize about the girl waiting for him. She was just a figment of his imagination.

On the other hand, his work with the Task Force was very real and demanded a lot of him. He determined to give it everything he had, leave that romantic nonsense to others foolish enough to believe in love.

Though he went to bed he couldn't sleep. At one point, he stepped outdoors. A light still burned in a room somewhere on the second floor of the hotel. He wondered whose room it was.

Max spent the night packing and getting

ready to leave. At daylight he drove up to the hotel one last time.

As he walked into the dining room, Kate was sitting at the table. She frowned at him.

'I guess no one else's up yet?' He inquired.

'I wanted to have a talk with you.' Kate said. 'You've had a change of plans?'

'Yeah, I'm catching an early train.' From her unusual coolness, Max sensed Kate knew all about what had happened between Claire and him. 'Here're the keys to the gatehouse.' He tried to give them to Kate. She ignored his out-stretched hand so he placed them on the tablecloth by her coffee cup.

Max crossed the room to the breakfast buffet and poured himself a cup of coffee before taking a seat across from Kate.

'Before you leave, I'd like to tell you a story,' she said.

'Oh?' His mouth turned dry. He didn't know what to say.

'This is a true story, about a little girl who lost both of her parents when she was very young.' Kate's gaze remained locked with his as she talked. 'First, her mother died in a skiing accident then her father committed suicide.'

'Who're we talking about here?' As if he didn't know. Max had to admit this was an unusual approach. He'd expected Kate to

312

lecture or scold him, not tell him stories.

'That doesn't matter, not at this point.'

'Okay, go on.'

'The little girl and her brother had servants to care for them, though a nanny or governess is not the same as having your own mother or father.'

'If you're talking about Claire, she told me already,' Max said. 'So don't waste your time.'

'Just a moment,' Kate replied. 'The little girl was five years younger than her brother. He was her only living relative except for an uncle who lived in London.'

'Where were you then?'

'I wasn't in the picture yet.' She heaved a deep sigh before continuing. 'The little girl would get frightened at night and would cry. Sometimes her nanny heard and came to her, other times she didn't. All the child had was one brother who adored her in his own way.

'When she was old enough to understand, her brother started telling her that it was the two of them against the world. He said it over and over until she believed him.'

'I don't know why you're telling me this.' Max tried to sound unimpressed with the pathetic story. Though he pretended indifference, his heart began to ache for the child Claire had been. Not that it was any excuse for what she did later.

313

'If you'll be patient, you'll see.' Kate appeared to study him with those peculiar green eyes of hers. 'When the little girl turned thirteen, her brother got into bed with her one night. She didn't know what he wanted. He raped her and told her if she didn't do what he wanted in the future, he would leave her, like their parents had. Then she'd have no one.'

'My God.' Surprised and shocked, Max drew a ragged breath and fisted his hands, yearning to punish Charles. 'To treat his own sister that way. He must have been a brute.'

'You can see why I'm so angry. It's not just your rejecting Claire. It's remembering what Charles put her through for all those years.' Kate wiped away a tear.

Max's own anger toward Claire faded. From the moment of their meeting, he'd been impressed with her decency and honesty. He should've known she would never condone anything morally wrong. Tears of shame ran down his cheeks as he met Kate's steady gaze again. 'And I blamed Claire.' His first instinct was to rush upstairs to her room and beg her forgiveness.

'Charles had two obsessions, Claire and King's Grant,' Kate mused. She could have been thinking aloud except he was with her.

'When he found he'd lost both, he didn't want to live.'

'How long did he force her to have sex with him?'

'When Claire turned eighteen and received an inheritance from her mother's estate, she started locking her bedroom door and told him to leave her alone. Before that she was a minor with no income of her own. When I married Stephen, she was almost sixteen. She told me later she was afraid to tell Stephen.'

'You would've believed her, wouldn't you?'

'If you knew me better, you wouldn't dream of asking that. Claire's the little sister I never had.' Kate's expression turned fierce. 'There's nothing in this world I wouldn't do for her.'

'Does that include talking to me?' Whose idea had it been, Claire's or Kate's?

'I thought you should know the truth before you left.' Kate returned to the past. 'Claire was too ashamed to come to me. As if I'd ever blame her for Charles's perversion.'

'What I don't understand is why she put up with it.'

'She had no choice. She was emotionally and financially dependent on her brother. Charles took advantage of that dependency. Claire was his victim, not a willing participant.'

'Will she ever forgive me?' Max's arms ached to hold her, kiss away her tears.

'Before I came downstairs this morning, I stopped by her room to ask her if she wanted to see you before you left. She didn't. She sent you a message. Do you want it?'

'Yes, please.' He held his breath, hoping and praying.

'She never wants to see you or hear from you again.' Kate seemed to be watching for his reaction.

Max slumped in his chair. 'I deserve that. Maybe later?'

'All I can say is when Claire makes up her mind about something, she doesn't change it.' Rising from her chair, Kate said, 'I'm sorry.' She patted him on the shoulder, passing his chair on her way out of the room.

As if in a daze, he found his coat, put it on and left the hotel. While he went through the motions of driving to the station and parking the car, parts of Claire's message echoed in his head, 'never again, never again, never again.' He'd lost her.

Boarding the shuttle train, Max didn't look back. There was no longer anything for him there.

★ ★ ★

Locked in her bedroom upstairs, Claire heard Max's car start up outside. Part of her yearned to run after him. She dug her fingernails into the drapery by the window, not wanting to admit she still cared. If she denied her feelings, in time they'd wither and die.

What was wrong with her? Was she destined not to love and be loved? Charles and she shared the same genes. He had been warped and abnormal, maybe she was the same way. Kate had tried to reassure her last night, telling her it had been Max's fault they broke up, not hers.

At a light tap on her door, she dropped the curtain. There wasn't anything to see now that his car was gone. 'Yes?'

'Are you all right?' Kate's voice sounded anxious.

Claire opened the door and let her aunt enter.

'Don't be angry. I told him everything.'

'What was his reaction?'

'Max was angry, extremely angry with your brother. And he wanted to know if you'd ever forgive him.'

'You gave him my message, didn't you?'

'Yes, just what you said.'

'Not in his lifetime or mine.' Claire's chin went up.

Kate sighed. 'I hope you know what you're doing. Lots of things can happen in a lifetime. Like loneliness and regret.'

'Don't mention him again.' Claire ordered Kate.

When her aunt tried to hug her, she stood rigid, not able to tolerate kindness. Sheer will power held her together. Later, when she was alone, she'd cry. For now she didn't want anyone to see how much she grieved.

'Why don't you come downstairs? I'll get the children up and we can all have breakfast together.'

'No, thanks. Take care of Nicky and Kayla. I'll see you later.' She held the door open until Kate left the room.

Claire just wanted to be alone. If her aunt kept talking about Max, she might give in and start having foolish ideas, like it wasn't too late to catch him at the station. It was taking all of her strength to stay in the house until he was gone.

The telephone rang downstairs. Mattie must've answered since it only rang a couple of times. Or perhaps it was a wrong number.

Claire dressed and went downstairs. As she entered the kitchen, the housekeeper was on the telephone. Mattie handed her the phone.

'It's me,' said a voice Claire would never forget. 'I know you won't talk to me. I just wanted to say how sorry I am. I botched things for us by not believing in you. It will be on my conscience the rest of my life.'

Max's voice was low and she could feel his sadness. She wanted to speak to him, to say anything that would let him know she forgave him. No words came to her frozen lips.

'Good luck to you, Claire,' he said at last. A click on the other end of the line and he was gone.

She laid the phone back in its receiver. 'Max wanted to say goodbye.' Looking upward, her gaze met her friend's.

'Poor child.' The housekeeper took Claire in her arms and held her close, rocking her like she was the twins' age.

Struggling to hold back her tears, she moved away. 'I'm going out.' Claire located her coat in the hall closet. 'Tell Kate I'll be back in an hour or two.'

She drove down the hill to the Windermere station. Of course the shuttle had departed. Then she drove hard and fast over the twisting, turning road, pursuing the little three-car train, all the way to Oxenholme. She'd take this as a sign. If it was meant for them to be together, he'd still be there waiting for the train to London.

Of course she was too late. The British Rail train had come and gone. Claire stood on the station platform, staring down the trestles while dead leaves blew around her feet. The bleak sky overhead appeared almost as somber and hopeless as her heart.

She kicked the leaves on her way back to the car. *That's that. The two of us . . . it would have been a big mistake anyway.*

Claire felt frozen. Would she ever be warm again?

Her next stop was a place she'd vowed to never visit again.

Morcambe Bay was emptying as she parked the car. In a few minutes nothing was left except vast expanses of pale, wet sand and debris the sucking, greedy tide hadn't taken. While gulls wheeled and cried overhead, Claire sat on a damp log, thinking.

Perhaps she wasn't meant to be happy. Some people never achieved happiness. Was it because they didn't deserve it or was happiness random, just something that happened?

She drove back to the hotel, arriving cold and sad.

Kate came to the door, took one look at her and hugged her close. This time Claire let her aunt embrace her, in fact she clung to Kate and wept, her body shook.

'Come into the kitchen while I make us a pot of tea,' Kate said when Claire was calmer.

'Then we're going into the library to get you warm.' Her aunt stepped out of the room and Claire could hear her whispering to Mattie.

Soon the two of them were seated in the snug library. Kate lit a fire and in a matter of minutes the room was comfortable. Before Claire knew what was happening, she was wrapped in a quilt the housekeeper had made long ago, her feet buried in Kate's pink fuzzy slippers. The hot tea warmed Claire and she sighed.

'Where did you go?' Kate wrinkled her brow. 'I was worried.'

'Down to Oxenholme. His train had already left . . . '

'You'll hear from him again.' Her aunt nodded assurance.

'I still haven't forgiven him.'

'I know, darling. I know.' Kate patted her hand.

'I just wanted to say goodbye.' Claire blinked hard.

'You were gone a long time. Did you go somewhere else?'

'To the Bay. I haven't gone there since . . . '

'That must be a grim place on a day like this,' Kate began.

'It is,' Claire said. 'Not a place to take tourists.' It was amazing to find she hadn't lost her sense of humor.

'I'm going to say something I should've said long ago.'

She must've looked apprehensive since Kate took her hand and squeezed it. 'Now you just listen. Maybe this will help.'

Claire had to smile. 'You're so good to me.'

'What happened to Charles was due to the kind of man he was. You didn't cause your brother to grow up emotionally twisted. You didn't cause his unhappiness. It was all Charles. There was nothing you or anyone else could have done.'

'Are you sure?' How long she'd waited to hear those words.

'I'm sure. Now let me say one more thing and we'll not talk about it again, at least not today. You sent Max away. This morning I told him everything and he broke down and wept for you. Do you have any idea what that means?'

Claire shook her head.

'Max's a strong man.'

'Like Nick,' Claire added.

'Yes. And I would say one who doesn't show his emotions easily. For a man like that to weep openly . . . He cares very much for you. If you still love him, let him know.'

'It's too late. Even if I wanted to get in touch, I couldn't. I don't know where he is. He's gone.'

29

For the first few days after Max's departure, Kate, Nick and Mattie spoke to Claire in the hushed tones people use to patients convalescing from a terrible illness. She also caught them talking about her when they thought she couldn't hear.

The children were too young to understand her loss. They treated her as they always had, like their 'Cuz' who, though larger and older than they, was still a good playmate.

As a consequence, Claire sought out Kayla and Nicky's company every chance she had. Time spent with them helped ease her pain.

She sat at the dining room table reading the local paper one morning after breakfast.

'Can we take a walk?' Kayla asked when the cartoons ended.

Through the dining room window, Claire could see the side yard. At that moment the hotel flag was blowing stiff in the autumn wind. 'If you'll wear your warm coats with the hoods,' Claire replied, finishing her cup of tea, 'We might take a short walk. Why don't you invite your mommy to go with us?'

Kate was too busy so Claire helped the

children put on their warmest coats, slipped into her own, and the three of them set out. She held Kayla's hand while the little girl's more adventurous twin Nicky skipped down the path ahead of them. It was a pleasure to observe their childhood so much happier than her own. Out of the blue an idea presented itself to Claire. She considered it with care.

That night at the dinner table, she addressed Kate and Nick. 'If you don't mind, I'm going to leave The Folly to Kayla and Nicky when I'm gone. Maybe one of them will want to live there.'

Nick and Kate exchanged glances then Nick replied. 'We appreciate the thought, Claire. Still, wouldn't you want to leave it to your own children?'

'I will never marry,' she said firmly. In her heart, Claire knew she'd missed her chance. She'd never love another man the way she loved Max. If only she hadn't let her wounded pride and stubbornness get in the way. Now she couldn't even reach him. He hadn't left her his address in London, and she had no idea where his next assignment would take him.

'Don't be so sure.' Kate sent her a warm smile.

Although Nick and Kate didn't encourage

her, Claire proceeded. She made an appointment to have her will prepared.

The following day, she entered the law offices the Stanhopes had used for generations. The old brick building that had been built during her grandfather's youth still appeared impressive.

Claire stepped up to the reception desk where a thirtyish woman was busy transcribing, her back turned to the door.

When she turned around, the receptionist flashed a beautiful smile that lit up her whole face. 'Can I help you?'

'Claire Stanhope to see Mr. Mallory.'

A frown crossed the other woman's features. 'You're the lady who called yesterday about a will?'

'Yes, is there a problem?'

'You hung up before I could explain. I guess you haven't heard. The older Mr. Mallory had a stroke and is now in a nursing home. His son, Keith Mallory is taking over his father's practice. At least he will when he returns. At present Keith's on his honeymoon, on a Mediterranean cruise with his bride.'

'I see.' Claire felt let down. She'd hoped to get the matter settled right away. 'I guess I'll have to ring you up later.' She turned to leave.

The receptionist got to her feet. 'Wait, please. I didn't mean no one here could help you today. An solicitor friend of Keith's is filling in for him. He'll be glad to see you.'

The outer door opened. 'You're just in time,' the receptionist called to the well-dressed man who entered. She gestured to Claire.

Seeing a familiar face, Claire blinked in surprise. 'Percy? I didn't expect to see you here.'

Nick's former solicitor appeared pleased to see Claire. Percy April took her hand and held it until she gave it a tug.

'Daphne here left me a message that one of Mr. Mallory's clients needed a will. She didn't say who it was.' Percy led Claire into his temporary office. 'Let me help you with your coat.' He was beside her before she knew it.

Once he'd hung her wrap on a hook beside the door, Percy guided her to a comfortable-looking armchair near his desk.

Claire took a seat, waiting quietly for him to settle in his deskchair. The moment he appeared ready, she spoke. 'As I said before, I need to make a will. I think everyone should have one, don't you?' His constant smile made her nervous.

'Hmmmm? Oh, yes, quite true.' He played

with the pen in his hand, doodled on a pad of paper on top the desk blotter. 'How's your uncle?'

'Fine, thanks.' Claire told him what she had in mind. 'I want my property to go to Kayla and Nicky Connor on my death.'

'I hope you aren't ill.' His gaze became apprehensive.

'Not at all.' Claire smiled slightly. 'I'll come right to the point. I'm single and don't intend to marry. It's possible one of the children will want to live there when I'm gone.'

'In a village like ours, everyone knows everyone else's business,' Percy mused. 'There's been talk about you and that FBI agent. Might I ask if you're still seeing him?'

'Actually,' she began, tempted to tell Percy it was none of his business. Claire hesitated. Not wanting to sound rude, she simply replied, 'No, I'm not.'

'You're a young, lovely woman,' Percy said appreciatively, 'Even more attractive than when you were a girl.'

Though the compliment was flattering, her muscles tensed. Why did his few simple words of praise put her on guard?

'Would you have dinner with me tonight?'

'I'm sorry. I have other plans,' she said right away.

'Lunch today?' He persisted.

'Why don't we take care of the will?' She put him off, hoping he wouldn't ask again. She'd just lost the man she loved. She wasn't in the mood for socializing.

Diverted, Percy asked a few questions about The Folly and her personal income. That done, he gazed at her across the desk. 'As soon as the document's transcribed, I'll bring it to you for your approval. By the way, I'll need the children's full names and their date of birth.'

'Let me check on their middle names. Their birthday is April 18th, that I do know. They were four years old last Spring.' Claire got to her feet, ready to leave.

Percy brought her coat and helped her with it. The way his hands lingered on her shoulders, the simple gesture came close to turning into a caress. Then he escorted her to the reception area and would've escorted her to her car except for an incoming telephone call he had to take.

They shook hands at the door and Claire escaped before Percy could again ask her to go out with him.

While driving back to Kings Grant, Kate wondered about the solicitor. Percy was handsome, if you liked overly-groomed men. He reminded her of the male models in clothing catalogs Charles used to receive in the mail. Mid-thirties and well-educated, Percy lived alone in a mansion on the lake that he'd inherited from his doting mother, one of the grande dames of the Lake District. To the best of her knowledge, he'd never married. Claire wondered why.

As she turned into the hotel driveway, she admitted his conduct bothered her. Percy was a little too eager.

He was nothing like Max. Maybe that was a good thing. Right now, she needed a friend, not another lover. The question was would Percy be satisfied with friendship?

★ ★ ★

That same afternoon Max sat studying the information he'd been given in a small meeting room at Scotland Yard. Random thoughts of Claire floated across his mind and he struggled to push them aside. *Think about her later.*

Presuming he'd be on his way by now, it had been a pleasant surprise to learn his next investigation was near London.

The woman he was to investigate had a flat on The Isle of Dogs. On the surface, Tansy Carlisle seemed an honest, law-abiding citizen. It was possible she was none of those things.

A disgruntled ex-boyfriend had reported her to the London police. Because of its international scope, the local authorities had turned the accusation over to Scotland Yard.

Tansy flew from London to several major American cities including New York, Chicago and Los Angeles and back on a regular basis. A graduate of one of London's most prestigious schools for nannies and holding impeccable references, she escorted small children from England to their wealthy parents in the States.

If her rejected lover hadn't turned spiteful and wanted to get even, Max's Task Force at the Yard would never have been aware of the petite, demure brunette. But when they heard the accusation, his group became most interested in interviewing the ex-boy friend and hearing more about his suspicions.

According to the man, Tansy was involved in a black market ring whose commodity was children stolen and sold to the highest bidder via the Internet. She didn't actually steal the children, someone else did that. Using her 'TLC Infant Escort Service' as a front, Tansy was suspected of transporting children to buyers.

Max shuddered. He'd met all kinds of criminals through his work with the Federal Bureau of Investigation and the International

Task Force to which his own agency had assigned him, though no cases like this.

If the Yard's suspicions were correct, this woman had to be a heartless criminal. Kidnapping someone else's child was bad enough. Being involved in the sale of a child was worse.

Max closed the folder and sat back in his chair, thinking. Next he must learn where Tansy lived then find himself an apartment or room nearby. The Task Force needed evidence of criminal activity on her part before they questioned Tansy.

Unfolding the London Times he'd bought outside his hotel, Max glanced at apartment listings for the Isle of Dogs. Though it was too late that day to visit any of the offered flats, he'd make a few telephone calls.

Max tucked the folder into his briefcase and shrugged into his overcoat. Turning off the fluorescent lights, he closed the door as he left. On the ground floor, he checked out at the front desk. They had his hotel phone number if they needed him. He walked the several blocks to the hotel, wondering what Claire was doing at that moment. Would she ever forgive him?

★ ★ ★

Viewing King's Grant Hotel through his new set of expensive binoculars, a chuckle escaped Percy's lips. Claire had no idea how lovely she was. And soon she'd be his.

It had been years since he'd first caught a glimpse of her in the village. Even then, she'd been accompanied by her watchdog brother. Percy sensed it wasn't the right time for them to meet.

He hadn't realized how much he wanted her until she returned from Devon. He'd forgotten how sensual and exciting a woman could be until he saw her again. One glance confirmed Claire was still all he wanted.

Though she might not accept him as her suitor at first, she would soon enough. This time nothing would keep them apart.

From her sad demeanor the last few days, Percy suspected someone had disappointed Claire. Never mind. He'd bring smiles to her pretty face. And as soon as she realized he was the man for her, they would be together, forever. He smiled and put down the binoculars. It was getting too dark to see anything at the hotel. Tomorrow he'd proceed with his plan.

The next morning, as soon as the shops opened, he dialed the most exclusive florist in town and ordered two dozen red roses. The clerk at the florist shop assured him that the flowers were perfect. What message did he want on the card? He smiled and dictated a few words.

★ ★ ★

Claire walked down the staircase that same morning, passing through the dining room on her way to the large, sunny kitchen. Kate stood at the stove, cooking breakfast.

She came up behind her aunt. 'Good morning.'

'Sit down and talk to me while I finish these,' Kate responded, placing strips of cooked bacon on a paper towel to drain. 'What's on your agenda today?'

'Nothing much,' Claire said. 'I don't guess you have time to go shopping. There's a new ladies apparel shop in the village.'

'Of course I do.' Kate seemed pleased. 'Is it possible you're feeling a little better?'

Claire nodded. 'I don't know how you all could stand being around me. I've been moping for days.'

'We understand you've been sad, dear.' Kate hugged her. 'The important thing is to feel better. And I think you are.'

Her aunt was right. Claire felt less depressed, though she'd never get over Max.

'What shall we shop for?'

'Maybe a new dress or two. I need something pretty.' And something she hadn't worn with Max. Perhaps if she pretended happiness, one day she'd achieve it.

The whirl of a vehicle coming up the drive caught their attention. It stopped outside. Kate peered through the front window of the kitchen. 'Did you order something?'

'No. Maybe Mattie did.'

The front door opened and a deliveryman stepped inside. 'Hello,' he called. 'Is anyone here? Lakeside Florist has a delivery for Miss Stanhope.'

'What in the world?' Claire eyed Kate. 'Did you and Nick send me flowers?' She tried not to get too excited. Was it possible they were from Max?

'No.' Kate shook her head.

Claire hurried into the hotel reception area where the delivery man waited. 'I'll take those.'

'If you'll sign right here.' He handed her a pad and pen.

She quickly scribbled her name. 'Thank you.'

'Anytime.' The young man smiled at her.

'Goodbye.' She held the door until he left.

'I think you made a conquest,' Kate said.

'Help me open this box, won't you?' Claire carried the long white floral box into the dining room, placing it on the table.

'Wait. I'll get scissors.' Kate ran into the kitchen, reappearing a moment or two later.

Snipping the ribbon, Claire opened the box. She folded back the green florist paper and glanced down at a mass of beautiful, red roses. 'I wonder who sent them.'

She found a card and read the message in silence.

'Well?' Kate seemed curious.

'This is the strangest thing. All it says is, 'See you in my dreams.'' Claire frowned. 'What does that remind you of?'

''See you in my dreams, hold you in my dreams . . . '' Kate stopped. 'It's part of an old song. Who'd send you flowers with a message like that?'

'Your guess is as good as mine.' Apprehension touched Claire. It didn't sound like Max. Did she have a secret admirer?

★　★　★

Nick took one look at the vase of roses and whistled. 'Those better be for Claire or Mattie,' he said, teasing Kate as they cleaned up the kitchen after supper. Claire had volunteered to give the children their baths and read them a few stories before bedtime. Mattie was having dinner with an old friend.

'I don't have a secret lover, if that's what you're implying,' Kate said. 'Someone sent them to Claire. There was no signature, just a strange message.' She showed Nick the card.

Nick didn't comment, though he looked thoughtful.

'When you called home from the office today, you mentioned wanting to talk to me about something?' Kate preceded Nick up the stairs to their room, hoping it concerned the vacation brochures she had tucked in her husband's briefcase.

'Maybe it wasn't such a good idea.'

'Go on. Now you've got me curious.' Kate waited.

'Well, remember I mentioned my new assistant at work?'

'How could I forget? You've been talking about nothing else for the past week or so. What has he done now?' Nick had been praising the new assistant he'd hired to replace his second in command who'd left when Nick was reinstated.

All she'd learned so far was Scott Eastland was American, single and thirty-two. If he was unattached and a nice person, perhaps Claire would like him.

Once they were both inside their room, door closed, Nick volunteered, 'I asked Scott to have dinner with us and he accepted. He said anytime, just let him know.'

'At least you didn't ask him for tonight,' she said.

Nick's smile was sheepish.

Kate knew that look only too well. 'I got it. He's coming tomorrow night?'

'I can postpone, if you'd rather.' He slipped his arms around her and kissed her cheek.

Kate stood in his embrace, just where she wanted to be. *Dear God, don't let anything else happen to my man*, she prayed. Ever since that scare with Nick's false arrest, she often found herself in need of reassurance he was safe. She played with his shirt collar. 'No, that's fine. I'm sure we can manage.'

'Good girl.'

'Is Scott engaged or anything?'

'I dunno. You can ask him.' Nick unbuttoned the top buttons on his uniform shirt, slipping it over his head while he moved toward their bathroom. It was clear he was ready to trade his police uniform for more casual clothes.

'I guess Percy must've sent those flowers,' Kate mused. Nick's former counsel had called Claire several times that week.

'How did she respond?' Nick came out of the bathroom, barechested, wearing his favorite jeans.

Kate shrugged. 'She wasn't upset or

excited. I suspect Percy is more interested in Claire than she is in him.'

'Didn't she tell you that she thought he liked her earlier?'

'Yes, I think she did.' Kate patted her hair. 'Well, maybe that's what she needs, a few new men in her life.'

'Yeah. You don't need any.' He hugged her again.

'You're right about that. You're more than enough for me.'

'Thank God for that.'

His earnest expression was so endearing, Kate was tempted to lock the door and lure him to bed. She smiled. Once the children were asleep, the evening had definite possibility. After knowing, loving and living with Nick for five years, she hadn't missed a certain glint in his eyes.

30

Max shivered as he exited his hotel that morning. The chilling wind prompted him to turn up his overcoat collar and walk briskly in the direction of the station. He was in luck. A Docklands Light Railway car stood waiting down the tracks.

With scant knowledge of the Isle of Dogs where his latest suspect lived, Max had searched the Internet the previous evening. Now he had a basic knowledge of the locale. The Isle was an island formed by the Thames and the West India Docks. Some historians believed the name derived from Henry VIII's keeping his hunting dogs on the Isle when he was in residence at the Greenwich palace. They would be brought to him by boat.

While the fast, efficient light rail carried him to his destination, Max reviewed what else he'd learned. From what he'd read, the Isle of Dogs was undergoing a great commercial change. That included many new restaurants and musical comedy clubs. The residential neighborhoods were also changing. Several luxurious high towers now intermingled with poor neighborhoods.

Max disembarked at the Docklands Station and soon located Tansy's address in a high-rise apartment building.

The swank glass-and-chrome structure had an expensive air about it. If Tansy's place of residence was any guide, transporting children to their parents in the States must be a lucrative business. Or maybe her ex-boyfriend's accusations were based on fact. Maybe she did traffic in stolen children.

Stepping inside the building, Max asked for directions to the building's rental office where he found a fortyish platinum blonde in a dark green ultra-suede suit chatting on the telephone. As he entered, the agent sent him a swift, appraising glance. She motioned for him to take a seat before continuing her telephone conversation. From her obvious lack of interest, Max got the impression she didn't think he qualified as a prospective client. He'd dressed casually so perhaps he didn't appear prosperous enough to live in the elegant building. He waited.

'May I help you?' The agent asked a few moments later, her tone indicating she didn't expect she could.

'I'm here on business from the States and need to find an apartment for a few weeks,' he said. 'From what I've seen so far, this area of London intrigues me.'

A raised eyebrow and frosty smile signaled her displeasure. 'Please don't refer to the Isle as London,' she requested in a chilly voice. 'Those of us who live and work here think the Isle is a special place. It has its own identity and history.'

'I stand corrected.' He bowed his head. 'Would you know of any vacancies on the Isle? I'm particularly interested in this location.' He aimed to rent a flat in the building, as close to his suspect as possible.

If Tansy was the monster her ex-boyfriend believed her to be, Max would be doing the world a service by putting her out of circulation.

'I'm sorry. We have a long waiting list,' the agent said. 'The best I can do is take your information and add your name.'

'Even for a couple of weeks?' Max shrugged. 'Thanks anyway.' It would've been the perfect location. He headed for the office door.

'Wait a minute. I keep forgetting one flat.' The agent flipped through a rolodex on her desk. Seconds later, she paused. Heaving a deep sigh, she sat back in her chair and looked in his direction.

'There's a furnished studio apartment near the top of the building. The occupant has gone to New York to visit family. She asked me to rent it for a month. That lets out most people. Almost everyone wants at least a six months lease. I don't know if that would work for you. It's rather small, I'm afraid.'

'It might be just what I need,' he said. 'Size doesn't matter. I'll be at work most of the time.'

'Fine. Before I take you up there, let me say living spaces on the Isle are quite the thing at present. So the rents are a little pricey. I'm trying to prepare you so you won't be shocked. Wait until you see the flat and hear about the services that we provide our tenants. Then make up your mind. Also, don't hesitate if you see what you like. There's a whole legion of people hungry for a unique place to live.'

The way she spoke, Max glanced around, almost expecting the legion to storm through the office door like a herd of thirsty elephants headed for a scarce waterhole.

The agent opened her desk drawer and brought out an ornate key. 'Come with me, please.'

Max followed her from the rental office. First, she stopped to speak to the people at the Information Desk. A tenant had lost her key, thought she had dropped it down the mail chute in her corridor. After glancing over her shoulder to be sure Max was still with her, the agent made a note of the problem and started off again. Her high heels clicked on the ornate marble of the hall until they reached the elevator. She stepped inside, holding the door open for Max.

'Here we go.' With the tip of one frosted sculptured nail, she pressed a button and they rose.

The elevator stopped once on the forty-fifth floor so a young woman who appeared familiar could join them. Max smiled. The woman didn't look in his direction. When they reached their destination on the forty-eighth floor, the woman preceded them off the elevator, vanishing into one of the apartments.

Glancing around, his first impression was a narrow hall and several closed apartment doors. The agent's high heels clicked down the hall. She stopped at one apartment and inserted her antique-looking key, opening the door. 'Come along.'

Max had been trying to see if there was a name on any of the apartment doors. None were marked.

The agent ushered him inside the apartment, turning on ceiling lights in each room as they walked through. The window blinds were all closed.

His first glimpse revealed nothing extraordinary, just a smallish living room furnished in black leather and glass followed by a Pullman-style kitchen with a built-in bar for dining, about big enough for one person if he moved with care. The bedroom was also small, a few pieces of furniture with the king-size bed taking most of the space. There appeared to be sliding glass doors to a balcony behind closed drapes. He wondered if the Task Force would cover the rent.

'This is why it's so expensive,' the agent said. She pulled the vertical blinds to one side. 'Look here.'

In the distance loomed London Bridge and the Houses of Parliament. As if on cue, the sun chose that moment to shine. The river shimmered in the new found light.

'Beautiful!' He thought of Claire and wondered if she'd like the view as much as he did.

'Thank you.' The woman seemed pleased at his response.

'What would my rent be?' Max queried the agent.

'There's an olympic-sized pool on top of the building, heated in the winter of course.' The agent said, ignoring his question. 'And a jogging track, also.'

'Of course,' he echoed.

'There's also a five-star restaurant and a complementary dry cleaners pickup and maid service once a week.'

Max was growing disturbed. How much, lady?

The agent must have sensed his anxiety since she consulted a notebook she'd brought along. '3000 Euro-dollars per month.' She purred, saying the figures.

He did some quick math in his head. The question was how much the Yard would pay. And how long it would take him to gather evidence on his suspect. 'Can I give you a deposit and have you hold the flat while I check with my company?'

The agent agreed, though she cautioned him that he must sign a contract in twenty-four hours or lose the flat and deposit.

Using his cell phone, Max was able to locate his superior at the Yard. He explained the situation and reassured the man the flat was necessary. Surveillance would be much more difficult if he had to live in another building. He received permission, though it was reluctant.

Max had placed the brunette on the elevator. Tansy Carlisle must live on the same floor. The only difference he'd been able to see in her appearance was a more severe hair style in her photograph. Today she'd worn her dark hair loose on her shoulders. He'd also noticed the number of the apartment she entered. The set-up couldn't be better. She lived two doors down the hall.

Bringing his clothes plus snacks and bottled water, Max moved in later that day. He was ready to follow Tansy whenever she left her apartment.

Later he found her dressed in jogging clothes at the elevator. Max made a mental note of the time. Tansy must use the track on top of the building. The next day he met her, leaving her apartment. They rode to the top together.

Soon he learned her routine. Jogging followed by a light breakfast in the restaurant then back to her apartment. Later she'd come out with a collapsible shopping cart, headed for the shops nearby. He'd follow along behind, not too close.

She didn't appear to be engaged in any suspicious activity. Max kept tailing her. The second day he noticed another man who seemed interested in Tansy. Max's inner radar was activated. Was the guy a stalker? There were weirdos who'd fixate on a pretty woman and follow her wherever she went.

The next day Tansy didn't go shopping. Max waited inside his living room, his door ajar so he could hear if she came out of her flat. Thoughts of Claire drifted into his mind at times while he was waiting for Tansy, he pushed them away.

Once he almost lost her, she moved so fast. He caught up with her downstairs. Again the strange man trailed Tansy. If he noticed Max, he gave no indication.

That day the man caught up with Tansy. From his position down the street, Max saw her stop and the two seemed to have a confrontation. Then she walked on while the man entered a shop.

Max was about a half-block behind Tansy when a car sped down the narrow street. The vehicle slowed as it neared the sidewalk where she was strolling.

At the last moment, Max realized what was about to happen. He broke into a run. Too late. A shot rang out and Tansy fell to the pavement. The car sped away. By the time he reached her, a small crowd had gathered around her body. Max took her hand, feeling for a pulse. There wasn't one.

Hours later, the police picked up her ex-boyfriend who broke down, confessing he'd paid to have her killed.

Max hadn't known Tansy so he didn't grieve for her, personally. He did regret not moving faster. Perhaps he could have saved her life.

The case was closed when the ex-boyfriend admitted he'd lied to the police and Scotland

Yard. Her crime was rejecting him.

The Task Force gave Max time off. As soon as he was free, he packed a small suitcase and bought a train ticket to Bowness.

He couldn't go through life haunted by his memories of Claire and how they'd parted. He must see her one more time. The question that he longed to ask was always on his mind. Would she forgive him? In a day or so, he'd find out.

31

Claire slipped into her new silk dress. The multicolored print was brighter than her usual preference. Still, her aunt had convinced her the dress was becoming. She'd wear it that night when Ron, her new friend took her out to dinner.

She reflected on how they'd met. Nick had invited his new assistant for dinner last night. Prepared to spend several hours being polite to a boring stranger she'd never see again, Claire had been more than a little surprised to find she was having a good time.

Ron was an amiable man, an American who knew no one in England except the people in his department. And he made it clear he already had a girl back home. Before she knew it, Claire was chatting with the man, telling him all about the Lake District.

When Kate called Nick from the kitchen, requesting help with the dessert, Claire found herself alone with Ron.

She felt comfortable with the man and found herself opening up to him. 'I'm just getting over a bad experience,' she confided.

'A relationship I had didn't turn out the way I hoped.'

'I've been down that road once or twice myself,' he said. 'You'll recover. Give yourself some time.'

'I will. In the meanwhile, I can't get involved with anyone else until I get over it.'

'Of course not,' he said. 'I guess I've been lucky. Shelia and I have been together for two years now. She's waiting for me back in Boston.'

'Thank you for being so understanding.'

'I hope you and I can be friends while I'm here, Claire.'

'You know, I think I'd like that.'

The following day Percy called again. Without any encouragement, he continued to ask for dates. Claire reminded herself that Percy had once tried to help her.

For that reason she felt she owed him an occasional date. Kate told her that she was foolish to date the man if she didn't like him. In private, Claire agreed, yet she still went out with him on occasion. She found herself liking him less and less. He was too possessive, reminding her of her brother. Percy kept pushing her to make a commitment.

There was also the matter of the flowers she'd received. Percy insisted he hadn't sent her the roses. She wasn't sure she believed him though why would he lie?

Claire wished she'd never agreed to date Percy April in the first place. Unless he changed, she'd soon have the unpleasant task of telling him they should limit their contact to business matters, like the will he was still preparing for her.

Before Ron left the previous evening, she'd agreed to accompany him to a lakefront restaurant she'd recommended. He picked her up in his new van.

She hoped they didn't run into the solicitor. Percy had asked her if she was seeing someone else. Reluctant to lie, Claire had admitted she was dating another man. She didn't say who it was and Percy didn't ask.

Following a couple of hours of pleasant conversation and an excellent meal, they left the restaurant. The parking lot was not well lit except for near the entrance to the restaurant. As they approached Ron's car, his mouth fell open. 'Damn.'

'What's wrong?' Claire wondered what had upset him.

'Look at the van.' He moved around the vehicle, swearing under his breath. 'Hell, somebody's slashed all four tires.'

A teenage gang? Somehow, it didn't fit the

setting. The busy season had passed, leaving the Lake District quiet and serene. The nearest large city was sixty miles away. Cities attracted a criminal element but Bowness and Windermere were small villages except during tourist season. 'You'd better notify the police.'

'I am the police,' Ron said, his face flushed with anger. 'If I ever catch the bastard who did this . . . ' Pulling his cell phone from his coat pocket, he called for a tow truck. Then he reported the incident to his department.

In a few minutes, a young constable arrived. The officer quickly assessed the damage. 'Sir, do you have any idea who could've done this?' He queried his superior officer. 'Has this ever happened to you before?'

'Never.' Ron scowled. 'Can you give this lady a ride home?'

'I'll wait with you,' she offered, not wanting to leave him.

'It's all right. There's no reason for you to stand around and wait.' Ron managed a slight smile. 'I'm sorry about this. I'll talk to you tomorrow.'

Claire thought about what had happened as she rode home in the patrol car. Her aunt met her as she walked into the hotel.

'You're home early.'

She explained what had happened.

'What a way to treat a newcomer in our community.' Kate sounded disgusted.

'Where's Nick?' He'd been home when Ron picked her up.

'He had to return to work,' Kate said. 'Do you remember the girl who was reported missing in Pennhurst?'

Claire thought a moment. 'The dental assistant who went to work and never returned home?'

'Yes,' Kate said, tersely. 'A woman's body has been found. It may be that girl.'

Claire recalled the news article had been in the Bowness Bugle a week or so ago, accompanied by a snapshot of an attractive eighteen-year-old with long blonde hair. A shiver raced through her and she wrapped her arms around her body. Who'd do such a horrible thing?

★   ★   ★

From a grove of cedars from Kendal Road, Percy had watched unseen as Claire left the hotel earlier that evening. He'd spied on Kate's dinner the previous night and recognized Claire's escort this evening as the same man who'd come to dinner. That annoyed Percy. They didn't invite him for a meal.

Turning on his car's ignition, he followed them, at a discrete distance of course.

While Claire and her friend enjoyed dinner in a restaurant overlooking the Lake, Percy lurked in the shadows of the parking lot. Having determined no attendant watched the guests' cars, he pulled a knife from his pocket. It was small yet razor sharp. He'd always been fond of knives for some reason. Maybe it was because they were quiet, not noisy like guns.

Percy's pride still stung with rejection from last week. He'd asked Claire to go to a performance of the local symphony and she'd turned him down. The last few days she almost always had a reason not to see him. Her latest excuse had been Nick's new assistant was coming to dinner and Kate was counting on Claire's being there to help entertain him.

Percy was trying to be patient with Claire. She was young and didn't realize who he was. That didn't mean he was going to be patient forever.

The new man she was seeing would soon learn he was asking for trouble. He shouldn't have intruded into their relationship.

Percy checked the restaurant once more. When a middle-aged couple exited the building, he ducked behind Claire's date's van. They were engaged in conversation and didn't notice him as they headed for their own vehicle. As soon as they drove off, he got to work.

As soon as he was done, he returned to his own car and drove away. Traveling down the road, Percy chuckled, envisioning the man's dismay when he returned to his vehicle.

It was possible Claire's date wouldn't connect his ruined tires with her, not right away. Meanwhile, Percy would come up with something else to convince the man to stay away from Claire.

★ ★ ★

Nick rubbed his tired eyes. As he entered King's Grant Hotel, he caught himself looking over his shoulder.

Kate was sitting by the fire in the living room.

He leaned over and kissed her. 'You didn't have to wait up.'

'You know I don't sleep well alone.'

Sitting down on the sofa by her, he reached down and removed his shoes. A deep sign escaped him.

'Your expression was so serious as you entered the room. What happened?' Kate's eyes showed concern.

'We think we've found the missing dental assistant.'

'Do you have any idea who killed her?'

'Not yet. Our labs will be working all night.' He put his arm around Kate and gathered her close. 'Every time I see something like that, I'm thankful you're home safe.'

'Maybe an old boyfriend,' Kate mused. 'Someone she dropped, someone who wanted to get even?'

Kate liked talking with him about his cases. Nick realized he shouldn't tell her as much as he did, yet at the present it was important that they all stay alert. Though there was no reason for a killer to focus on his little family, a madman didn't always act in a rational manner. Right now every woman in the county was at risk.

'This wasn't the work of a sane person, Kate. The woman was butchered. I've never seen anything like it in my entire life.' He glanced at his wristwatch. 'Where's Claire. Is she home yet?'

'As a matter of fact, she is,' Kate reassured her husband. 'Ron's van tires were slashed while Claire and he were dining in a lakeside restaurant tonight. A constable brought Claire home while Ron waited for a tow truck.'

'Claire needs to stay close for a few days. And I don't want you or Mattie driving around by yourselves either. Until we catch this nut case, you stay home as much as possible.'

'All right.' Kate kissed his cheek. 'It's been a long day. Why don't we go to bed, Nick?'

'Are you tired?'

'Not that tired,' she responded, smiling. Getting to her feet, Kate held out her hand. Nick took it and they went upstairs together, walking quietly through the still house. In the room they'd turned into a nursery, they stopped to look in on their children, Kayla was curled up on her bed, her favorite dolls taking up more space than she did. Nicky sprawled, hugging his new race car.

'Don't wake them.' Kate whispered. Nick nodded and followed her down the hall to the privacy of their room.

* * *

Claire was clearing the table after breakfast next day when the kitchen telephone rang. 'I'll get it. That may be for me.' She ran to the kitchen and picked up the phone.

Following a brief conversation, she rejoined the housekeeper and the children at the table. 'Ron wants to take me on a picnic tomorrow.

357

I told him I'd go if he'd let me furnish the food. He's living in an efficiency apartment. Besides, I don't think he knows a thing about cooking.'

'Poor lamb.' Kind-hearted Mattie was quick to pity those who couldn't cook. 'Tell me what you want to take and I'll prepare it. I know you and Kate planned to work on winterizing the gardens today. With Chris and Diane in the States visiting her family, you've got a lot to do. This pleasant weather won't last much longer. It's almost the end of October.'

Kate came into the room yawning. 'You should have woke me. It's going on nine o'clock.' She poured herself a cup of tea and sat down at the dining room table.

'There wasn't any need,' Claire said. 'We've all eaten. I thought you might like a little extra sleep. Weren't you up late, waiting for Nick?'

'Yes. He was off early as usual this morning?'

'Of course. Oh, Ron called. We're planning a picnic. I told him about the lakes around here and he wants to visit Wastwater.'

'That's kind of a remote area.' A cloud of doubt crossed Kate's face. 'I guess it's all right. Ron will take care of you. Just don't go wandering off anywhere by yourself for a few days. Nick wants all of us to stay close to home until they catch the person who k-i-l-l-e-d the dental technician.' Kate spelled the word to avoid alarming the children.

Mattie stopped polishing the already shining buffet. 'What's wrong?' She queried Kate.

'Nick didn't go into specifics, just said it was a brutal murder,' Kate said.

'Do they have any idea who he is?' Claire didn't like not being able to come and go as she pleased.

'No, just be careful. You too, Mattie.'

The housekeeper nodded. She reached out and hugged Kate then Claire put her arms around both of them. For a moment they all clung to one another. Warmed by her bond with the two other women, Claire was again glad she had returned to Bowness.

32

The skies were still clear the next day as the housekeeper watched Claire packing a picnic basket. 'You'd better take a heavy jacket and an umbrella in case of rain.'

Claire smiled. 'We'll be fine. Ron checked the weather forecast and there're no storms headed this way.' Having said that, she added a selection of cookies and several bottles of water and closed the basket.

Thanks to Mattie, they had enough food for at least three days. Claire had promised to call the hotel once they reached Wastwater.

'What time is he coming?' Kate asked, entering the kitchen.

A vehicle stopped outside. 'That sounds like him now.' Claire looked out the side window in the dining room. Seeing Ron in his van, Claire slipped on her coat, lifted the picnic basket into her arms and headed for the door. 'I'll talk to you later,' she said. Waving to the others, she left the hotel.

Ron smiled pleasantly as she settled herself in his van. 'You can be navigator,' he told her.

Claire nodded. It was good to get away for a few hours. As much as she loved her aunt and Mattie, she needed a little breathing room. On occasion Kate still treated Claire like a kid sister and the housekeeper often forgot she was a grown woman.

'Just take the A595. When you see the Gosforth exit, get off there and follow that road. It'll take us most of the way. I'll give you more directions later.' She made herself comfortable and watched the scenery.

It'd been years since she visited Wastwater. The last time had been with Charles. Thinking of her brother, her feelings were as always mixed, sorrow and anger. Claire sighed and leaned her head against the passenger window.

'What's wrong?'

'Nothing, nothing at all.' The smile she flashed seemed to satisfy Ron since he said no more, just concentrated on his driving. The road became less traveled as they left the more populated area around Bowness-Windermere and proceeded westward toward the Irish Sea.

Claire alerted Ron before they reached the Gosforth turnoff and minutes later, she advised him to go to the left at the Greendale signpost. At the second layby he pulled off the road onto an unclassified road that took them right to Wastwater.

Today the lake seemed benign. The

mountain face on the shoreline on the other side shone in the sunlight.

'Where do we park?' Ron asked.

'See those grassy areas?' Claire pointed to off-the-road parking marked by stones. 'You can park over there. Remember to be extra careful when we leave. Some people put their cars in reverse and hit the stones. You don't want to damage your van.'

He grimaced. 'After what happened the other night, I sure don't want any more problems.'

'Did the police locate the person who slashed your tires?'

'No, that guy's long gone.'

They left the picnic lunch in the van and went exploring. The ground was soft and sometimes boggy as they walked toward the lake. There was a relatively steep drop to the shoreline.

Ron studied the mountain across the water. 'There's something eerie about this place. Can you feel it?'

Claire looked around. She shrugged. 'That's because we're the only people here,' she explained. 'You should see it in the summer. It's mobbed with picnickers, tourists, climbers, scuba divers and people sunbathing. This late in the year, it doesn't attract many visitors.'

'I imagine the water is cold.'

'Even in summer. I remember reading that Wastwater is colder than most seas. Divers like it. It's England's deepest lake.'

'Why don't we head back to the van and get the lunch?' He suggested. 'I noticed a good spot near the water where we can sit and eat.'

Claire followed him back to his vehicle and watched as he got out an old blanket for them to sit on. Claire handed Ron the basket. 'If you'll carry this, I'll take that blanket.'

'That's a fair trade.' He chuckled good-naturedly. 'I'll take the food anytime.'

An hour later, they'd feasted on the baked ham, salad, fruit and chocolate cake Mattie had prepared for their outing. 'Shall we save the cookies for later?' Claire inquired.

'Fine with me. Did you ever call home and let them know we got here all right?'

She shook her head. 'Thanks for reminding me. I better get in touch before Nick calls out a search party.' She tried several times to use her phone. 'That's something else I forgot, to charge the battery. May I use your phone?'

'Sure.' Ron reached in his jacket pocket and came up empty. 'Well, it looks like you're not the only absent-minded person here. I must've left my phone back in the van. Let me walk back and get it.' He paused before asking, 'Want to come?'

'No, I'll clean up our mess while you're gone.' She watched him until he was out of sight. Then an unseen bird called from the other side of the lake. Its sorrowful cry sounded so lonely, Claire shivered. Don't start getting spooked, she told herself. You've been out here before and it's quite safe. Besides, Ron will be back soon.

Claire busied herself, picking up trash and putting it in a plastic bag to empty into the large waste receptacle near the entrance to Wastwater. Then she took out her compact and proceeded to freshen her lipstick and comb her hair.

Not wearing a watch had its disadvantages. As Claire tried to estimate how much time had passed, a dark cloud passed over the sun. The light dimmed and a slight breeze began to blow over the surface of the lake. She'd go and look for Ron except she didn't want him to think she was afraid of being alone.

A few minutes passed and she relented. Carrying the basket, Claire walked back up the trail. As she approached Ron's vehicle, she called his name. No response. The only sound she heard was the whisper of the wind. She turned and glanced around, hoping to see him approaching from the other direction. She saw no one.

Trying to remain calm, she reasoned that she couldn't stay there indefinitely. In a few hours, the area would be pitch dark. Maybe Ron was inside the van, looking for his phone.

Claire called his name again. Ron still didn't appear.

Perhaps he'd become ill and was resting. With that in mind, she positioned her face against a window and tried to see inside. A black object rested on the front seat. Through the tinted glass, it resembled his cell phone.

Claire tugged on the car handle on the off-chance he hadn't locked it. Much to her surprise, it opened.

Without hesitating, she slipped inside the van and locked the door. Switching on his cell phone, she was relieved to see a green light flashing on its surface. 'Thank God.' She punched in the hotel's number.

Nick answered on the first ring. 'We were becoming concerned about you. Are you all right?' His voice sounded worried.

'Sorry, we were so busy looking around and having lunch, I forgot. Then my phone battery died.'

'Where are you, Claire? Is Ron there? Let me speak to him.'

There was something wrong with Nick's

voice, or maybe the cell phone distorted the sounds. He sounded tense. It wasn't like him to get upset because she was late calling. 'What's the matter? You don't sound like yourself,' she said.

'Let me speak to Ron,' he said again.

'That's what I was about to tell you. Ron walked back to the van for his cell phone after mine wouldn't work. When he didn't return, I came after him.' Looking outside, Claire took a deep breath. In an hour or so, it'd be dark. 'He's not here.'

'All right. Listen to me. First, lock the van doors and don't open them for anyone except Ron. Where are you?'

'At the first parking lot inside the main entrance to Wastwater.' What was going on? Why didn't Nick tell her?

'We're on our way.'

'Wait. What happened?'

'The crime scene investigators were able to lift a thumbprint off the dead girl's body.'

'Have they been able to identify the owner of the print?' Claire strained to hear Nick's answer.

'Yes, it was — ' The line went dead.

Claire stared at the phone, then a sharp knock on the van door startled her.

She whirled around. Through the closed window, she saw a familiar face.

★ ★ ★

Nick slammed down the phone. 'I've got to get out there. Ron's gone missing and Claire may be in danger.' Grabbing his jacket, Nick headed for the door.

'Wait.' Kate called after him. 'I'm going with you.' She followed her husband to his car and jumped aboard right before he raced down the driveway. 'Don't you think you should get reinforcements? We don't know . . .'

Before she finished speaking, Nick punched in the constabulary's number. 'This is Superintendent Connor. Send two police cars to Lake Wastwater right away. Ron Eastland, the Assistant Superintendent, vanished out there this afternoon while he and my niece, Claire Stanhope, were having a picnic.' He paused to listen to the person on the other end of the line. 'Right. I'll meet you there. Also, pick up Percy April. We want to question him in regard to the dental technician's murder.'

Turning off his cell phone, Nick glanced at Kate. 'I don't know what we'll find at Wastwater. You stay in the car once we're there. All right?'

'Yes, unless I can help Claire.'

Strong-minded woman, he thought to himself but felt glad for her company. He hoped Claire was all right. If Percy April was out there, God knew what would happen.

* * *

Max watched the fleeting countryside, impatient for the train to reach Oxenholme where he'd leave BritRail and take the sprinter train to Windermere.

Rehearsing what to say to Claire, Max thought his words sounded artificial and stilted. Not one for flowery phrases, he decided the best approach was to just tell her the truth.

When she'd told him about her abnormal relationship with her brother, he'd overreacted and hadn't given her a chance to explain. At this point, all he could do was beg her forgiveness and hope she'd let him back into her life.

Too tense to sit still, he paced the length of the passenger car. This was turning out to be the longest journey of his life.

At last the train stopped at Oxenholme. Max jumped off and walked over to the smaller track where the sprinter would come in. Checking the schedule posted on a bulletin board by the tracks, he groaned aloud. He'd forgotten it was off-season. The next train wasn't due for two hours.

He glanced around for a taxi, then he remembered it was a Sunday. There was limited taxi service provided by a Kendall woman. But the lady didn't work on the weekends. Max entered the station and bought a local newspaper from a coin-operated stand.

★ ★ ★

Claire stared through the window of Ron's van. Were her eyes deceiving her? Percy motioned for her to open the door. She remembered Nick's warning. Surely, he hadn't been thinking of Percy. She released the lock.

'Are you all right?' He slid into the driver's seat.

'I guess.' Claire couldn't get over the coincidence of finding him there. 'Are you up here with friends? I didn't notice any other cars.'

'My car's over there.' Percy motioned vaguely toward another parking area in the distance. 'I saw you walking by yourself and followed to make sure you're all right.'

His earnest, worried expression, coupled with her anxiety about being left alone, brought tears to her eyes. 'Oh, Percy. It is good to see you.' She grabbed his hand and held on.

He reached across the seat and patted her arm. 'It's all right. I'm here now and I'll take care of you.'

'Nick's new assistant Ron and I came out to Wastwater for a picnic,' she explained. 'When I remembered to call Kate, I tried to use my cell phone. It didn't work. Ron volunteered to retrieve his own phone from his van. Now he's disappeared, and I don't know what to do.'

'Why don't we get in my car and drive around a bit? Maybe we'll find him.'

Why hadn't she thought of that? Good old Percy. Maybe she'd misjudged him. 'I'm sure that's a good idea.' Claire let Percy lead her to his own vehicle.

'There now,' he said, helping her into his car. 'You'll have to give me a description of your friend. I haven't met him.'

'Ron's tall, has dark hair, I don't know. He's a Yank.'

'Do you like him, Claire?' Percy leaned toward her.

'He's just someone to talk to, that's all.'

'Of course.' His smile seemed relieved. 'Well, in the future, perhaps you should talk to me.'

'I'm glad we're friends, Percy.' She returned his smile. 'I'm sorry we haven't seen more of each other. Something always comes up.' His gentle treatment was making her feel guilty. She'd avoided him. Today his presence was comforting.

'I'm the one you should be seeing. Remember that. The others don't matter.' He hesitated. 'In fact, I've been making plans for us. I'm a wealthy man. We can leave here today and go anywhere you want. Rio, Paris, the States. How about Hawaii? I'd love to have a picture of us on the beach at Maui.'

'You have an active imagination, Percy.' Claire laughed nervously. He must be kidding. 'I couldn't just pack up and leave. My family is here.'

'We can send them a cable when we reach our destination.' He concentrated on driving for a few moments.

'Oh, sure. I can imagine my aunt and uncle's reactions to that.' She chuckled. Percy was teasing her to take her mind off her worrying about Ron. 'I haven't seen anyone else. Is there another road around the lake?'

'No, that's it.' Percy examined his wrist-watch. 'I guess we better get going so we can catch the train. I thought we'd drive to Oxenholme and leave my car there.'

'You're not serious? Even if I wanted to run away with you, I don't have my passport or any clothes.'

'That's no problem,' he said in an

371

reassuring tone. 'We'll have Kate send your passport to our hotel in London and I'll buy you tons of clothes.'

'Maybe you should take me back to Ron's van so I can wait for him to come back.' Percy's wild story and strange behavior were beginning to trouble her. Was he on drugs?

'Be quiet,' he shouted. 'You are going to do what I say starting right now.'

Claire tried to open her car door. It was locked. She pounded on the door. 'Please let me out.'

'Just sit back and relax. We'll be at Oxenholme in an hour.'

'At least let me leave a note for Ron so he'll know I'm all right.' Claire tried to stay calm. She mustn't upset Percy.

'There's no need for that,' he said. 'Ron wouldn't be able to read it if you left one.'

'What did you say?' Fear clamped down on her chest until she couldn't take a deep breath.

'Don't worry about him. He's not important.' Percy stared at her. 'Say it. He's not important.'

Thinking he had experienced a nervous breakdown, Claire decided to humor Percy until she could escape. 'He's not important,' she repeated docilely. The first chance she had, she'd escape from him.

Claire's obedient behavior seemed to soothe Percy since he reached over and patted her knee. 'Good girl. You and I are going to be so happy. Wait and see. Just remember, do what I tell you.'

Claire waited. When they reached the station, there'd be someone to help her.

As they drove into the Oxenholme car park, the place appeared almost deserted. There was one man sitting in the station, reading a newspaper. She stared at his back, willing him to turn around and notice her.

Percy unlocked the passenger door and let her get out of the vehicle. Clutching her arm, he led her in the direction of the British Rail platform.

The man turned around. His gaze locked with Claire's.

'Help me.' Claire screamed and struggled to free herself from Percy's now bruising grip on her arm.

Max strode out of the station and hurried after them. As Percy half-dragged her away, Claire's heart hammered fiercely in her chest. If Percy forced her onto the British Rail train, she was afraid she'd never get away from him.

Max tackled Percy from behind and punched him hard.

Percy let go of her and ran toward the British Rail platform. He didn't take time to use the bridge to the other side of the tracks. Instead, he ran across them.

In his haste, Percy dropped the briefcase he'd been holding. The case sprang open, releasing a cascade of paper currency onto the tracks. He scrambled to retrieve his funds.

The engineer of the on-coming train blew his horn and slammed on the brakes. It was too late. The locomotive screeched as it hit Percy. Claire heard a muffled scream then the train rushed by them.

Sickened by what had happened, she buried her face in Max's coat. From the safety of his arms, she asked, 'Is he . . . ?'

'Don't look. He's beyond help.'

Claire raised her head and stared at Max. It was like a dream. He'd appeared just when she needed him the most. She touched his cheek. 'Why did you come back? I didn't think I'd ever see you again.'

'To beg you to forgive me. Hearing about your brother shocked me so much, I responded without thinking. The next morning Kate told me the whole truth. I should've known you would never do anything like that of your own free will.'

'He took advantage of my innocence, Max. I'm sorry I can't be the girl of your dreams.' Had he just come to apologize? She didn't think she could bear his leaving her again.

'Are you kidding? You're exactly my dream girl.' He gave her a quick hug. 'You told me you'd waited for me in your heart. That's what counts.'

As Max kissed her, Claire realized she never would have been able to love another man as she loved him. 'Yes, I waited for you. And here you are.' Feeling safe and cherished, she leaned against him. 'You'd better call the police. Then, will you take me home?'

'Yes.' Concern wrinkled his brow. 'I love you and want to be with you for the rest of our lives. And when I have an assignment, I'll hurry back as fast as I can. Wait for me?'

'You know I will.' Tears of joy blurred her vision.

He kissed her and held her close while in the distance sirens sounded, announcing the imminent arrival of the police.

Epilogue

Two weeks later, Claire lounged under a beach umbrella, watching the waves break gently on the shore at Aruba. She glanced across the table at Max, her husband of two days. They'd been married in a small, private ceremony at Kate's hotel. 'It's so peaceful here. I'm glad you suggested coming to the Caribbean for our honeymoon. We both needed to get away.'

He nodded. 'The important thing is we're together.'

'That's right,' she said, smiling. Then a more solemn thought made her frown. 'I'm still puzzled over Percy April. What made him turn bad?'

'That's a question for a psychiatrist. From what I've heard, Percy's mother adored him, gave him everything. He still turned out twisted.'

'The day I met him, he made me uneasy. I had no idea he'd become a killer.'

Max nodded. 'The dental technician may've reminded Percy of you. And Ron could've seemed a threat because you were dating him. They both became Percy's victims and there could've been others. Nick's people are reviewing the missing persons file.'

'What would I have done if you hadn't been in that train station?' Even now, thinking of that day frightened Claire.

'Nick was already on Percy's trail,' Max told her. 'Percy wouldn't have evaded the authorities much longer.' Getting to his feet, Max stretched and looked down at her. 'That's enough about the past. Why don't we go to our room, shower and take a nap before dinner?' He smiled.

Claire gazed at him thoughtfully. 'The first time we met, you infuriated me. If anyone had told me then, that we'd be married, I'd have laughed.'

'Stranger things have happened,' Max said.

'But no nicer things.' She became more serious. 'Thank you, Max. You've made me very happy.'

'I never thought it possible to experience so much happiness,' he replied. 'After my parents died, I built a wall around my emotions. Then you came along and changed my life.' He kissed her cheek. 'Shall we go?'

'I'm with you.' As he led her into the coolness of the hotel, Claire silently added one more word. *Always.*

We do hope that you have enjoyed reading this large print book.

Did you know that all of our titles are available for purchase?

We publish a wide range of high quality large print books including:
Romances, Mysteries, Classics
General Fiction
Non Fiction and Westerns

Special interest titles available in large print are:
The Little Oxford Dictionary
Music Book
Song Book
Hymn Book
Service Book

Also available from us courtesy of Oxford University Press:
Young Readers' Dictionary
(large print edition)
Young Readers' Thesaurus
(large print edition)

For further information or a free brochure, please contact us at:
Ulverscroft Large Print Books Ltd.,
The Green, Bradgate Road, Anstey,
Leicester, LE7 7FU, England.
Tel: (00 44) 0116 236 4325
Fax: (00 44) 0116 234 0205